Silence

R. P. Poe

*The beginning of atonement
is the sense of its necessity.*

- Lord Byron

This book is dedicated to Charles J. "Charley" Crosson, lover of books, friend, kindred spirit, and to my wife Diane, who makes all things possible.

One

San

I've known some folks say they hear God talking right to them but I never have. Not that I didn't try more than once when I got myself into a situation and thought my time had come. I reckon I've seen too much of the bad side of this world. Folks that have seen what I have don't much expect to hear from the higher power.

My friend Linder Wertz says I have a dim view of this life and the people in it. He says you spend your time around death and meanness, it will sour you on people but I tell him that law enforcement is about upholding the law so that death and meanness stay where they belong. Where Linder looks to God to know what to do, I look to the law and I've told him so more than once when my temper got the best of me. He can make me madder than anyone I know. The law is one thing I can believe in, maybe the only thing. Lately, I've had a hard time believing in much else.

Now, I was raised Catholic and we went to church nearly every week, so I can't plead ignorance of things religious. My grandfather passed out programs every Sunday morning, and my two aunts volunteered in the church kitchen any time there was a wedding or funeral. I hate to think what they might say if they heard me talking like this, but there it is. I suppose it's a good thing they're no longer with us.

My mother, father and older sister were killed when a trucker fell asleep and crossed the center line. I was eight months old. My aunts, Gert and Mattie, were a good deal older than my mother and never married, so they took me in and raised me as their own. Linder lived right next door. Growing up, he was as close to a brother as I'll ever know.

Linder's good-for-nothing father left before he was born and was never seen again. His mother had to work the swing shift at the Rock, the granite quarry used to build the Capitol, so the aunts ended up raising him too. We were a fine pair, I have no doubt. I don't know how Gert and Mattie managed.

Linder was always thin and awkward-looking. He tried all the sports, mostly because I played, but he was never good at much of anything. Except, that is, for archery. His slight frame and good eye were perfect for it. He went on to win the state championship for his age three times over. He might have really made a name for himself if he hadn't happened to go out hunting when he was about sixteen. It was something the men in the community did for fatherless boys.

True to form, Linder killed a white tail buck outright with his first shot. I believe he only went because he was asked and never gave it much thought until he saw that deer fall. I was standing right next to him and I could see right away he was distraught. Linder always was of the sensitive type, caring for hurt animals and people. He later told me it ruined the sport for him to see a living thing end so quickly at his hand. He put up his bow for good that day. Gert and Mattie did their best to convince him to take up the sport again but he would have none of it.

About a week before Gert died – she would never let anyone call her by her given name, Gertrude – Linder and I called on them. She and Mattie had always been in good health considering they were in their eighties and they seemed alright that day, although Gert did mention she couldn't shake a stomach bug.

"I just knew I should have thrown out that venison Charlie Timmons brought over. It was well over a week old, but you know how I hate to waste good food. Now that I think back on it, I should've just given it to the pigs and let them have the stomach ache." She placed a hand over her middle.

They had some young man living out back and helping them fix up the place. He took care of the pigs and did other chores. The last time I visited, I noticed they had moved him to one of the extra rooms inside the house. I was surprised by that but kept it to myself.

Something else bothered me. Gert was not one to complain. I knew it was likely she was feeling a good bit worse than she let on. But I knew she'd argue if I mentioned it, so I let it go. We got to talking about their days teaching half the kids in the county, most of them old as me by now, and I forgot all about it - until later.

Not twelve days passed and they were gone, one right after the other. Mattie died a week to the day after Gert. Doc Nowak, their doctor, said it's not uncommon for people that age to die in a short proximity if they were very close. Gert and Mattie had lived their entire lives together, so that did make some sense. Still, he couldn't give an exact cause of death. He just said they got a virus and died. They were in their eighties and it happens, he said.

Now, I was a Ranger for many years and when things don't add up I have a sense about it. It just nags at me like a rock in my boot and I have to do something. No matter that I'd been away from the law for some while. It's an old habit and one hard to shake. And I couldn't get used to the idea of them passing so fast like that. They were the last of my family. So, I went to see Doc Nowak.

Two

Linder

Santana Nitakechi Turner, or San to his friends, was always one you could count on for a clear head. For as long as I could remember, his mind seemed to work like the gears of a well-made watch, the sort my grandfather kept on a chain in his front pocket. What with the clocks in cell phones and computers nowadays telling time, some say watches like that are past their time. Some said San was past his as well but I knew better. He might have left the law but the law never left him. His mind would only tolerate what fit, as in one puzzle piece snapping into another just so. Anything else was unacceptable.

Close was always good enough for me. The same could never be said of San. It got on his nerves to no end that I wasn't bothered when things didn't fit just right. When I told him I was more interested in the big picture than the details, he looked at me like I'd lost all my faculties at once. We two were opposites in that way. Any inconsistency, no matter how small, and he worked at it and worried it until he had it figured.

But when his wife, Janie got hurt his mind went cloudy. I believe the only thing he ever feared in this world was losing her. He tended to her night and day, and it was all I could do to get him out of the house for even a short while. When I did pry him away, he was so distracted and distant that our conversations would lag and eventually cease altogether. Independent to a fault, he was never one to ask for anything and so he was more than a little reluctant to accept help. He just couldn't be away from her. It nearly did him in.

After she passed, he was quiet and sullen. Not that he was ever much good at serious conversation. But he had been known to occasionally hold forth if he had a bottle of decent Scotch and a subject that held his interest. I count those as some of my favorite memories. Eventually his sharp mind came back. Then we argued until all hours about the law and religion, like we had before. Him being an ex-lawman and me a pastor, that's not too surprising.

Still there was an edge to him that hadn't been there before. It was as if, in losing Janie he had lost the gentler side of himself. He was always no-nonsense, especially when it came to the law, and as a young man he could be as hard-nosed as anyone. But over the years he became more tolerant and understanding of the effect hardship has on a person. It was Janie that softened him. She had lost her mother at a young age and her father was never able to get over the loss. He drifted from job to job, never properly caring for his family. Janie was the one that took care of things. They lived hand to mouth mostly.

After they married, San came to see what life had been like for her as a young girl, taking care of her father and growing up at the same time. All that and her sweet nature softened him. But the ease San had with people seemed to vanish after she died. He wasn't comfortable in his own skin and you could see it. The only time I would see that familiar relaxed way with people was when he was with his two aunts. Though he would never say it out loud, they were all the family he had left in this life. On any given day he might be withdrawn, irritable and not fit to be around but visiting them would bring back his gentler side, if only for a while. I could see it in the way his eyes relaxed and brightened a little when they called his name.

So when he told me he didn't believe they had died of natural causes like the doctor and everyone else said, I understood why he might think so. In spite of my experience with funerals and grieving, I admit I can't imagine what it must be like to lose everything that makes this life worth living in one stroke, more or less. Janie, Gert and Mattie died within two months of each other. Truth is, when I let myself stop and think about it, what had happened to San was beyond belief. It was no surprise he held the law in such high regard. It was one thing he knew he could count on.

But this idea of his worried me. And it was clearly important to him to be right about it, as if he was somehow responsible and needed to make it right. How he could feel responsible for the deaths of two women in their eighties was beyond me. On the other hand, I understood how he could feel responsible for Janie's death. He was at the wheel when it happened. Although the trooper said he had little doubt that it was the fault of the poor weather conditions, especially considering San was driving under the speed limit, I knew San would see it differently. He would never allow himself the consideration he gave others. On top of everything, he walked away without a scratch. That made it even worse.

For a while, I was hopeful that the ordeal of caring for Janie those months might make some difference. I think it did help for him to have something to do. But seeing her lying there, not knowing if she was suffering or at peace just added to the score. I tried to get him to talk about it more than once with no luck, and eventually I stopped trying. It only seemed to make things worse.

Something else worried me. He had gone to carrying his gun in the glove box of his car. As a ranger, he had always carried a pearl-handled, chrome-plated .45 automatic. It was something he was known for. But he was meticulous about firearms and never carried the pistol when off duty. He said it was bad practice to carry a gun for no reason. I decided he believed he had a reason. So, when he told me he was going to see Doc Nowak, I knew I had to go along.

6

Three

San drove the long gravel drive leading to his aunts' house and stopped his car. He sat looking over the solid one-story built by their father from a Sears and Roebuck mail-order kit around 1920. Paint flaked off the columns flanking the wide porch, and a few weeds had sprouted between the hedges, but otherwise the blue and white house appeared to be in good condition. Even the navy shutters held their color. The place still looks lived in, he thought. Beyond, buffalo grass and cedar spread over the five acres of sparsely wooded ranchland that made up the property.

Across a barbwire fence, scattered lines of Hereford cattle stretched up and over the distant ridge, their broad orange and white faces looking at him with mild interest. To the right, bluish hills seemed to pile into themselves above the thin silver line marking the Lander River. As boys, he and Linder spent their summer days fishing the river, swimming and sliding down the low spillway next to the town dam. If they caught any fish, Mattie and Gert would inevitably pan fry them along with onions, peppers and new potatoes. Those times are long gone, he mused.

He walked through the tall grass to the back of the house, and on to a guest house attached to the garage that had once been the residence of a ranch hand they hired to care for their forty-acre cattle lease. The aunts had fancied themselves ranchers and had done reasonably well until keeping up with the lease became too much. They were visibly disappointed the day San announced he was choosing law enforcement over ranching. They never said a word but he could see he had let them down. The memory stung even now.

Unable to shake the feeling he had failed his aunts both in life and in their deaths, just as he had failed Janie, his mind filled with their image and he struggled to accept they were gone, though he knew it was true. What he could not change he might at least understand, he thought. There must be something that explains what had happened to them, and in turn to him, something that connects the dots and makes some sort of sense. He wondered what he might have missed.

The door to the small apartment stood ajar, which he found puzzling as he stepped through into the dark room. Once his eyes adjusted, he surveyed the one bedroom kitchenette. Papers were strewn over the table and countertops, and drawers and cabinets left open, as if someone had been looking for something. He picked up letter, finding it addressed to the young man his aunts had hired to care for the place.

He stared at the envelope as if it might tell him something. Sent from a bank in the Panhandle, the return address listed a route number near the town of Red Rock, Oklahoma. The papers inside explained the process for transferring funds electronically. Why would a young man want to waste his time in a dead-end job working for a couple of octogenarians, he wondered? And the move into the main house seemed odd, unless he was after something. A nagging idea just out of San's consciousness kept trying to intrude, interfering with his thoughts.

He looked up from the letter, sensing someone in the building, listening as the sound of gravel underfoot, barely audible, sounded from beyond the door. That the house, visible from the highway, might attract a vagrant crossed his mind before car door slammed shut. An instant later, tires slinging gravel peppered the building and he turned, running out the front door just as a blue sedan sped up the drive and out the gate. A trail of dust hovering behind made it impossible to identify the make or model, much less the license plate. Probably just kids, he consoled himself. The car well out of sight, he dismissed the notion of following and instead left for his appointment with Dr. Nowak.

San angled to the curb and waited for Linder to climb in. He was in a foul mood, the blue sedan adding to rather than answering his questions.

"What's taking you so long? Get in and let's get moving." He barked.

"What's your hurry? Last I heard, you had a lot of time on your hands." Linder eased into the seat.

San frowned. "Thanks, Linder, for reminding me. I don't like wasting time in any case. I have a lot of questions for old Nowak."

"You know what they say, 'He who hurries cannot walk with dignity'." Linder recited.

"What? Have you gone senile?"

"It's an old Chinese proverb."

Linder could see the tension on San's face. He glanced around the car for the chrome-plated pistol.

"Now don't start with your quotes. I've got to think. I was just at Mattie and Gert's and I scared up a two-legged rabbit in a blue sedan."

"You think it was kids looking for a place to smoke or a burglar? That house is out there all by itself." Linder tried to keep him talking, hoping it would ease his mind a little.

"It's hard to say. The thought of a transient crossed my mind. I can't rule out juveniles either. In my younger years, I would have taken out after him but I just let him go. I suppose I'm just..." He left the thought unfinished.

"What were you doing out there?"

"I needed to think before talking to the doctor. I thought seeing the aunts' place would help but I didn't expect to find an intruder. The apartment out back looked to have been searched and the door was open. It might have been the blue sedan or someone else."

9

"Maybe kids looking for spare change or something to pawn."

"It's possible. No way to know."

"Does being out there make you think of Mattie and Gert?" He wanted to keep the conversation going.

"Hell, Linder, what do you think?" He shot Linder an irritated glance.

"Alright, that was a stupid question, but there's nothing wrong with talking about them now and then."

"No, there's not." His voice softened. "But I need you to help me think through this talk we're going to have with the doctor. He says there was nothing out of the ordinary, even considering they died within a week of each other. How do we get him to reconsider?"

"What happens if he reconsiders? Are you going to have them disinterred to do an autopsy?"

"Hell, Linder, why don't you just get straight to the point? Besides, it's not that easy. Some of their friends might object. I don't want to upset these old folks without good reason. I'm just looking for something that makes sense. So far, nothing does."

"They were old and they died. That doesn't make sense?"

"Are you going to help or not?"

"Okay, I've spent a lot of time visiting sick people in hospitals and talking to doctors, so let me get the conversation started. Then you can jump in. We want to get a clear picture of how it went from a medical perspective." He paused to consider what he was about to say. "What are you going to say if he brings up the fact you are no longer in law enforcement?"

"Damn it, Linder, why would he bring that up? And for that matter, why did you?"

"Because you're sounding like a Ranger."

"That has nothing to do with my aunts and that's what I'll tell him."

"But it's not like you left the Rangers because you wanted to. He knows that."

"It's not his business, or yours either." He pulled into a small parking lot and stopped abruptly. "Let's go."

They walked to the low orange brick building and through the green metal door, stopping at the small receptionist's window. A young woman looked at San from behind the glass, impulsively tucked her dark hair behind one ear and slid the window open.

"We're here to see the doctor. He's expecting us." He figured she was barely out of her teens.

"Do you have an appointment?"

"Like I said, he's expecting us."

"Your name?"

"You won't find it on your calendar, but he knew we were coming by. The name is San Turner."

"I'm sorry, you need an appointment to see the doctor."

"What? Just tell him San Turner is ..." The phone rang before he could finish.

"Excuse me." She picked up the receiver.

"We don't have all day."

Linder walked up to the window just as she set the phone down.

"Hi Father Wertz, how are you?" She broke into a broad smile.

"Alright if I go on back, Jasmine?"

"Sure, Father, I'll tell him you're on your way."

Linder grabbed San by the elbow and pushed through the double doors.

"Friend of yours?"

"I see her in church every Sunday and I talk to a lot of doctors, like I said." They walked down a narrow hallway, painted an off-shade of purple. "Remember, let me get this started."

They entered a wide office framed by two large windows looking out on a small garden. Framed diplomas and certificates covered one wall, across from an

11

expensive-looking mahogany bookcase. Behind a broad oak desk sat Dr. Nowak, red-faced and frowning. His neck appeared several sizes larger than his collar, spilling over like an oversized muffin.

"Hello Alvin." Linder reached across to shake his hand.

"Father," he nodded, "we need to make this quick. What can I do for you?" He shifted awkwardly in his chair.

"I need you to tell me what in the hell is normal about two sisters, my aunts, dying within a week of each other." San blurted out.

"Pardon me?" The doctor turned a darker shade of red.

Linder gave San a cool glance. "What he is trying to say is that we're interested in your medical opinion of the cause of their deaths, in order to gain some closure. You know a sudden loss like that is quite a shock."

The doctor seemed to relax a bit. "I've already given my opinion. They got a virus that, because of their advanced age, resulted in their deaths due to complications. Severe dehydration is not uncommon in older adults and can be deadly at such an age. Unfortunately the one passed the virus to the other and it happened very quickly." He leaned back in his chair as if he had nothing more to say.

"I see…" Linder paused.

"That's it? That's all you've got to say? What virus was it? How do you know it was dehydration? Why wasn't an autopsy done?" San stepped toward the desk.

The doctor leaned forward and managed a stiff smile. "This sort of thing happens all the time with folks in their eighties. It's not standard practice to do an autopsy unless there's strong evidence supporting it. In this case, there was no such evidence." He placed his elbows on the desk. "And, I don't like it when someone questions my medical judgment, even an ex-lawman. Keep in mind you are no longer in the Rangers."

"I don't need you or anyone else to tell me what I am or what I'm not. It's none of your damn business."

"Alright." Linder placed a hand on San's shoulder. "San just wants to be sure he has done right by his aunts. Are there any other possibilities, from a medical standpoint, that might explain this?"

"Linder, I'm surprised at you. It's not like you to cause trouble." A white speck of spittle formed on the right corner of his lip. "I see nothing to suggest another medical cause. But going back to what you said earlier. It *is* a shock to lose two family members together like that." He faced San. "And if I remember right, you lost both your parents at the same time."

"I was not even a year old. I don't see the connection."

"And you also lost your wife a short while back, I understand, and your job. That's a lot to lose. Depression is a serious condition. It can interfere with our thinking, make us think something happens when it doesn't or doesn't happen when it does. It can significantly cloud our judgment. Not only that, it can make us distrustful," he paused, "or feel responsible for things that are not our business. Guilt is a powerful thing. It goes with the territory, but depression is nothing to be ashamed of." He gathered the papers on his desk and put them in his briefcase. "Gentlemen, I have an appointment with my stock broker, so I'll have to cut this short."

"You have to go?" Linder looked at him in surprise.

San took another step forward. "That's fine, we're done here. But you're wrong." He gestured with his index finger. "You're wrong about me, you're wrong about what happened and you're sure as hell wrong about my aunts. They were good people, none better, and you knew them for a long time. A man with any self-respect would want to know the truth about what happened to them. But you go on and count your money now. That's bound to be more important than any two old ladies." He turned and walked out.

"Good Lord, San!" Linder threw up his hands and followed.

Four

San

I started a journal after Janie was gone. I had always been clear-headed, but all of a sudden I couldn't think worth a damn. I knew I needed to do something. I figured that if I could get my thoughts of her out of my mind and onto paper, I might could think straight again. Gert taught me that. She said if you get the bothersome things out on the table, you can make some sense of them. And with all that had happened, I had a lot to sort through.

For a time, my mind would go round and round with the idea of Janie being gone, like some kind of wild polka. As crazy as it sounds, the house still felt like it always had, as if she was in the other room and might come around the corner any time. I'd find myself expecting her to call any moment, or I'd hear her voice somewhere just out of range. More than once, I thought I saw her in a crowd. It was almost like I'd forgotten the last few months. But, then the other part of me that knew better would step in. When that happened, I'd go into a dark humor and eventually my mind would just shut off. Sooner or later, I'd have to snap out of it and get on with whatever needed doing. I still have trouble thinking about her. My mind clouds up and I can hardly recall her face without looking at a photograph. That disturbs me more than I can say. So, I tried putting it down on paper.

When I was a young man I loved to read and for a time even fancied myself as a writer. Gert did her best to encourage me. As an English teacher, she took special care with that side of my education. Her love of books is probably what got me to thinking I wanted to write in the first place. That and the stories she and Mattie would tell about growing up on the old place, back when her father ranched the three hundred acres he owned, before he sold two hundred of them to send his two girls to teacher college.

At dinner, Gert would ask me what I was reading at school and really wanted to know what I thought of a book. Other times she'd go on and on about her favorite novels, hoping I'd decide to pick one up. More than once I did just that. So one day I decided to try my hand at writing, mostly to please her. With her encouragement, I put a lot of time and effort into the task but I didn't have the knack for it. Eventually, she stopped asking and I gave it up. In any event, I never had the patience for it though I knew my quitting disappointed her.

Gert and Mattie never married and, although you'd never know it from their gruff manner in the classroom, they had a soft spot for children. I figure they might have adopted if I hadn't come along. It wasn't the custom back then for unmarried women to adopt, but they were not the type to worry about custom, and were as likely to go their own way as not at any given time. When they set their mind to something, that was it. Starting the ranching operation after they retired raised a few eyebrows in the town, but they paid no mind to the comments and even went to a bank in Austin after the local bank turned down their loan for no good reason. And when some religious types wanted *Huckleberry Finn* removed from the library because they didn't like the language, Gert and Mattie worked day and night to fight it. That was the way they were.

I suppose a little of that independent streak rubbed off on me, maybe more than a little. After Janie passed on, I returned to work full time. While I was out, the office had hired a new man to replace my old boss, who had up and retired out of the blue. I had seniority and might have been up for the position under different circumstances, but it didn't work out that way. The new man was young and had big ideas about changing things. Before I knew it, we had locked horns on how to do this or that. My short temper didn't help. The final straw came when he stepped in and reassigned the younger officers I supervised without telling me. I had to hear it from them. I went straight to his office and cussed him good. I was fired later that same day for insubordination. He was looking for a reason to get rid of me and I gave it to him on a plate. Not real smart, not my finest hour, but there you have it. So, there I was with plenty of time to fish or play golf but instead for some reason I couldn't explain I started a journal.

I reckon a man needs to make sense of his life and all that happens, both good and bad. But I could find no understanding in a God that would allow the suffering and trouble I could see all around. There was a time when I was caring for Janie that I would ask God to make her well and bring her back to me. All I got for my trouble was nothing, not a word, not a feeling, not a sign, only silence. Silence like that has a weight to it, a heaviness that wears on you. Most people think there's nothing to it, just emptiness, but that's not true. That sort of silence fills the space around you, every inch and every hour, until there's no air left to breathe.

I could make no sense of what had happened to her, to us. Instead, day in and day out I was angry, damn angry and there's no future in that. So, after working on the journal for a time, I decided to do what I could in this world and let the rest go. But it wasn't that easy.

Five

Linder pondered the situation as he walked out of Dr. Nowak's office and on toward the car. The last time he had seen San this hot-headed they were young men. It wasn't like him. Normally he was cool and rational, as predictable as sunrise. But recently his temper would flare without warning and he'd do or say something that he regretted later. It was as if they had switched roles. Linder was now the moderating force. Although uncomfortable acting as the voice of reason, he could see no alternative. He tried to collect his thoughts.

He slid into the passenger seat and looked at his friend. "That went well."

"I hope you feel like a drink." San turned the ignition.

"Well, you haven't completely lost your mind. Where are we headed?"

"Curly's Cue." He turned onto the highway, heading north.

"I take that back, you have lost your mind. Why Curly's, of all places? I haven't been there in years."

"There's an old boy I need to talk to and I'll bet my salary he'll be there."

"You don't have a salary, remember?"

"Don't get nitpicky on me. I'm going to need your help with this."

"Who are you hoping to find?"

"The guy's name is Sammy Chuicotl. We call him Sammy Chico. He claims to be some kind of Mexican Indian, I can't remember the tribe. It doesn't matter. A lazy wet back is no different than a lazy Indian."

"You sound like a redneck." Linder frowned at him.

He had never understood how San could talk that way when his father had been born in Mexico. Maybe it was because the family had disowned San's father when he eloped with an American girl. After San's parents died, no one in that family would have anything to do with him except for his great grandmother. She came to visit him right up until she passed on. She was the only person that ever called him Santana.

San ignored him. "He's just this side of the law most of the time. Then again, he knows the other side and he hears a lot. He'll share it with you for a price, unless it's too dangerous to tell."

"Nice guy."

He looked over at Linder and continued. "A long time back, the sheriff's office was on the lookout for this guy that Sammy wouldn't touch. They called him Wyatt Earp because he had a thing for the old long-barreled .40 caliber pistols. Those cannons could kill an elephant but they were so unreliable you'd be more accurate throwing the thing than firing it.

"Old Wyatt had been in and out of prison, and when he was released he came straight here to find his girlfriend. First, he assaults his girlfriend's father at his store. Keep in mind he hadn't been out a week. Then, before the sheriff can find him, he beats up his step-father with his mother right there to make sure he gets it right. So, he's clearly going back to jail.

"I get involved by accident – that's another story – so I go ask Sammy where to find this guy. He looks at me and says he might as well shoot himself as tell me because it would amount to the same thing. He said the guy had the devil in him or some such Mayan mumbo-jumbo and he'd have nothing to do with finding him. I was annoyed by his attitude so I told him that we'd find this guy sooner or later and there's nothing to stop me from saying it was Sammy that turned him in. His face turned almost white. That's something for a Mexican Indian and told me how dangerous this guy really was.

"Finally, Wyatt goes to his girlfriend's house and assaults her brother pretty bad when the brother tries to protect her. Then he starts walking to his truck for the big pistol so he can finish the job. Not taking any chances, the girlfriend's mother pulls out a twelve gauge and shoots him before he reaches the truck. Shot him right in the back. It took him a week to die but they never filed charges on her. I reckon everyone was glad to be rid of him."

They pulled into a gravel parking lot and up to a faded yellow shack built on short wooden pilings, the sort used near the coast. It gave the impression the place might flood at any time. A red neon sign flashing the word "Lounge" was the only indication of activity inside the windowless building.

San pushed through the door. Linder followed, glancing back out the door and hoping no one had seen him go inside. Trying to avoid notice, he had taken off his clerical collar and put on a jacket to cover his black shirt. The room, dark and cool, no longer contained the single pool table that had given it a name. A thin layer of cigarette smoke hovered near the dingy ceiling. Several patrons sat at the bar and against the far wall, their faces lit by blue and red beer signs overhead.

San turned to him, speaking softly, "Sammy's at the far end of the bar. He's the one with the long hair. Our story is that your house was burglarized and I'm helping you out, trying to find out who might have done it."

They sat at the bar as a waitress came through a side-door carrying a tray of beers. She looked at them, turned and called back through the door, and a short figure with a thick beard stepped through the door, his face shaded by a greasy cap. His thick arms seemed unusually long for his size. He looked at them from under his cap for a moment.

"Don't I know you fellers?"

"Hello, Curley. My friend and I will have a beer."

"Any particular flavor? Wait a minute." He reached into the top pocket of his overalls, pulling out a pair of reading

19

glasses. "Why, San Turner, I didn't even recognize you. You haven't been in here in a dog's age."

"You got that right Curley. Things have happened since, that's for sure." He nodded toward Linder. "Remember my running-buddy, Linder Wertz?"

The man pulled at his gray beard. "Why, yes, you're the one that couldn't hold his liquor. I remember."

"What?" Linder frowned.

"That's right. I can't see so good anymore, but the memory's still working fine. You got plastered right here and made a pass at the waitress and half the women in the place. We were lucky to get you out with no trouble."

"I don't remember that." He turned to San.

"See, that means it really happened. If it hadn't, you'd remember." He patted Linder's shoulder.

"San, you haven't changed a bit, just older is all. You want the usual, I guess."

"You do have some kind of memory, Curley."

San turned away from Linder and stared down the bar. He tapped his finger on the dark wood and waited.

"What do you want, San?" Sammy Chico turned to face him.

"It is Sammy Chico, Linder. I thought it was but I wasn't sure."

He moved down the bar, next to San. "Like hell you weren't. Why are you here?"

"I just want to talk. Can't two old friends talk for a while?"

"We're not friends. Besides, I heard you're not a lawman anymore so what would we have to talk about?"

"My friend here had his home broken into and I'm just helping him out a little. It was a mid-sized blue sedan, unknown make or model."

"Why should I give you anything? You're just a person, like anyone else. You don't have no authority over me anymore."

20

San laughed. "Sammy, I didn't have any authority over you before either, except for those twenties I'd pass you under the table. You didn't seem to mind that, if I recall."

"Oh, you always had something on me you could use if you needed to. If I were a betting man, I'd say you have something in your back pocket even now. But I don't want your cash. I don't know nothing about no blue sedan or burglary."

San sipped his beer. "Sammy, you're not sounding like a friend. A friend wants to help. A friend wants to do the right thing." San tapped the bar with his index finger.

"Like I said, we're not friends. Besides, I don't know nothing about no blue car."

"Son, you need to adjust your attitude."

Linder was worried by the change in San's voice. "San, I believe him. Let's move on."

San held up his bottle and studied it. "Linder, do you know how many stitches a bottle like this can make if it's slammed against someone's face?" He turned to look at Sammy.

"San, I mean it. We don't want trouble." He glanced at Sammy. "Let's get out of here."

"These new bottles break real jagged. I saw one tear up a man so bad they couldn't piece his face back together. He never looked right again."

Sammy wiped a drop of sweat off his upper lip. "Okay, jefe, okay, you win."

Just then the front door burst open as if it had been kicked, and a thin man with a shaved head entered, quickly surveying the dim interior. He seemed to spot what he was looking for and walked briskly across the room to the far corner. Linder turned to watch.

"Get your skinny ass up, woman", the man yelled, "right now!" The loud slap of hand against skin followed. A woman fell to the floor.

"San, there's a kid." Linder grabbed his arm.

"Where?" San set down his bottle and turned.

The man kicked several times as the woman cowered beneath a table. Next to her crouched a young girl. San thought it strange that she made no sound. Then the man threw the table aside, grabbing the woman by the hair.

Before Linder had a chance to say more, San leapt from his seat, walking directly toward the man. Linder followed, looking for an alternative plan as the man, still holding the woman by her hair, bent towards the child. She hid behind a flimsy wooden chair, staring at him.

"What are you looking at, freak?" he said slowly. "I know you can't hear me but you know what I say. Your mom is going with me. You stay here."

"You leave her alone!" The woman screamed.

"Shut up bitch." He dropped her, turning his full attention to the girl.

"You heard the woman, leave the kid alone." San stepped behind the man.

The man turned to face him. "Stay out of this old man. It's not your business and you're likely to get yourself hurt."

"I'm not afraid of little girls." San smiled.

"A funny man."

"Or of overgrown juveniles who like to pick on them."

He reached out and took hold of San's collar. "You're not too smart, are you?"

Linder stood by, not knowing what to do. The man towered over San. Linder again looked for the waitress or bartender or any sign of a phone he could use, instead spotting Sammy Chico slinking out the side door. Wishing that he had brought along his cell phone, he studied San, now calm compared to a moment earlier.

The two men stood for a moment looking at each other. Then in one motion San lifted the man's hand from his collar, twisting counter-clockwise and causing him to lurch forward as he kicked him in the jaw and then used the same foot to knock the man's legs from beneath him. The man landed hard. Still holding his hand, San bent the man's thumb inward. He placed his other hand firmly behind the man's elbow.

"Now, you probably never finished high school but if you had you'd know that an elbow goes only one way. Sort of like the thumb." He twisted the man's hand slightly and he let out a yelp. "If you try to make it go the other way, it'll break sure as the sun rises. Now if I'm you I have to ask myself if I want an arm that works or one that is good for next to nothing." He leaned into the man's elbow.

"Let me go man. I didn't mean any harm." He grimaced. "What are you, some kind of cop?"

"Something like that. You need to leave these people alone. Do I make myself clear?"

"Nora, honey, I didn't mean it. It was just my bad temper getting to me again. You know I won't do it any more. Tell him, honey." He managed a twisted smile.

"She's not the only one you owe an apology."

"You mean the retard?"

San gave his arm another twist. "You need to learn some manners, son. That's no way to talk to your child."

The man cried out. "You'll break my thumb!"

"He's not her father. He just can't handle that she's deaf." The woman sat down and rubbed the bruises on her legs. "He doesn't bother her much. Mostly, he ignores her."

"Tell him to let me go. I'll leave and not come back. Tell him." The man pleaded.

"You can let him go now. He won't bother anyone."

"You can press charges. You have plenty of witnesses." San thought she looked to be in her late thirties or early forties, a good deal older than the man on the floor.

"No, I'd rather leave it be. He has a lot of problems of his own. He's not a bad man."

"Linder, call the sheriff. I'm not letting this one walk out of here. I'll press the charges myself."

23

"I already took care of it." Curley called from the bar. "I can't understand why they're not here already. Damn authorities, never around when you need them."

"Why do you have to press charges?" The woman walked to where San was standing. "I told you I want to leave it be. He's not a bad man."

"Where I come from, you treat people with respect, and there's no excuse for hitting a woman." He gave the man's hand another twist. "But, if he did anything to hurt your young one, I'd hunt him down myself", he smiled down at the man, "seeing as how we're friends and all now."

"Let him go." She grabbed San's arm.

"You can't mean it. You're going to let him treat your daughter that way and get away with it?" He shook off her grip.

"Let him go you son of a bitch!" She yelled. "You cops are all pig bastards!"

San studied her face. Her green eyes had flecks of blue and the determined look of a survivor. "Pig bastard? Now, that's a new one. Alright." He let go of the man's hand and stepped away.

"Come on, Dewey." She bent down to help him up, just as two deputies walked through the door.

"There he is over there." Curley pointed the officers to the man. "They may not press charges, but I will. This is the last time he gets to come in here and cause trouble and then get off free and clear. A man can't do business with that kind of nonsense going on. Get him out of here."

The deputies escorted the man out the door, followed by the young woman. The young girl sat in the corner, unmoving. Linder walked to her and sat down in the opposite chair. She studied him for a moment. Linder was surprised that she looked so different from her mother. She had straight black hair, braided into thick plats, and dark eyes. Although small, she appeared to be about ten or eleven.

24

"She's a pretty little girl, wouldn't you say so Linder?" San stood at Linder's back.

The girl smiled.

"She heard you, San."

"You mean she can hear after all?"

"She read your lips. She picks up a lot, considering how dark it is in here. My guess is she's pretty bright."

She got up and walked to San, taking his hand. He knelt, looking into her face, and she pressed his hand to her chest. San looked to Linder, his eyebrows raised.

"She's saying 'Thank you', San."

"I think you're right. How in the hell do you know that?"

"I just do. Talk to her, San."

San looked at her again. "Oh… well… I just happened to be here."

She looked up and past him, then ran towards the door where her mother stood. She turned and waved, and then they were gone.

"Linder, she had me tongue-tied before I had a chance to think. How do you like that?" He looked towards the door. "I would have liked to talk with her."

"Maybe you'll get the chance some day. Either way, you've made a friend."

"I guess that's one thing good we can take from this wasted day. Hell, Linder, I can't remember when I've spent more time and effort to find out not a damn thing. You're riding around with a cursed man. You know that don't you?" They walked through the door and on to the car.

"By this time, I think I know it."

"Don't get the wrong idea. I'm not through with this. I have another avenue to try. I'll tell you about it on the way to dinner."

"Dinner? But, I've already spent half the day on this wild goose chase."

"That's right, and now it's time for some eats. By the way, dinner's on you."

25

Six

Linder

When I was about twelve or so, Gert came to me and asked if I'd help her with a new student. She told me he was deaf. She said she would have asked San but he was never any good at helping people. He had no patience for it. Besides, he was preoccupied with football right then.

"I'm sorry to have to ask you, Linder, but I need someone to help and I think you're our best hope. This boy is smart, he's real smart. He's the top student in Mattie's math class and she's thinking of moving him into Algebra. That's two years ahead of where he should be. But he's having a tough time in English. I can see he's working hard, reading the assignments and doing the work. It's just that he doesn't understand what he reads, not completely anyway.

"I've been trying to get an interpreter for the deaf but they're next to impossible to find in a small town, out away from everything like we are. And his parents refuse to send him to the deaf school in Austin. He can read lips and he communicates using a little note pad he carries. I believe that with the right sort of assistance, he'll do fine. I know you'd be a big help to him."

I was more than a little flattered that she would come to me. No one ever asked me to do anything. In fact, it seemed no one ever noticed me at all. I was no good at sports. I was a fair student when I put my mind to it, but there were plenty of good students and even some outstanding ones she could have asked. My mother never took much interest in school and almost never talked to the teachers. Working nights and sleeping most of the day six days a week didn't leave her much time or energy for anything after work but a bottle of Scotch and the television.

So, getting asked to help do something important was an entirely new experience for me. I was still puzzled as to why Gert chose me. Plenty of others would do anything for her. We all loved Gert, although we were a little afraid of her too. She had a serious quality about her that would get your attention, especially when she got that certain look on her face. She passed that quality on to San. You could see it clear as day. Gert must have sensed my surprise, because she made a point of giving me her opinion.

"You know, Linder, there are a number of students I could ask to help with this. They understand the material well enough. But I'm asking you because you have something they don't. You have the heart for it. You see someone in trouble and you have to do something. You can't help yourself. It's a part of who you are. I wish San had more of it but he's not made that way. So, I'm asking you because I know you'll do a good job and won't settle for anything less."

No one had ever talked to me like that, not my mom or any other teacher, not anyone. It was like she had opened a door to a mirror and said 'Take a look Linder. This is who you really are'. The world all of a sudden seemed very different.

It turned out that Willy Bishop – I called him Billy Wishop for fun – was as smart as Gert said. He could run circles around all of us in the math department. But his parents were also deaf and used sign language at home to talk to each other. Sign language is different enough from written language that Willy had fallen behind in English class. He had learned to read lips at school because he could hear some when he was younger, but ear infections eventually caused him to lose what little hearing he had. He had been able to get by in school because of his lip-reading ability. Otherwise, he would have had no choice but to attend school in Austin.

Willy and I worked out a system that included lip reading and a sort of short-hand note system not unlike the texting kids do with their cell phones these days. By the end of the year, he had improved noticeably in all his classes. We had become good friends as well.

Oddly enough, his father got a job at the deaf school in Austin, so they had to move at the end of the school year and Willy ended up attending school there after all. I was sorry to see him go. We had a lot in common and he even talked me into teaching him to shoot with a bow. Knowing Willy had given me both a friend and a sense that I was good at something. Before then, I didn't think I could do much of anything very well.

Later that summer I was moping around feeling sorry for myself and San asked me what was wrong. I did my best to explain and he surprised me by saying he always knew I had a knack for making people feel welcome and understood, even those that are 'a little odd', as he put it. I took it as a compliment and our friendship seemed to change at that point. San was who he was and I was who I was, and we both understood that.

Seven

Linder waited by the car while San returned to ask Curley a question. He had declined to accompany San, instead taking the opportunity to consider the situation. Just as he feared, San's anger had come uncomfortably close to creating a real problem. If not for the diversion of the woman and her child, there was no telling what he might have done.

Linder had nearly always become confused and agitated when a situation became a problem. He never knew quite what to do until it was over. Contemplative by nature, he was accustomed to long hours reading professional journals or researching the particulars of an illness before visiting a church member in the hospital. He preferred to be prepared and would avoid entering into an unknown situation if at all possible. On the other hand, San had no qualms about taking action whenever necessary. In fact, he now seemed to have a renewed energy in spite of his dead-end talk with Sammy Chico. Linder could see it in his faced as he trotted towards the car.

"How about some barbeque, Linder? I could eat a whole pig right now, tail and all."

"You're sure happy about something. I can't imagine what, considering that big guy could have put an old man like you in the hospital."

"Big Jim's brisket would do just fine. That okay with you?"

He was accustomed to San ignoring comments he didn't like and decided to let it go. "Fine, San. What did Curley have to say?"

"We'll talk about all that in a minute. I need to ask you a question."

"Okay if I don't answer it?" He replied, annoyed at the way San controlled conversations.

"Earlier, you said Gert's and Mattie's house may attract transients because it's way out there by itself. I got to thinking that it might be a good idea to have somebody live there so there's less chance of vandalism or vagrants moving in. It's one way to keep an eye on it, assuming the people living there can be trusted."

"Was there a question in there?"

"Now don't get all ornery on me, Linder."

They pulled up to a low red building with a corrugated tin roof, the entire left side a screened-in room with a gravel floor and picnic tables arranged in two short rows. Beer ads and high school football schedules covered the walls here and there below an assortment of stuffed animal heads, mostly deer. A dusty bobcat stood in one corner. They ordered and sat at a rust-colored wooden table scattered with grease stains and carved initials.

San picked up a sauce-covered rib and looked across the table at Linder. "How about you tell me if you know anyone that lives up around Baby Head Mountain."

"I thought you wanted to talk about renting the house." Linder paused and then continued. "There are a number of things to consider, like whether you want to be a landlord, how you'll arrange the lease, what you'll charge for rent, those sorts of things."

"I thought you wanted to hear what I found out from Curley." He smiled. "Linder, do you always make your meal-time conversation this boring?" He held up his hands. "Don't answer that. Alright, professor, tell me what you think I should do with the house."

"San, you've entered a new period in your life."

"I'm already sorry I asked."

"Seriously, a lot has happened. Things are different now and you have a lot more choices that you used to. That means freedom to do things differently but it also means deciding how you're going to do things, what's worth doing and how you want to spend your time. People need to spend their time on what's meaningful to them."

"Hell, Linder, you sure like making things as complicated as possible. Can you just give a simple answer to a simple question?"

"I'm just saying to give it some serious thought. For instance, you could sell the house. Or you could sell your house and move there. Or, of course, you could rent it. It's yours to handle however you like. Now that I think about it, a change like that might even be good for you."

"I reckon the answer is no, you can't give a simple answer."

"Yes I can. I think it's a good idea to have someone living there."

"Thank you, Lord. Now eat your brisket and listen up."

"No problem there."

"I went back in to talk to Curley because I thought he might've heard something useful. Bartenders tend to overhear a lot if they have a mind to, and I know Curley likes to know what's up with his customers." He leaned forward. "So, he tells me that he heard talk of a blue sedan over near Cherokee, near Baby Head mountain, and that lying Sammy Chico is the one he heard talking about it. Sammy was talking on his phone so Curley couldn't hear much else but he was sure about the car."

"So, you want to go snoop around over there?"

"I thought you might know someone we could go pay a social visit to, see if they know anything useful."

"I do know a widow by the name of Doris Shuerman but she must be near ninety by now and wouldn't be much help."

"Just let me be the judge of that." He snapped back.

"But San, it'd be a waste of time."

"Can she talk?"

"Yes, her mind is sharp as a tack but that's not the problem."

31

"Linder, just because I'm no longer in the law enforcement business doesn't mean I've forgotten how to talk to people. That's enough hobnobbing, let's go." He stood and began walking towards the door. "Don't forget to pay on your way out."

They drove the crushed granite county road that skirted Baby Head Mountain, throwing up a cloud of reddish dust that hovered briefly and then disappeared on the light fall breeze. Just past a low water crossing, a green and white house came into view at the top of a broad meadow. To the right, several out-buildings hugged the steep hillside just beyond a small orchard of peach and pear trees, their leaves intensely yellow in the bright sun. San drove through the gate and parked in the shade of a sprawling live oak. He noticed the garage was open and there was no car in view.

A wide porch stretched across the front and around one side of the compact house, casting the tall windows in deep shadow, its broad set of stairs bordered by thick columns that marked the beginning and end of the porch rail. San noticed the roof held octagonal slate tiles he had seen only once before on a turn-of-the-century home near Pontotoc. The owner, an old German farmer, had shot his son-in-law for selling a family heirloom.

San was out of the car and up the steps before Linder had unbuckled his seat belt. He hurried to catch up, arriving at the front door just as San finished ringing the doorbell.

"She must be old. I've had to ring the bell twice."

"Well San, it's likely to take her a minute. She's not one to hurry, in any case."

Just then the door opened and a small voice came from behind the screen door. "Yes, can I help you?"

"Hello Doris, it's Linder Wertz. I've come for a visit."

"Why Father, it's so good to see you. Please come in. Can I offer you some coffee?"

"No, thank you, we won't take much of your time."

Linder opened the door and they stepped into a small portico that opened onto a large living room. The curtains were drawn, making the room unusually dark for the time of day. Off to one side and obscured by the deep shadows, a small, bird-like woman waited with her hand slightly outstretched. Linder took her hand and gently shook it, and then helped her settle into a nearby chair. San had already seated himself on the couch. Linder pulled a chair up next to her and leaned forward.

"I've brought a friend with me, Doris. His name is San Turner."

"San Turner? Could you be Gertrude's and Madeline's boy?" She sat up straight in her chair.

"It's been a long time since I thought of myself as a youngster, but I'm the one."

"I was so distraught at their passing. We had known each other our whole lives, you know. They were good people, finest kind."

"Thank you for saying so. In a way, they're why I'm here." San had trouble seeing her clearly in the dim light. "Someone recently broke into their house and I'm hoping to find who that might have been. I'm looking for a blue sedan. I believe the owner may live around here."

"I see. Oh, I remember now. You are an officer of the law." She frowned. "But how can I possibly help you?"

San avoided correcting her and continued. "If you have seen that blue sedan, it would be very helpful to know where and when."

She turned to Linder. "Why, Linder, you know I've been blind as a post for years."

San jumped up. He looked from Linder to the woman and back. "Well, I do apologize, Mrs. Shuerman. I have a habit of getting an idea in my mind and then going after it without thinking it through. You can ask Linder about that. I'm the one that dragged him up here to waste your time." He started toward the door.

"It may not be a waste of time after all." She put her hands together in thought. "When you lose your sight your mind makes up for it to some extent. My hearing, my intuition and my memory are what I rely on nowadays, and I believe I may have something for you."

"I would appreciate any help you can offer." San remained standing.

"After Gertrude and Madeline passed, a young man who knew them came by to call. He said he had worked for them and they had mentioned me once or twice as a friend who had lost her sight. He wondered if I might need a boarder who could help around the house in lieu of rent." She held up a bony finger. "Now, in visiting with him I'm sure he said he had a blue car, a four door. I'm sorry, he never mentioned the make. He said he was looking for a place to live around this area because he hoped to get a part-time job at the children's home over in Cherokee."

San sat back down and leaned toward her. "Yes 'mam, that is very helpful. Did he say anything else that you can recall? Even ordinary comments can sometimes be useful."

"Well, the more I talked with him, the more uncomfortable I became. My sense was that he was after more than just an inexpensive living arrangement. He played up to me just like a traveling salesman and I've never tolerated the hard sell.

"It wasn't just that. I sensed some violence about him, a cowardly type of violence, but violence just the same." She put her hands to her face. "I just couldn't see how Gertrude and Madeline could have been very safe with a man like that nearby."

"Doris, what became of him?" Linder looked across at San.

"You may think I'm a little bit crazy, and maybe I am, but when I realized what I was dealing with I ushered him out of here but quick. He gave me the jitters although I never let on to him." She smiled.

San stood again. "Well, I appreciate your help Mrs. Shuerman."

"Please sit down, son. And call me Doris."

San looked at Linder in question. "We've bothered you enough today. We should be moving on."

"I have something else for you if you'll have a seat."

"Alright." San puzzled at how she could tell he was standing. He settled back into the chair and waited.

"I mentioned earlier that my hearing helps me where my sight does not. What I didn't tell you is that my husband was a mechanic for thirty years. His auto repair shop was in the buildings out back of the house." She pointed over her shoulder. "I've always had a naturally curious mind, so I asked a lot of questions and learned a good deal about the way cars work and how to go about diagnosing a problem. It's not unlike diagnosing an illness, so it's a process of ruling in or out possibilities." San shifted in his seat and she chuckled. "Don't worry, Mr. Turner. I have a point and I'll get to it soon."

"Yes 'mam." San looked at Linder and shook his head.

"When a car's transmission is on the way out, it will make a high-pitched whine as it tries to shift from one gear to the next. That's the first thing I heard when the young man came around the curve, just past the low water crossing. Based on the type of sound, I'd say it's a General Motors vehicle, probably a Chevrolet between fifteen and twenty years old. So, that car will end up in a repair shop soon, if it hasn't already. Now, how do you like them apples?" She let out a laugh and slapped her knee.

"Doris, I can see why you and my aunts were friends. They always appreciated a sharp mind and a good laugh. That will help, no doubt. I appreciate it."

"You can go on now if you need to, although I've enjoyed talking with you."

"I've taken up too much of Linder's time for one day so we'd better be going."

She stood and turned to Linder, holding out her hand. "Linder, please try to come back for coffee sometime when we can have a good visit."

"I'll do that, Doris."

"Mr. Turner, it has been a pleasure."

"Same for me. Please call me San." He shook her hand.

"I hope to see you again. Let me know if I can be of assistance any time." She waved as they went out the door.

After they were out of sight of the house, San stopped the car and gave Linder a long look. "I bet you had yourself a good laugh watching me stick my foot in my mouth back there."

"I tried to tell you."

"You never told me she's blind."

"You never gave me a chance. You yourself said when you get an idea you pursue it without thinking."

"Oh, that was just talk so she wouldn't be offended." He waved off the thought.

"Oh, is that what it was?"

"Never mind, I need you to help me with one more thing."

"I heard you had wasted enough of my time."

"The time hasn't been wasted. But I need to put an ad about renting the house in tomorrow's newspaper. We'll need to hurry."

"So, you've decided to rent the place?" Linder was surprised he had made a decision so quickly.

"Not exactly. I'm going to rent the house and live out back. That way I can keep a close eye on things and take care of whatever needs fixing. Plus, I need the income. Otherwise, I'll have to go out looking for work. We retirees don't like that thought." He turned to look at Linder. "You gave me the idea so I guess I should thank you."

"Not at all, I'm glad I could help."

"I didn't say I *did* thank you, I said I *should* thank you. I'm still thinking on it." He chuckled.

"Well, you're welcome anyway. And, you're not retired. You got fired, remember?"

"With you reminding me every other day, there's no way I'm going to forget. By the way, what time do you want me to pick you up tomorrow?

"Some of us don't have rentals to bring in money and so we have to work."

"That's no problem. I'll pick you up after work. We need to check out auto repair shops, the sooner the better."

"San, I have other responsibilities." he countered.

"Nothing this important. You'll have plenty of time to do boring stuff later."

"What I do is not boring."

"So, I'll pick you up at five sharp." He pulled to the curb.

"I thought you wanted me to help you place the ad." Linder got out and closed the car door.

"You're too busy, remember? Don't work too hard, Linder." He called out the window as he left.

Eight

San bought a newspaper and drove to his aunts' house. He barely had time to check the ad before wheels sounded on the gravel driveway and a car door opened and closed. He surveyed the living room where he had spent much of his boyhood. He had moved the more valuable furniture to the garage, replacing it with the sturdy but plain furniture Gert and Mattie had originally purchased to outfit the guest quarters. He planned to use what he needed to furnish the apartment once he got around to moving in. He had not realized the process would move so quickly.

What would Gert and Mattie have thought of renting, he wondered? They loved the house and had always lived there, yet they did have lodgers in their later years. Frugal to a fault, he decided they would approve, especially considering his current financial situation. He was determined to find a renter that would take proper care of the place inside and out.

As he took one more look around, his eyes fell on the wide limestone fireplace, heavily blackened by years of use. Suddenly, a Christmas day came back to him in vivid detail. A blue norther had blown in the night before and the brisk wind howled off and on in the flue. He had awakened to the sound of a truck and trailer. Just as he was slipping on his boots, Mattie appeared in his doorway, motioning him to follow without a word and then stopping him in front of the fireplace, bright with a roaring fire.

"Warm yourself up now, honey. It's cold out." She squeezed his shoulder. She left before he had a chance to ask any questions.

A moment later, Gert called for him to come to the kitchen. She and Mattie stood at the back door. "Come along now, San. It's Christmas you know."

"Of course I know it's Christmas. What are y'all up to?"

They both smiled and motioned him out the door, where standing on the gravel drive was a young horse, a chestnut-colored Bay with four black socks tethered to the trailer with a bright red halter. A man San recognized as Mr. Weisenhunt, a distant neighbor, stood by.

"Well, go on, it's yours." Gert nudged him out the door.

A knock at the door pulled him from the memory. He opened the door to a woman with reddish-brown hair. Although obscured by the rusted screen, her face looked vaguely familiar. He pushed open the door.

"You." It was all he could say. Before him stood the woman from Curley's place.

"You've got to be kidding me." She turned and walked down the steps as if to leave and then turned around again. "Look, I'm sorry about the way I acted at Curley's. I've had trouble before with the police, very bad trouble. It was a long time ago, but I haven't forgotten it."

A flash of anger crossed her face, and then she dropped her head. She looked as if she might cry. "The truth is, I've been thrown out of my place. My boyfriend got into it with the landlord...again. I need a place to live right away or my little girl and I will be on the street. You can't imagine how frightening that is. Will you consider renting to us, please?"

San stood in the doorway without responding. She looked up at him for a moment and then turned to leave. He watched her walk toward the car, opening the door before turning back towards him, her eyes wide.

"My daughter's not here!" She yelled. "She was with me but she's not in the car."

She began running around the side of the house. San could see that the rear car door was open. He hurried around the other side of the house, meeting up with the woman at the back porch. Checking the guest quarters they found the door still locked, the girl nowhere in sight.

San turned to her. "What's your daughter's name?"

"It's Nina."

"Nina." He repeated. "Well, she's around somewhere. Let's split up. I'll go up the hill. You head down the driveway. It wouldn't be good for her to get near that highway."

"Nina!" San called out.

"She's deaf, remember?" The woman called over her shoulder.

"Right. I knew that." He shook his head.

San circled around the garage and past the neglected stables, the weathered wood a rich gray in the bright sunlight. He thought of his horse again. She had been an even-tempered yearling filly, and they later bred her. He raised the foal from birth and kept them both until he left for college. Somehow, it seemed only a short time ago.

Something up the hill caught his eye. He could see the girl near a herd of cattle that stood just across the fence line. They had stopped grazing and were facing her attentively as she slowly walked towards them. A bull nearby snorted noisily and stomped the ground, kicking up a cloud of dust. It wouldn't do to aggravate him, San thought, fence or no fence. He trotted up the hill, keeping a close eye on the agitated bull. The girl noticed him and turned, smiling broadly. He motioned for her to stop.

"We don't want that bull to get too nervous. He might forget there's a fence." He made sure she could clearly see his face.

She stepped back and walked to him, taking his hand before he realized what she was doing. They stood watching the cattle, who soon returned to grazing the tall blonde grass. The girl was mesmerized. After a moment, San tugged at her hand and she looked up at him.

"Your mom is worried about you. We had better go find her."

She nodded but held tight to his hand as they walked down the hill and past the garage and stables. It was an odd but pleasant feeling to hold a child's hand, he thought.

They rounded the front of the house just as the woman came walking up the drive. The girl released his hand and ran to meet her.

"Where was she?" The woman bent down to face the girl. "You scare me when you go off like that without letting me know. Please don't do it again." She looked up at San. "I think she likes it here."

"She was having a visit with the cows across the fence." He gestured up the hill.

"She has always liked animals but we've never lived where we could have any. It's hard to find a place that will allow it."

"Raising an animal is a good way for a youngster to learn responsibility."

"Well, we need to get going if we're going to find a place to live. Otherwise, we'll be sleeping in the car." She winced.

San looked back at the house and then faced the girl. "Nina, would you like to live here?"

She turned to her mother and signed frantically. The woman smiled and silently responded.

The girl looked at San and nodded.

"Well Nina, I guess we're going to be neighbors." He looked at the woman. "That is, as long as your tall friend with the bad manners doesn't ever show his face around here."

"Don't worry about that. He and I are done for good. Did you say we're going to be neighbors? Where do you live?" The woman surveyed the surrounding area, no house in sight.

"I have a house in town but I'm planning to sell it and move into the guest quarters out back." He nodded in the direction of the garage. "This house has been in my family for three generations. My grandfather built it. I plan to see that it is well taken care of."

Hearing himself talk, San realized for the first time the importance the old house held for him. He had always taken the place for granted.

"Oh." She tried to hide her misgivings.

"Don't worry. I'll keep my nose out of your business. My only concern is that the house is cared for properly. Will that be a problem?"

"Oh, no." She held up both hands. "We'll take good care of it. We'll treat it as if it belonged to us."

"It's a might big for just two, but it's a small house by most standards. My aunts lived here, just the two of them, for a good many years once I was out of the house and it suited them fine. Will you be able to manage the rent?"

"I work at an insurance company in town. We should manage alright."

"Would you like to take a look before you make up your mind?"

"What am I thinking? Of course I want to see it." She laughed. "I've been so worried about what would happen to us if we couldn't find a place. I haven't been able to think straight all day. I've never been evicted and it's a shock, I can tell you."

"I'll show you around then." He gestured towards the steps. "I just realized I don't know your name."

"It's Nora O'Quinn. Please call me Nora."

"Nina and Nora." He mused. "Just call me San. Where are y'all from?"

"A little town way up near the Panhandle called Quanah. It's almost in Oklahoma. Ever hear of it?" She signaled for Nina to sit quietly.

"I can't say that I have, and I've seen a lot of this state." They went inside and slowly walked through the house. "What brought you to this part of the world?"

She stopped and looked at him for a moment. "I guess it won't hurt to say since you've already seen Dewey in action." She took a deep breath. "I had to get as far away from Quanah as I could. An ex-boyfriend broke my jaw

42

with a baseball bat. It wasn't the first time he hit me but it was the last. I finally decided I wouldn't let him do that ever again, so I left for good. I had to sneak out in the middle of the night."

"That sounds serious."

"I'm no good at picking men, I guess you could say."

"You could say that. It can be hard on a child."

"Nina was away when it happened. Thank the Lord."

"I don't see much to thank the Lord or anyone else for when you're lying in a hospital bed."

Her eyes widened. "You don't often hear people around here talk like that."

"You're right, that was wrong of me. I have no business bringing up religion when you're trying to decide whether or not to rent the house. It's a bad practice. Maybe the house isn't what you're looking for."

"Oh no, I hope I didn't say anything wrong. Please, we do want to move in." She sounded alarmed. "I hope we can bring our things over today. We don't have much of anything, really. Would that be okay?"

"That's no problem. We'll settle up after you and Nina have a chance to get yourselves situated." He stopped and turned to her. "One more thing. I won't be a bother to you and I expect the same. I'm used to my privacy and I want to keep it that way."

"Oh, you won't even know we're here."

He pulled a key from his coat pocket. "I have something I need to take care of this evening so here's your key. I'll check in with you tomorrow afternoon."

"Thank you so much, San."

"You don't have to thank me. It's a fair arrangement and I'm counting on you to take good care of the old place. Let me know if there's anything you need."

He watched them drive away and wondered how this new situation would work out. Having had no children of his own, he scarcely knew how to act when around them. They were a puzzle and Nina's deafness only added to the mystery. Not only that, her mother seemed to repeatedly get herself into bad situations with men, situations that could prove dangerous to both her and Nina. He could not understand being careless with a child's safety and had no toleration for it.

Yet, in spite of his misgivings he had offered to let them stay. It was not like him to trust anyone so easily, especially a stranger, and he was at a loss to explain it. Maybe Linder was right and he was ready for a change. He looked down at his watch and realized he had little time left to finish preparing the house before he had to pick up Linder. They would have to move quickly in order to check all the auto repair shops in the area before they closed up for the night. He went straight to work.

Nine

San and Linder sat outside Pinkie's Auto Repair and Ranch Supply. The auto shop doubled as a feed store when there was a need. A grove of tall pecan trees, their leaves an intense yellow in the afternoon glow, surrounded the wide brick and rusted metal building. Linder studied the design. The arched doorway and stone lintels of the original brickwork gave the structure an odd and incongruous respectability. The metal addition had come as an afterthought, no doubt, probably much later.

Linder watched the owner, a large man in green coveralls, carry several fifty pound bags of cow pellets to a white pickup parked next to the loading dock. He held the bags on his shoulder as if filled with goose down. Pinkie came by his name rightly. His meaty face was a bright shade of pink, his nose and ears nearly purple.

San went over his notes in silence, scratching off every auto shop on his list except for this one. They had yet to find anyone who recalled seeing, much less working on, a blue sedan. A sense of futility began to creep into his consciousness.

"Well, let's go see what Pinkie has to say." San said listlessly.

"Something will turn up sooner or later. I believe Doris knows what she's talking about, San." Linder opened the car door.

San considered the comment for a moment. "I would not underestimate her, no sir."

They pushed through a metal shop door and found Pinkie standing behind a grimy counter littered with crumpled and coffee-stained receipts. Out-dated calendars featuring shapely women in low-cut coveralls covered the wall behind the counter. Pinkie punched at a dingy calculator with one finger, deep in concentration.

"We won't take up much of your time." San declared. "We're looking for a blue sedan, probably a Chevy with a bad transmission. Have you had one in?"

The big man continued to punch the calculator for a moment and then looked up. "A blue Chevy sedan? Are you a cop or something?"

"More like something." San leaned over the counter. "This is not, I repeat not, a social call. We're trying to locate the owner of a blue sedan that needs transmission work." He spoke very slowly. "Have you seen the car?"

"Why do you want to know?" Pinkie stood back and folded his arms.

"Look here, son." San blurted.

Linder stepped to the counter. "The car was seen leaving his mother's house." He nodded toward San. "Someone, maybe the owner of the car, broke into the house. Nothing was taken so the sheriff is not interested."

"Why didn't you say so in the first place?" He glared at San. "We haven't had the car in here. But I saw a car like that pulled over by that lady deputy day before yesterday over near Baby Head Mountain."

"Did it look liked he was being ticketed?" San asked.

"The deputy was writing something so I think it's likely."

"Alright Linder, we'd better go." San turned. "We appreciate your help." He called over his shoulder.

Linder shook the man's hand and placed a business card on the counter. "If that car should come in for some work, will you give me a call?"

"No problem." He looked at the card. "What are you going to do now? That new sheriff was in the other day looking for an ex-mechanic of mine and he's a piece of work. Getting anything out of him will be a trick."

"That's good to know. Thanks."

46

Linder walked towards the car, studying San as he sat huddled over his notes, deep in concentration. He seemed a bit more relaxed with something to occupy his mind. Linder worried what would happen when they reached a dead end, as they surely would sooner or later. He opened the door and slid into the seat.

"I believe a deputy I know works this shift. We'll head over to the sheriff's office to see what she knows." San set the notes on the seat and turned the key.

"How far are you going to take this search of yours?"

"As far as it goes." He frowned. "Linder, are you wanting to quit already?"

"No, but there other things to attend to. For instance, what did you decide to do about renting the house?"

"You're not going to believe this. I just rented it to that woman from Curley's place."

"You mean the woman with the skin-head boyfriend? I don't believe it, San. You're too hard-nosed to tolerate anything as messy as that."

"I said you wouldn't believe it. I was right." He turned onto the highway.

"How could that happen? It's hard to imagine." He shook his head and then looked up. "Wait. Did her little daughter have anything to do with it?"

"Do you really think I'd rent that house to someone who won't take care of it?"

"Was the girl with her mother?"

"She was there. Her name is Nina. Her mother's name is Nora. They got evicted thanks to the boyfriend."

"San, you do have a heart after all." He slapped his leg.

"Hell Linder, she needs a place and I need a renter. It's as simple as that."

"Yeah, well, whatever you say, San."

San pulled into the gravel lot surrounding the county court house. Except for several corner windows on the second-floor, the building was dark. To the right, the stone clock tower glowed a dusky ochre in the fading light of

47

dusk. Teenagers milled outside the shops lining the town square, waiting for the small movie theater to open.

Linder followed San to the side of the court house and down a steep flight of stairs to the basement entrance. A gray metal door led to a dimly lighted hallway that wound through a maze of offices. San waved a greeting to a juvenile probation officer still at her desk. They came to another set of stairs and climbed the three flights to the second floor sheriff's office, where a young deputy sat in a room full of desks arranged back to back. She looked up and smiled.

"Look what the cat dragged in. San Turner, I thought you had better things to do than hang around the court house after hours. Are you just bored or did you come to meet our new sheriff?"

"I seem to recall hearing something about a new man. But seeing as how no one can replace Weldon Jung, I have a hard time working up any interest in the subject." He grinned. "Besides, I came here to see you Jules, and here you are.

"Here I am, alright."

"Now Linder here, he bet me a beer that you'd be down at Rosie's drinking coffee and eating sopapillas. He claims you can't stay away from Rosie's sopapillas."

"He did, did he?" She looked at Linder and smiled.

He thought she looked familiar but was unable to place her face. Her broad forehead and dark, slightly upturned eyes gave way to a slim, no-nonsense mouth in spite of her smile. She gave Linder the impression she could go from a belly laugh to deadly serious in a split second, her good looks notwithstanding.

"Nice to meet you." He nodded at San but continued facing her. "See what I have to put up with? Try not to encourage him and maybe he'll go away."

"You're just mad that you owe me a beer."

"Tell the nice deputy why you're here, San."

"It was your idea, why don't you tell her?"

48

"My idea?" He looked from her to San and back. "Okay, we're trying to locate the owner of a blue sedan, probably a Chevy. The car was seen speeding off from the house San's aunts lived in and we'd like to know why. Pinkie, the mechanic, told us he saw you stop a car like that over near Cherokee."

"I'm not in the habit of giving out information to just anyone but I'll make an exception for you Linder, in spite of being a friend of our man San. Just don't tell the sheriff. He's a straight by the book man if there ever was one.

"It was last week some time. He was a young guy I didn't recognize in a beat up Chevy. I jotted down his license plate to run it through a check but I didn't ticket him."

"Why did you stop him?" Linder sat down across from her.

"I was behind him and he swerved onto the shoulder a couple of times so I pulled him over. He said a bee flew through the window and he was trying to get rid of it without getting stung. Once I got a look at him and heard his story, he seemed so pitiful I sent him on his way." She smiled. "You have a nice face, Linder, a kind face."

"Was there anything memorable about him?" Linder smiled back.

"Nothing other than he could talk a good game, in a pitiful sort of way. He'd make you feel sorry for him in a heartbeat if you let him but I think it was all for show. He didn't want a ticket." She looked to San. "Sorry I can't give you more, San."

"Maybe I could look through the reports from the other deputies while you and Linder talk archery." He turned to Linder. "Jules has taken up archery. Someone told her it'll improve her accuracy with a pistol. I don't believe it myself but I'm old school when it comes to firearms."

"You're old, that's for sure." Linder winked at Jules.

49

"I'd like to hear your thoughts, Linder. But I don't know about those records, San. Sheriff Wilder is strict about protocol."

"The sheriff doesn't need to know."

The door opened and a tall, heavy man walked into the room dressed in a brown business suit. His belly partially hid a belt buckle the size of a small plate, and his pock-marked face held no expression. He looked over the room as if there was no one in it, ignoring San and Linder. His eyes eventually focused on Jules.

"Are you in the habit of having parties on the county's time, deputy?"

"No sir, Sheriff Wilder. Mr. Turner was asking if I'd seen a car that was poking around his aunts' house. I wasn't able to be of assistance."

"We don't have time for social calls." He turned to San. "Mr. Turner, we haven't met but I've heard plenty." He didn't offer his hand. "If you have a question, you can direct it to me. I'll thank you to leave my deputies alone."

"Alright." San stood. "My elderly aunts died within a week of each other and I don't think it was a coincidence. I want to know what you're going to do about it."

"Unless you have evidence to the contrary, they died of natural causes and you're wasting my time. I know all about your misguided theories. This isn't the first one, as I understand it. Now, unless you have some new information, I'm a busy man." He turned to leave.

"I don't like your attitude." San started after him.

"File a complaint. Nobody will listen." he called back as he left the room.

Linder stood and stepped in front of San. "Let it go, San. You're not helping yourself by arguing with him."

"Hell, he won't listen anyway. Let's get out of here." He walked out the door.

Linder turned to Jules. "I'm sorry. We didn't mean to cause you any trouble."

"It won't amount to anything. Tell San not to worry." She paused. "I'd like it if you'd give me some archery pointers sometime. I heard you were once a crack shot."

"I wouldn't be much help. I haven't touched a bow in thirty years." He looked at his hands.

"It's just like riding a bike...and sex." She smiled. "I read all about it. It'll come back to you in no time. Anyway, you know way more than I do even if you haven't been practicing."

He looked toward the door, feeling his face redden. "I'd better get going."

"I'm off tomorrow, how about meeting at the range about four-thirty?"

"Don't get your hopes up."

"Great, I'll see you then."

Linder turned and made his way out of the building.

Ten

San watched Linder emerge from the basement stairs in the dull glow of the court house lamps. It had grown colder and shadows now seemed to lunge here and there before a brisk wind. In the distance, the faint flash of lightning outlined the treetops.

He was at a loss as to what to do next. He wanted to continue but could see no ready options, and the hope that the blue sedan had held appeared to have vanished. He felt trapped. The feeling that he had somehow failed Gert and Mattie returned, and a bitter taste caught in the back of his throat. For a moment, he thought he might get sick.

Linder climbed in and closed the door, whistling between his teeth and rubbing his hands. He looked up through the window at the trees rattling overhead.

"That wind has a bite to it." He knocked on the glass with his knuckle. "And those pecan trees are really taking a beating. I wish we'd get some rain out of this."

"I apologize for wasting your time, Linder." San stared into the darkness. "I hoped there might be something to that blue car but it was a rabbit trail just like you said. I'm fresh out of ideas." He rubbed his forehead. "I can't stand the idea of quitting on Gert and Mattie."

Linder looked at his friend for a moment. "Let me buy you a beer, San and let's talk it over."

"No, I've wasted enough of your time." His voice was slightly more than a whisper.

Linder tried to keep him talking. "You're always wasting my time. That's nothing new."

"See what I mean?" He held the steering wheel with both hands.

"Now, is this fair? I go with you to your favorite dive, Curley's Cue, and watch you mix it up with a twenty year old as if you think *you're* still twenty. And now, you won't let me take you to my favorite bar."

"I never said Curley's is my favorite anything." He frowned. "We went there for a reason."

"Oh, I could see how much fun you were having. Come on and admit it. You just wanted an excuse to go."

"Hell Linder, it was strictly business."

"You conduct all your business in bars now?"

"Maybe. So which bar is it?" He held up his hand. "Wait, let me guess. It's that fancy place, Harlan's House. Am I right?"

"No, it's Club Winnipesauke."

"Club Dub?" He grimaced. "Do they even sell beer in there?"

"Get moving and let's find out."

They pulled into a crushed granite lot and parked under a flashing neon outline of a tomahawk. The building crouched beneath two thick pine trees that carpeted the walkway with fragrant needles and gave a vague impression of entering a forest. The windowless orange brick exterior led to a bright entryway that seemed several times too big for the building. Chainsaw-carved wooden Indians stood on either side of the red door.

Once the door closed behind them, they stood waiting for their eyes to adjust to the dim interior before entering the main part of the room. Red velvet wall paper covered the walls from floor to ceiling. In one corner a parquet dance floor sat next to a curving, ornate bar with a unframed mirror covering the wall behind.

San sat at a corner table while Linder walked to the bar and then returned, smiling.

"What are you so happy about?" San grumbled.

"It's time we had something decent to drink."

"What's wrong with beer?"

"Not a thing. But the times call for a thinking man's spirit."

"Ah, hell. What now, Linder? You know I can't tolerate those sweet mixed drinks."

A waitress in a fringed buckskin dress and beaded headband set two drinks on the table and left.

"Don't tell me you won't partake in the nectar of the gods San, single malt Scotch whiskey."

"Now you're talking." San held up his glass. "This, I can tolerate."

Linder studied San for a moment. "What's this about quitting on Gert and Mattie?"

"I have to admit Linder, you don't forget much."

"Let me guess. You think you're letting them down if you don't get to the bottom of how they died. Am I right?"

"Let me ask you something, Linder. When we were kids, did you ever imagine that you'd end up a preacher in the same little town where you grew up?"

"San, I'm not a preacher, remember? I'm no good at preaching. That's why I'm the pastoral care minister. That's why I know all the hospitals and doctors in the counties around here."

"Alright, so you're a pastor. Did you ever think you'd be doing that or anything like it?"

"No, not at all. I dreamed of being a scientist. I thought that I'd discover the cure for some dreaded disease." He chuckled. "Of course, I was no good in math, so that was that."

"Gert wanted me to be a writer. I tried but I didn't have a talent for it. The high school principal's brother served as a secret service agent and he came to the school one day to speak to our Government class. That's all it took and I was hooked. I dreamed I'd travel the world protecting the President and other big wigs in Washington. Just thinking about it made me feel important." He shook his head. "Instead, I ended up a public servant in the same part of the world where I grew up."

"You did alright, San. You don't need to be famous to do some good in the world."

"I don't believe in complaining. But I'm not young anymore and I wonder what I have to show for all that time."

"A lot of what we do is not something you can point to and say 'I did it', but that doesn't mean it's not important. Ask that little girl at Curley's place. What's her name?"

"Nina." San said absently.

"Like I said before, a lot has happened to you that's hard to make sense of. It takes time."

"There's not enough time in the world for me to ever understand why someone like Janie had to suffer like she did; or Gert and Mattie. What sort of a god makes that happen? What god makes a little girl watch her mother get kicked senseless?"

"God speaks to us in ways that are sometimes difficult to understand, San. It's part of the mystery of faith."

"I don't hear anything." He glared at Linder. "Try telling that to Nina."

Just then the door opened, briefly flooding the room in bright light. San turned to see Jules standing near the door rubbing her eyes. After a moment, she walked to their table and sat.

"Hello again, Linder." She smiled and sat across from him, then turned to San. "I thought that was your car out there. It looks like the same cruiser you drove as a Ranger."

"That's because it is. It was time to trade it out for a new one so I bought it. Does the law in this county have a problem with that?"

"I'm sorry about the sheriff, San. Don't take it personally, that's the way he is."

"You mean the friendly type."

"Sure. If Linder hadn't stepped in you would have had a real friendly talk with him, I suppose." She laughed.

San frowned. "Do you want something to drink or is this business?"

"I did some checking. That young guy that lived at your aunts' bought a car not long ago from a place over in San Saba. He paid cash. The guy said he had a big wad of bills. He couldn't have made much as a boarder so I'm wondering where he might have gotten that money."

"What type of car?"

"Blue Chevy sedan. Why else would I be here?"

"So, it's likely it was him out at the house." Linder added.

"Anything else, Jules?" San ran his hand through his hair.

"He told the guy that sold him the car he was heading for the Panhandle, where he has family. He said he was leaving in a couple of days, as soon as he got insurance for the car. He mentioned the State Farm agent in San Saba. That was four days ago but may be worth checking. I'd say he's gone by now but I'll keep an eye out and let you know if anything turns up. "

"You're a peach, Jules."

"You're not supposed to talk to an officer of the law like that. But I don't mind if it's the right person and I'm off duty." She smiled and looked at Linder. "I need to go. Linder, don't forget about my archery lesson tomorrow."

They watched her leave. "Linder, you better have another drink. You'll need to keep your strength up."

Linder ignored the comment. "Aren't we going to see about the insurance?"

"It sounds like your archery lesson is more important than my trip to San Saba so I'll have to go it alone." He waved to the waitress.

"Did I really agree to give her a lesson?" He rubbed his temple.

San looked at him. "Linder, it doesn't matter. Jules is not a woman to be toyed with. If she wants a lesson, it's a lesson she'll get."

Eleven

San

I've been thinking about children lately, or what my grandmother from Mexico called "mijas", thoughts I haven't had in years. It's a puzzle. Janie and I never had kids. It wasn't that we didn't try or want to. Early on, we decided to wait until the time seemed right. After we'd been married a few years, I was promoted and we reckoned it was time. But Janie started having some female problems so we had to postpone things for a while. It all seemed to drag on.

After a couple of years of this or that setback, all of a sudden she was pregnant. It seemed to happen right out of the blue and she was happier than I'd ever seen her. She was never one to show her feelings easily. She seemed to glow from the inside, her dark hair as long and thick as a horse's mane. All her checkups were good right up until the delivery but the baby was stillborn. It was a shock even to the doctor. Janie was beyond consoling.

I never would have believed a person could go from good to bad in such a short order but there she was right in front of me and not a thing I could do for her, at least not anything I could see. I had always been able to take care of things one way or the other, and I knew she counted on me that way, but there was nothing for me to get a hold on. I couldn't bull my way through it either, like I was prone to do. I just had to wait and stand by her. That was one thing I knew I could do and I reckon it helped in some small part. Still, I felt I had failed her.

Little by little she began to pull out of it although it seemed to leave her changed somehow. We eventually got back to a routine and she went back to teaching. At least then she was around the little ones. She got pregnant once more a few years later but had a miscarriage early on and that was all she wrote. She went through another spell but then seemed to resign herself to not having children. She never would talk about it, at least not to me. I can't say that I was real keen on talking about it myself.

I had my own struggle but didn't let on much. I reckon Janie knew, and probably Linder. He's always wanting to talk about this or that so I doubt I would've noticed. And Janie was caught up in her grief. But underneath all my effort to help Janie, I was angrier than I could say to see her suffer and our dreams of a family drift away like smoke on a windless night.

I would take walks late in the evening, after Janie had taken one of her pills and was finally able to sleep. I'd walk and walk and try to think through what had happened. I couldn't understand a god that would allow it. There was never a finer person than Janie. Seeing all she went through made me mad at the world and everyone in it, and I blamed God for her bad fortune. I felt bad about it and knew it would upset Gert and Mattie if they knew, not to mention Janie. She had taken to church-going more than ever, as if all that praying would change a thing. But there was no answer to any of my asking and I reckon I just gave it up.

That time eventually became just one part of our life together and faded into the past. Janie and I were luckier than most because we got on so well. I'd heard tell of folks splitting with each other after losing a child. But we'd always rather have each other's company than anyone else's. Between working, taking care of Janie's animals and keeping an eye on Gert and Mattie as they got on in years, there seemed to be little time for much else.

Still, that was the start of my drift away from things religious. It didn't happen all at once like the movies will make you think. It was a piling up of things, little things, week to week, month to month, year to year, until one day

I realized I had no use for it anymore. I had finally stopped to listen and decided I didn't understand a word of it, not a word. None of what the preacher said made a lick of sense. I understood that people ought to treat each other right, but I couldn't see that it was necessary to believe in the Bible to do that. And all that religion gave me nothing to understand the pain and suffering I saw. For a man raised in the church his whole life, that was a dark day and I had not a soul I could talk to about it. But there it was.

Twelve

As Linder stepped through the door leading to his office, the church secretary motioned him over with a wave of her hand. It was the time of week he set aside for his pastoral counseling responsibilities, which usually involved problems with marriage, finances or wayward children. Marta Zelinski, prudish and widowed, typically avoided involving herself in the concerns of Linder's clients and rarely even spoke to him. He had decided she considered him unimportant in the church social hierarchy, which was more or less true. She made no attempt to hide her preference for attending to the needs of Reverend Bell, a task she clearly considered to be the truly important work of the church. Linder looked at her long face and struggled to put out of his mind the thought that she resembled an old greyhound.

"Father Wertz, there is a very distraught woman waiting in your office. She did not have an appointment and I told her she would have to come back at the properly scheduled time but she refused to leave. She became so upset, I worried the ladies working on Sunday's flower arrangements might hear. It wouldn't do to expose them to unseemly behavior.

"I thought it would be acceptable to put her in your office. She has a young child with her, a beautiful girl. Those little brown ones can be darling when they're young. Unfortunately, they grow up and get pregnant or arrested." She shook her head slowly.

Linder frowned but let it pass. "What's her name."

"Well, she was so difficult I never got a name."

"Alright." He turned and walked to his office.

He paused at the door, gathering his thoughts, and then stepped in. The lights were off and the room nearly dark but he could see the silhouette of a woman on the couch across from his desk. She did not look up. He scanned the room for the girl and found her to his left beside the low bookcase, thumbing through a book. He waited a moment and then flipped the light switch. They both looked up at once.

"Hello again." The woman managed a crooked smile.

Linder stared at her for a moment. Her face was so swollen from crying he momentarily failed to recognize her. He looked over at the girl and instantly remembered her from Curley's. He smiled at her.

"It's Nina, I think. Is that right?" He spelled her name in sign language.

The girl nodded and shook her closed hand, the sign for "yes".

He turned to the woman. "And you're Nora, I believe. San told me your names."

"He talked about us?" She raised her eyebrows in surprise.

"Just that you're renting his house. Is that why you're here? Is there some problem with making the rent?"

"Oh no, I'm so relieved we have a place now." She shifted uncomfortably and glanced at her daughter. "Is there some place she could go read while we talk?"

"Sure."

He opened the door, motioning to Nina to follow. After a minute, he returned and sat across from Nora, waiting for her to speak. She glanced around the room, he thought, as if looking for an escape.

"She doesn't need to hear this." She turned to him again.

"I understand. We have a day care down the hall. She'll be fine."

"It's just that I want her to have a normal childhood, if that's possible. I don't want her to be scared all the time." She began to cry softly.

"Everything we discuss is confidential so try not to worry." He handed her a tissue. "So, why are you here?"

"They called me this morning at work." She dabbed her eyes.

"Who called?"

"I'm sorry. I'll try to be clear. The parole board called me. They told me my ex-husband is going up for parole this afternoon. He's been in prison for six years and now I'm afraid they're going to let him out."

"If you're divorced, he has no reason to contact you."

"You don't understand. He doesn't need a reason. He was dealing drugs and I testified against him. That's the reason he's in prison. It's because of me." She brushed the tears from her eyes.

"And you're wondering what to do?"

"He doesn't know where we are. But I'm afraid someone will tell him."

"You're concerned with your safety and Nina's. That's understandable. Most people would be concerned."

"I'm not afraid for myself so much as for Nina. I know what he's capable of but I don't know what he might do."

Linder studied her for a moment. She seemed genuinely fearful yet seemed to be holding something back. He tried to focus but was distracted by her appearance. She was an unusually attractive woman, in spite of her emotional state. He green eyes glowed against her olive skin and auburn hair. But as he thought about it, he found the difference between Nora's and Nina's appearance bothersome and more than a little puzzling. He decided it was not yet the time to ask her about it.

"Have you contacted the sheriff's office? You may want to alert them. They also have victim services available. They can help you know how to manage these kinds of situations." He looked at her again for a moment. "Is he Nina's father?"

"No, but he knows he can hurt me by hurting her. That's the kind of person he is." She slapped the table in frustration. "I can't believe he's still controlling my life."

"If you want to feel in control you'll need to do something, take some action. The question is what."

"It feels better to talk about it."

"I know someone at the sheriff's office. I want you to ask for her, if you decide to contact them. Her name is Jules Lefebvre. I guess you're supposed to put 'officer' in front of that."

"A woman deputy." She commented.

"That's right. It might be easier to talk with her than one of the other deputies." He thought of another possibility. "Have you considered telling San?"

"Oh, please don't tell him." Her eyes grew wide with fear. "I'm afraid he'll kick us out. I don't want to be on the street. I could never forgive myself if I allowed that to happen to Nina."

"I won't tell anyone anything unless you ask me to. The only exception is if someone is in imminent danger of getting hurt. That's not the case here."

"I just want to be a good mother to Nina and for her to have a normal life. Is that so much to ask for?"

"No, it's not. What I meant is that it might be helpful for San to be aware of the situation. He could help keep an eye out, if necessary, that kind of thing. Forewarned is forearmed, but you have to decide who to tell and who not to."

"I'll think about it."

"Nina's a good-natured girl." He rubbed his thumb along his jaw, a habit when considering a difficult question. "You two have such different coloring, she almost looks like she could be adopted."

She stood suddenly. "Why would you say that? Of course I'm Nina's mother. It scares me that you would say that." She paced the floor. "You're not going to have her taken from me, are you? I'm doing my best to take care of her. Please don't take her from me. I couldn't stand it."

"Nora," Linder put a hand on her arm. "Please sit down. I didn't mean to upset you. It was just a thought that crossed my mind. When I was Nina's age I had a friend who looked so different from the rest of his family, he swore that he was adopted. It was nonsense, of course."

She sat. "Nina's father had dark hair and eyes."

"Of course, children often take after one or the other parent."

She looked intently at him. "The child protection people took her from me once. She was only three. It was after her father left and I was having trouble paying bills, so I worked two jobs. One night I came home so exhausted that I fell asleep on the couch before putting her to bed. She somehow managed to open the front door. They found her walking along a busy street before I even realized she was gone. I was terrified by what might have happened to her and even more by the idea of them taking her. It was the worst week of my life."

"You were doing your best, working two jobs. It's what single parents sometimes have to do."

She looked at her watch and stood. "I have to get back to work. I told them I wasn't feeling well but I can't afford to use much sick leave. I need to save it for when Nina's sick and I have to stay home with her."

"That makes sense." He stood.

"I'm sorry I barged in and messed up your schedule." She held out her hand. "Thanks for talking to me."

"Things happen." He took her hand. "You can come back any time. The secretary will get Nina for you. Tell her goodbye for me."

Linder watched her leave and rubbed his thumb across his jaw again. Her reaction to his comment about adoption seemed excessive. Then again, she'd had a bad experience, so sensitivity to any mention of adoption was understandable. There was something else bothersome he

64

couldn't put his finger on. In any case, she seemed to have had more than her share of bad luck, if luck was what you called it. A soft knock pulled him from his thoughts as his next appointment walked in.

Thirteen

The two lane road to San Saba cut through the limestone uplift and past mounds of pink granite, the coarse surface speckled with orange and lime-green hues of lichen. Stands of post oak and elm crowded the meandering fence line. To his west, San could see the outline of Smoothing Iron Mountain rising above the rolling hills, bluish in the late morning haze. Below the hills a thin church steeple glowed brilliant white.

He had meant to get to town early in order to talk with some of the locals but had slept late. It wasn't like him, he grumbled to no one. He slowed and turned off the road, pulling up to a low frame building that stretched under several huge cottonwood trees. The faded red siding had peeled in long, narrow strips. A wooden sign hanging from a rusted metal pole simply read "Eats". San stepped through the door and took a seat at the bar. Down the bar, several older men hunched over their coffee, talking in low tones.

A waitress pushed through a swinging door leading to the kitchen, grabbing a half-full coffee pot from the warmer. Wearing her hair in two thick braids, she had a green "Free Leonard Peltier" button pinned to her apron. Her low-cut blue shirt strained against the straps. She leaned against the edge of the bar and smiled at San, holding the pot at eye level. She wasn't bad looking, he thought, except for the large mole shaped like Africa just above her top lip.

"Do you want coffee, hon'?"

"Coffee sounds good."

"Breakfast this morning?" She poured the cup to the brim.

"That's all for now." He tapped his fingers on the counter. "There is something you could help me with."

"Anything for a good-looking man. They call me Sky." She held out her hand.

He managed a crooked smile and took her hand. "I was supposed to meet a man in town but I haven't been able to find him."

"What does he look like?"

"Young guy, dark hair. He drives a blue sedan."

"There was a young, good-looking boy in here the last couple of days. I hadn't seen him before then." She smoothed her hair. "Let's see, we have a pretty good view of the parking lot from here. I think he was driving a blue car. He was too pretty to forget. But I prefer my men a little older."

"Did he say what he's doing here?"

"I believe he said he'd be in town for a few days helping one of the older ladies in town with her finances. I didn't recognize the woman's name. He liked to talk about himself. I figured he must be some kind of accountant and didn't get much chance to talk with people."

"What time does he usually come in?"

"It was after the main lunchtime rush both days." She looked down the bar. "I better tend to the other customers. Call if you need something. Remember, Sky's the name."

San gulped his coffee, paid the bill and walked to his car thinking about what she'd said. The young man sounded like the same person Doris Shuerman described and probably the one his aunts had befriended. He thought it strange they had given the man room and board yet San had never actually met him. He always seemed to be away when San made a visit. San had been so preoccupied with work during that time it never occurred to him that the man might have been avoiding him. He wondered if the man could recognize him. Probably, Gert and Mattie had pictures of him all over their house. San shook his head, seeing it just another example of how he had failed them.

He pulled up to the address Jules had given him. The new brick building housed several businesses, including the local State Farm insurance office. He went through the door and asked to speak with an agent. The receptionist's heavy lipstick and painted on eyebrows made her look vaguely clown-like. San was about to sit when he heard a voice behind him. He turned to see Nora walking across the room. She stopped and looked about the room and then back at him, her face blushed and lined with concern.

"Is something wrong? Why are you here?" She spoke in low tones.

"I'm just here to talk to an agent."

"Geez, what next?" She grabbed him by the arm and led him into an office. "You scared me. I thought something bad had happened and you were going to tell me we need to find someplace else to live."

"There's nothing wrong." He sat. "I thought you worked back in town. Nice office, though."

"I'm a secretary with the other office but I'm filling in for someone here. I don't need any trouble." She whispered. "I don't want to lose my job."

"Are you always this nervous or is it just me?"

She leaned on the desk, head in her hands. "I'm sorry. I've had a lot on my mind. And I guess you do make me a little nervous." She looked up at him.

"There's no reason to worry about me."

"Okay, I'll try not to."

"I'm here because I'm looking for someone. I have reason to believe he may have come in here to get liability insurance on a late model used car, a blue sedan, one he recently purchased. Have you seen anyone like that?"

"You sound like the law. I heard you had retired."

"It's personal. I'm not asking for any confidential information on this guy, just whether you've seen him or the car."

"That's good. We can't give out personal information." She sat back. "I've been here for a week and I've been

68

working overtime to help out. I'm pretty sure no one with an older blue car has come through. It would have come across this desk so I don't think we've seen him. Are you sure this is where he was supposed to come?"

"It's the only possibility I have to go on." He stood. "You're reasonably sure he hasn't been in here?"

"I don't think he has come in." She smiled. "You're lucky I'm here. Someone else would probably have thrown you out."

"I can see how that could happen and I appreciate the favor. I'll see if I can find a way to pay you back." He turned to leave just as something flashed in the large, glass-covered photo to his right. He looked up to see the reflection of a blue sedan parked just outside the building, a hunched figure hurrying out to it.

"That's him!" He leapt out of the office and sprinted through the front door just in time to see the car speeding around the corner. He ran to his car, closely followed by Nora, and then stopped abruptly without attempting to get in.

"What is it?" She called.

He threw down his keys and paced in a tight circle. "Damn it to hell, the coward slit my tire." He pointed to a flat front tire. "He must have seen me through the open door. That's damn careless."

"How could you know what he would do?"

"I should've known. Hell, I've just lost my touch." He leaned against the car, arms folded. "There was a time I'd never let something like this happen and I wouldn't tolerate it in anyone else either."

"Are you going to go after him?"

"Are you offering to let me use your car?"

"If it would help."

"I'm joking. The little lowlife must be halfway to Oklahoma by now."

"Shouldn't you call the police or something?"

"They'd just waste my time and then wouldn't waste theirs on a case as minor as a flat tire."

"I wish there was something I could do."

San looked at her for a moment. "Are you just being nice to me because you need a place to live?"

"What? No, of course not. That's not a nice thing to say."

"The first time we met you didn't have much use for me, remember?"

"It was because I'd had a bad experience, a very bad experience, like I said. You reminded me of that time and I got angry. Besides, I didn't know anything about you then, at least not enough to have an opinion one way or the other."

"Still don't."

"I know more than I did then. I know you decided you knew enough about me to rent your house to me. That means you can size up someone pretty quick. Well, I'm not so bad at that myself. I know more about you than you think."

"I'm not renting to you, I'm renting to Nina." He smiled. "You just come with the deal."

"See, you have a heart but you don't want anyone to know."

"There are a lot of people who would disagree with you on that one. Linder, he's the one with the heart."

"And you don't like to see people treated wrongly. What you did with Dewey proves that. So, I'm sure there's a good reason you want to find that guy and his blue car."

"Maybe yes and maybe no. I'm just trying to find some answers to some questions."

"And you're determined too. I hope you find them."

"They aren't coming easy but not much does in this world. You should probably get back to work, Doctor Freud." He nodded at his car. "I need to get this car taken care of."

Fourteen

Linder

I was bothered by what San had said before Nora's boyfriend showed up at the bar. For too long, it needled me like some tiny thorn that I wished but was unable to ignore. San had taken a hard look at his life and wasn't sure he liked what he saw. That was understandable given the circumstances. The Bible is full of stories of pain and suffering and attempts to make sense of it. And there are no easy answers, regardless of what some churches preach.

I can't say that I've avoided my own doubts about the goodness of God when faced with the pain of losing someone close, someone like Gert or Mattie or San. Just because I understand the grieving process, doesn't mean that I don't experience it as well. So, when I heard the despair in San's voice that night, I understood what I was hearing - *and* I felt it.

I was married once, a long time ago. Her name was Paula. We had only been together a few years when she decided she was tired of being married, as if marriage was a coat she no longer wanted and could simply cast aside. Loyal to a fault, I never saw it coming. I had been at my first church, St. Francis Episcopal, for less than a year and I was still getting to know the church and its members when it happened. After she left, it didn't take long for me to convince myself I was a failure as a marriage partner and a man.

I can't imagine what I was like to be around but I know it couldn't have been pleasant. I felt like I had entered a desert that had no beginning and no end, a dark nothingness that offered little comfort. And I managed to push away the few people who offered support. I went on like that for too long. Then one day San showed up out of the blue. He said he wasn't going to let me feel sorry for myself anymore and he meant it. It was what I needed to hear. Thanks to him, I eventually came out of it.

But then, more recently, I had a young woman come to see me. She was divorced but that's so common it doesn't mean much these days, and she had a young child. On the surface she seemed perfectly unremarkable. But she had taken to hurting herself, making small cuts on the inside of her arms. She told me she had been abused for years by her step-father. He would come into her room nearly every night after her mother and sisters were asleep. He continued until she escaped the house by eloping.

After her divorce, she tried to talk with her mother and sisters about it but they refused to believe her, saying she just wanted to break up the family because her marriage had failed. It made no sense to her. She and her sisters slept in the same room and they had to have known.

She wanted me to explain how God could let a thing like that happen to her year after year. She wanted to know why the merciful and loving God she had heard of all her life would allow it and keep it from being real because everyone that mattered now denied it. I said the words I was trained to say but they felt hollow and unconvincing, despite my wish to help her. She never returned. A month later, I learned by chance that she had killed herself. I'd been unable to explain to her what I could not explain to myself.

Soon after, I began showing up late for work. And when I was there I'd find myself listening but not hearing the words, my mind elsewhere. I knew something had to change but I seemed to be stuck.

Finally, I took a month-long leave of absence. It took a while but I finally admitted to myself I could no longer go on as I had. When I returned, I told clients that I provided counseling but they would need to go to another pastor for spiritual guidance. It was the best I could do at the time.

So, I felt like I understood at least part of what San was going through. But more than his personal struggle, which could be a good thing, it was San's unpredictability that worried me most. He was acting like a man who had nothing to lose. I knew that kind of attitude could end up in disaster, especially if you've spent your life around violence and death. For someone like San, things that most of us can scarcely imagine are all too real. If he didn't find something he could believe in soon, I felt sure he would cross a line and there would be no turning back.

He showed up at my office late one afternoon, saying he was on his way to talk with the bank that handled his aunts' accounts. He asked me along to help him think through what he wanted to ask. I was worn out from a long day of hearing the problems of the world but went because I could see he needed to talk. In spite of wanting company, he was not in the best of moods.

"You ever have trouble sleeping, Linder?" He asked as soon as I buckled my seat belt.

"No, I sleep good. Just lucky, I guess."

"It figures you'd be of no help." He shot me a glare. "I'm not sleeping worth a damn. I can't figure it. I thought maybe you'd know some cure or something I could take."

"Maybe you should ask doctor Nowak."

"That's real funny. He'd poison me in a heartbeat if I gave him the chance."

"Insomnia can be a symptom of depression." I knew it was a mistake as soon as I said it.

"Damn it Linder, are you siding with that quack now? Nowak was just trying to avoid my questions and you know it." He slapped the wheel. "I have half a mind to go back over there and make him talk."

I knew what he said was partly true but I was also concerned about his mental state. I glanced around the car for signs of his gun, trying not to be obvious about it.

73

"What are you looking for?" He barked.

"Nothing." I mumbled. "Don't go see old Nowak and do something you'll regret."

"Hell, the old witchdoctor would find some way of avoiding me anyway. I'd just waste my time."

I thought it would be a good idea to change the subject. "Tell me again why we're going to talk to the bank?"

"I want to see if there were any recent changes to their account."

"Didn't you get all that information when their estate was settled?"

"I got the final statements, but the records at the house were a holy mess. At first, I figured it was just because they were getting on in years and couldn't keep up with things so well any more. But it didn't add up. They were both sharp as a tack right up to the end."

"What are you looking for?"

"A recent transfer of funds."

"You think the young guy who was living with them found a way to get into their account?"

"They didn't have much left. I thought it was because they were teachers and never got paid much." He laughed. "But then again, they could have been millionaires for all I know. There was never a person born more frugal than Gert. She could stretch a meatloaf for weeks, maybe even months and there was no such thing as throwing out leftovers in her house. I should know, I ate enough of them. That's why we had the skinniest pigs in the whole county."

San pulled up to a narrow brick building obliquely facing the town square and adjacent to the county courthouse. Across the top, a limestone façade read "Adlof 1907" in deeply chiseled letters. I stood for a moment looking across the cast iron bridge that spanned the nearby river and on to the arching granite bluffs beyond, their violet surface carved by countless floods. Just across the river, the white trunks of Sycamore trees glowed like bones in the afternoon light. It was a favorite spot of Paula's for picnics and I was captured for a moment by an image of her leaving the river, her long hair dark and shining.

"Linder, are you going to stand there all day or come inside?" San stood by the entrance.

I followed him under a stone archway and into the cool interior. Several wide hardwood desks, flanked by leather chairs, stretched in a semicircle in front of a paneled wall lined with office doors. Overhead, three antique crystal chandeliers hung from the original molded tin ceiling. A stamp of the bank logo covered each panel. San nodded to several of the men behind the massive desks, and waved a hello to one of the tellers. After a moment, a young woman approached us.

"Can I help you?" She brushed back her bleached hair.

"I'm San Turner. I called earlier today."

"Yes, Mr. Turner, one of our managers will be right with you." She turned and left.

"You mean you didn't just show up this time and expect everyone to drop what they're doing to help you?"

"I can be civilized if there's a need, although I try to avoid it whenever possible."

"No kidding."

"Mr. Turner." A voice came from behind us. "Over here."

I turned to see an attractive woman with dark hair standing in a doorway. There was something striking about her appearance, even though she wore a nondescript business suit. San stood staring as if she had just spoken a foreign language. She was busy signing a stack of papers held by a young man, occasionally pausing to wave us over.

"Try not to stare." I gave him a slight push.

"Not interested. We're here on business, remember?"

"You're here on business. I'm sightseeing."

San approached her and held out his hand. "Thanks for taking time to talk with me." He nodded at me. "This is Linder Wertz."

"Molly Christopher."

She shook both our hands but seemed to hold San's a little longer than necessary. Her gray eyes, slightly bluish in cast and turned down at the edges, seemed to glow in the dim light. Thick, dark hair framed her narrow features, contrasting sharply with her fair skin. In spite of my efforts, I found it hard not to stare.

"I understand you're interested in any recent account activity prior to the time you inherited your aunts' estate. Is that correct, Mr. Turner?" Her voice had a slight drawl, sounding a bit like a warm summer night.

"That would be correct. Ms. Christopher, I'd appreciate it if you'd just call me San. I feel old enough as it is without being called 'Mister'."

"Well, San, I'd hardly call you old." She smiled at him. "Will you call me Molly?"

"Molly, I don't believe I've seen you around town before." I interrupted. "Have you worked here long?"

San frowned. "Linder, can't you see she's busy. We're not on a social visit." He turned back to her. "Don't mind him. Now, were you able to spot any funny business with the account, Molly?"

She led us to her office where we sat in two gray leather chairs facing her desk.

"As a matter of fact, several weeks before you inherited there was a withdrawal." She leaned toward San. "By the way, I am sorry about your aunts. I understand they were fine people, well-respected in the community and former teachers. My mother was a school teacher."

"They taught for many years."

"I'm sorry for getting us sidetracked, San." She leaned back in her chair. "The account had five thousand dollars withdrawn. The transaction doesn't tell us anything about the reason for the withdrawal, but that's a sizable sum.

"Did they have any cash hidden away? Our older customers will sometimes keep large amounts of cash at home, even though we advise them not to. I believe it makes them feel less worried about losing all their savings if something happened to the banks. If I had lived through the Great Depression, I might feel the same."

"They had a few fifties stashed in a sock."

"There's also a note that they had made arrangements to make an electronic transferal of funds but there's no evidence of activity in this account. Let me check their savings account."

"There wasn't much in there, as I remember."

"An electronic transfer of a thousand dollars occurred a few weeks earlier to a bank in Red Rock, Oklahoma. That's near one of the reservations, I believe."

"It must be small, I've never heard of it." He rubbed his chin. "Why on earth would they do that?"

"I'm sorry, San but I can't tell anything looking at the account." She reached out as if she would have touched his hand, had it been on the desk.

"There's no reason to apologize, Molly. You've been helpful. I haven't always gotten help in trying to sort out what happened to my aunts. I appreciate it." He stood.

"You're probably wondering why I'm here." I held out my hand again. "So am I."

"You must be a good friend to be so patient."

"I have enough patience for both of us. It was nice to meet you." I shook her hand and stood.

She scribbled something on a business card and held it out. "Again, San, I'm so sorry about your aunts. I lost my mother last year and I know how it can be. Here's my personal phone number. You can call me anytime if you need help with these questions you have."

"That's generous, Molly."

"Or anything else." She shrugged.

We walked through the archway and out onto the sidewalk. After the dim interior of the bank, the bright sunlight seemed blinding. We stood for a moment, letting our eyes adjust, and I watched the traffic on Main Street move steadily toward the bridge. San studied the business card in silence.

"Just business, is it?" I watched his expression. "That sounded like more than business to me."

"What are you talking about?" He said absently.

Just then I noticed a blue sedan coming around the courthouse. A dark-haired young man was at the wheel. For a moment, my mind couldn't seem to make my mouth do anything. And though I had no way of knowing if it was the car San had been looking for, I wanted him to see it. I reached out and grabbed him by the arm.

"Blue car!" It was all I could manage.

He stood for a moment looking and then ran to his car. "Linder, don't just stand there, get in!"

I jumped into the passenger seat. Before I could buckle my seat belt, we were flying along the street, dodging pedestrians and running stop signs. The blue car was nowhere in sight. Just then, the car crossed the intersection half a block in front of us. San slammed on the breaks and turned, tires squealing. The car made an abrupt turn onto a county road, spraying gravel and kicking up a cloud of dust. It was clear the driver knew he was being followed and was doing his best to out-distance us but the small sedan was no match for San's car.

San pushed the accelerator to the floor and quickly came alongside. Dust obscured the driver's window. Without warning, a side road appeared out of nowhere between two barbed wire fences and the car turned away from us in an instant. San cursed and slammed the brakes, quickly throwing the car into reverse. Soon we were again racing through a thick trail of dust, the blue car just ahead but barely visible. San gunned the engine, passing the car, and then slammed the brakes yet again, sliding the car in the lose gravel. The blue car swerved, coming to a hard stop in the bar ditch.

I could hear the driver trying to restart the car through the billowing cloud. San jumped out, running around the

78

rear of the car and snapping open the door. By the time I got there, he was dragging the man from the car by the neck of his shirt. San sounded like some crazed maniac, yelling at the top of his lungs. The young man struggled to stand, yelling back in protest.

"What's wrong with you man, are you crazy? Let me go, jefe!" His long hair fell over his face.

"What are you running from, junior?" San threw him against the car without even bothering to look at him.

"I thought you were the law." He struggled to turn. "You can't do this, redneck. That's no cop car!"

I took San's arm. "San, this is not the guy."

"This is the car."

"Look at him."

He turned the man around and studied his face. He was young and Hispanic with a thin beard, nothing like the man San was looking for.

"Where'd you get this car, wet back?" San barked.

"San, knock it off." I pulled at his arm.

"I'm no wet back, you redneck bigot! Let me go." He sneered.

"It was stolen."

"No way. I bought it from some white guy two days ago." He looked from San to me and back, as if trying to convince us.

"Is that right?" San asked skeptically.

"I got the title and everything." He sounded worried. "Are you a cop or what?"

"What did he look like?"

"He was some young, wimpy-looking white guy. He looked like he was about thirteen, man."

San loosened his grip and turned. "Come on Linder, let's go."

"Sorry." I shrugged. "It's the car. We're looking for the guy that sold you this car."

"He said he was leaving town, that's all. I don't ask questions. You know what I mean. I'm not in trouble with the law, am I?"

"No, it was the car. It was a mistake. Sorry." I walked away.

"Yeah, well, this ride better be alright, man."

I climbed into the car and San sped off. We drove in silence for a while as the day faded into evening. I was too stunned to speak. I knew San had a temper but he'd always been able to keep it in check. I'd never before seen him so close to being out of control.

When we reached the highway, he pulled off the road and stopped, pausing for a moment to look both directions. He then pulled his pistol from under his shirt, carefully placing it on the seat. Nearby streetlights glinted off the chrome barrel. Leaning forward, he took a heavy cloth from under the seat, wrapped it around the gun and then stuffed them both back under the seat. The shock on my face must have been obvious.

"What?" He looked at me.

"You had your gun with you."

"I thought we finally had the guy we've been after. I needed to be ready for anything." His voice was matter of fact.

"It's not like you."

"I was too late. The bastard got away."

"San, you worry me. You chase after some innocent guy like a mad man. When you catch up with him you nearly lose it. And to top it off, you're carrying your gun, something I'd never have imagined. What worries me most is that you don't seem at all concerned."

"I just wanted to see the guy face to face." His voice was quiet now.

"That's what worries me."

"He's gone."

"San, tell me you'll try to be careful."

"Don't worry, Linder. I'm done with it." He pulled onto the road.

"I'm glad to hear it." I hoped it was the truth.

Fifteen

San carried a can of paint in one hand and a tool box with scrapers, turpentine and brushes in the other. He walked away from the house and up the gradual hill that led to the barbed wire fence bordering his property. Halfway between the garage and the fence, a tall well house stood off by itself, the red exterior faded to dull pink. The paint was cracked and peeling along the corners and around the doorway, but it was the color that made him decide to repaint. He could barely stand to look at it.

Having scraped and prepared the surface, he was ready to begin painting, his only hesitation that a brisk wind had come up overnight. It would make the job tricky but he had other problems to tend to and wanted to be finished with it. He had not realized the house needed so many repairs, yet he found the work satisfying.

He opened the gallon can and stirred, taking the time necessary to blend all the pigment, and then poured it into a small container. Selecting a brush, he slapped it against the corner of the house several times to loosen the hairs and then dipped it into the red surface. The paint went on with a smooth hiss, gleaming in the bright sunlight.

He had finished two sides and was about to begin another when he heard something nearby. It sounded like a small animal digging in the soft dirt and appeared to be coming from the opposite side of the well house. He slowly took several steps forward and peered around the corner. There, sitting on the ground with a small, paint-stained brush was Nina. She was totally absorbed in the painting and failed to notice him until he stepped beside her. She looked up and smiled.

"This is not a job for a little girl." He said slowly to make sure she understood.

She nodded, ignoring the comment, and went back to painting.

"This is just what I wanted to avoid. I knew it would be trouble to have a child around." He mumbled to himself. "I'm not about to be a free babysitting service. And they have me talking to myself, to boot."

He knelt next to her. She was studiously ignoring him so he waved his hand in front of her. She looked at him, frowning. He frowned back.

"Your mother will not be happy if you get any of this paint on your nice clothes."

She held both hands in front of her, as if taking great care with the paint, and again shook her head.

"But I don't need any help. Thanks but no thanks." He tried to smile.

She nodded, dipped the brush in the can and began again. He stood and looked up the hill, at a loss as what to do.

"Okay, I give up." He got her attention again. "Nina, hold on a minute while I get something to protect your clothes."

She nodded and San walked to the garage where he had stored some of his old shirts for use as rags. He briefly considered going on to the house and asking Nora to come get the girl, but there was no sign of her and for reasons he couldn't explain he decided against it. He selected a shirt and walked back up the hill against the stiffening wind. He stood by while Nina put on the shirt and happily picked up her brush.

He continued with the painting, checking on Nina now and then. Less than happy about the situation, he decided he would talk with Nora about it later. He should have known a woman like her would be trouble. She needed to do a better job of caring for both Nina and the house. On the other hand, he had to admit that Nina was surprisingly easy to manage for a child. She had taken care not to get paint on herself and had done a better job than most adults, including him. She had not asked for a thing the entire time, and he was almost finished. Still, he had no intention of socializing with his renters, he reminded himself. It was a bad practice.

After brushing on the last of the paint, he stood back checking for spots he had missed when he noticed an odd line of clouds overhead. For a moment, he puzzled over why they would be moving so quickly and it suddenly dawned on him that he was looking at smoke. He ran around the well house. The black cloud pouring over the top of the hill spread across the sky in a broad band. Although unable to gauge the fire's distance, the smoke racing past carried ashes and he was almost sure he could hear the crackle of burning trees embedded in the stiff wind.

He raced back around the corner and picked up Nina bodily with scarcely a pause, running down the hill as fast as he could. He called for Nora as he ran. By the time he reached the back porch, she was opening the door. Bewildered, she stood by as San set down Nina and bent over, gasping in between trying to speak.

"Grab your wallet and keys. We've got to get out of here." He opened the back door and pointed. "It's a range fire. A wind like this is deadly if we get trapped. We have to go now."

"Oh God, all of our things are here." She stood unmoving.

San grabbed her shoulders. "Nora, look at me. We have to go now. Where are your wallet and keys?"

She pointed to the counter. "There."

He handed her the keys and took Nina by the hand. "Follow me."

By the time they reached the front door, smoke was streaming by the house in a dense haze. San led Nina down the steps and into the back seat of the car. Nora had regained her composure and quickly slid behind the wheel. She turned the ignition, put the car in reverse and stopped.

84

"What's wrong?" San yelled.

"Aren't you coming?" She leaned out of the window.

"I'll be along. I have to hose down the roof first." He started walking back towards the house.

"You must be crazy. Come on and get in quick." She called above the heavy wind.

"You need to get Nina out of here now. I'll be right behind you."

Nora got out and ran to him. "San, it's not worth the chance. Come with us, please!"

"I need to do this, Nora. This house is all I have left of my family. But you need to get your daughter away from here. I'll meet you at the courthouse." He ushered her back to the car. "Now go!"

She got back in and sped up the drive, vanishing in the thick smoke. San ran to the back of the house, grabbing the nearest water hose and quickly turning the spigot. The ladder he had used to repair a window still leaned against the house, and he scrambled up it trailing the spewing hose. Believing he could hear the crackle of fire, he climbed onto the roof, peering through the choking smoke. No flames were yet visible above the crest of the hill so he still had no way of knowing with any certainty the speed or direction of the fire but it sounded close.

He had just finished dousing the roof when the first embers began to land around him, tumbling before the driving wind. He knew he had little time left. Sliding down the ladder while barely touching the rungs, he ran for his car parked just off the front porch. The highway was no longer visible. Starting the car, he took a long look at the house. Then he raced up the drive and turned towards town.

Sixteen

San drove over a mile before leaving the thick wall of smoke. To the west, fire trucks kicking up clouds of dust raced towards the blaze, the sun a reddish-brown overhead. Further west, layers of hills shimmered in the crystalline air, a stark contrast to the blackened rangeland now coming into his view, the dark stubble still smoking before the stiff wind. He drove to a vacant lot at the crest of a small hill and sat for a long while surveying the damage.

The wall of smoke stretching across the horizon held little hope his house had come through the blaze intact, and knowing he'd done what he could to protect it was poor consolation. At least Nora and Nina got out safely, he thought as he started the car and drove toward the town square. He found it surprising that he now felt somehow responsible for them. It was not what he'd had in mind.

He pulled up to the courthouse, scanning the square and the few cars parked nearby, Nora's car not among them. Neither she nor Nina was in sight. He went inside the building, searching one floor and then the other, circling the building twice. The thought that they might have tried to return to the house when he failed to arrive as agreed flashed through his mind and he was caught by a sudden fear. He rushed up the stairs and into the sheriff's office.

The dispatcher caught him as he came through the door, barring his way into the office itself. San explained that his house was in the path of the fire and his concern about Nina and Nora. The more he was delayed, the more he was gripped with a fear for their safety. The dispatcher, another of the new sheriff's office staff, held her ground. He had turned to leave when Jules walked through the door.

"San, you look like you walked straight out of a coal mine. On second thought, it's a raccoon you remind me of." She stood back to look at him, sniffed the air and wrinkled her nose. "Either way, you're a sight. Keep your distance if you would, please sir."

"Jules, I'm glad you're here. I need your help."

"Is the great San Turner asking me for help? The world must be about to end."

"Knock it off, Jules. That range fire south of town may have taken my house and I can't locate the woman and little girl who are staying there. They may be in trouble."

"You mean the woman that called in the fire?"

"How in the hell am I supposed to know who called in the damn fire?"

"You mean the woman who reported that you were fool enough to be out in that fire?"

"Damn it Jules, I had to try to save the place. I couldn't just let it go. But I'm afraid they went back to look for me when I didn't show." He stopped talking and looked at her. "How do you know all that?"

"You mean the cute little deaf girl and her red-headed mom that I just let off a block away, at the Episcopal Church around the corner?" She turned and opened the door. "Go on, then."

San stood confused for a moment and then started out the door. "Thanks, Jules."

She caught him by the arm. "We were just out there, looking for you. They were afraid you didn't make it out so I checked with the fire crew to make sure you did. The little girl was pretty upset so you'd better go."

"I'd better go." He turned and rushed down the stairs.

As he neared the church, San could see Nora standing outside the door in the shadow of the broad archway. She paced the wide sidewalk and then stood again scanning the street. Turning at the sound of his footsteps, she looked at him for a moment and then covered her face with her hands. He stopped at the curb not knowing what to do or say. After a moment, she spoke.

"When you didn't show up we didn't know what to do. I thought the worst, of course. I always do. I didn't say anything to Nina but I didn't have to. She can read me in an instant. She was so upset." Her voice was shaking. "I told her you were probably just delayed by something and would be here soon. But I couldn't stand it so we went to the sheriff's office for help."

"I was too caught up in trying to save the house to think straight and I just lost track of time. It's no excuse but it is the truth. Still, I should have known you would wonder what happened if I didn't come right along." He stepped onto the sidewalk.

"I've never been so terrified. The fire came out of nowhere. If you hadn't seen it…" She shivered at the thought.

"Range fires are like that. But it was selfish of me not to come here straight away."

"You got us out safe."

"I should have gone with you." He took a step toward her. "I'm sorry, Nora."

She stepped back. "You'd better tell that to Nina."

He looked into the building. "Where is she?"

"I'll take you." She took his arm. "I ought to be mad at you, but it probably wouldn't do any good."

"Probably not."

They walked down a hall and into a large room normally used as a gym but now set up as a shelter for families displaced by the fire. A row of folding cots lined the far wall. At one end, church volunteers in pink vests prepared dinner behind a serving window. San spotted Nina sitting at a table alongside several other children. Nora led him to her. They stood watching until Nina turned, looking at them briefly before running to San without hesitation. She stopped in front of him, frowning at him for a moment before taking his hand and pressing her free hand to her chest.

He knelt and faced her. "I'm sorry I scared you."

Leaning into him, she hugged his neck and then stepped back.

"I wasn't expecting that." He said, flustered.

Frowning at him again, she signed something San was unable to follow and laughed shyly. San looked to Nora.

"She says you look like a raccoon." She smiled. "I happen to agree."

"That bad, huh?"

"That bad."

Seventeen

San unloaded the bare-root apple, peach and pear trees from the trunk of his car and closed the lid. He had decided to reclaim the orchard and garden that Mattie kept for years. The original fruit trees had played out long ago and most were dead or dying. He studied the trees, noting that their bent and mangled trunks had the strange beauty of time itself captured. He found it mildly troubling to have such thoughts and tried to focus on the task at hand.

As he opened the orchard gate, he could again hear Mattie saying a garden is like heaven for the all peace it brings, her voice so clear he felt she might be standing right behind him. He struggled not to turn around. Mattie had always tended to become philosophical when in her garden, the way some people do after several glasses of Scotch whisky. The first time he heard her say it he had asked why she grew things in the garden that she could just as easily buy in town. It was his way of complaining about having to help.

When his great grandmother visited from Mexico, she often helped tend the garden. She said she missed having a garden, and working the rows offered a pleasant reminder of her childhood. After they had finished planting, weeding or whatever else that needed doing, she would sit in the cool of the broad pear and apple trees edging the small peach orchard, call him "mijo" and ask him to sit with her while she talked of the house in Guadalajara where his father lived before coming to "El Norte".

San finished digging the final hole and turned to find Nina holding the last of the trees. She handed it to him and stood watching. In the weeks after the fire she had taken to following him when he was working around the house and, although she was apt to show up at any time, he was still surprised when she would suddenly appear. He never seemed to hear her. As much as he tried, communicating with her was still awkward. He turned and bent to plant the tree and she knelt next to him, pressing the soil around the trunk with her small hands. When he stood, he noticed she was holding a book.

He waved his hand to get her attention. "What's the book about?"

She stared at him with no response. He was sure she had been able to read his lips. Finally, she frowned and signed the abbreviation she had given him for his name, the letter "s" held against her jaw.

"Oh, right." He awkwardly signed the only two words he could remember. "What book?"

Instead of showing him the book, she took his hand and led him to the dilapidated stable gate. She opened the book to a picture of a goat and took out a scrap of paper on which she had carefully printed "Can I please have one of these?" She pointed to the picture and then the corral adjoining the stables.

"You want a goat?" He laughed.

She frowned, grimly nodding her head.

"Okay, I didn't mean to laugh." He held up his hands. "A lot of folks around here keep goats. It has been a tradition in this part of the world for generations. Some have milk goats and others keep them for the wool. It's called Mohair."

She held out both hands to ask again.

"Have you asked your mother?"

"You ask her." She signed.

San was surprised that he understood her. "You want me to ask her for you?"

She nodded.

"Isn't that your job?"

She shook her head.

"You're the one that wants the goat."

"You ask her." She signed again.

"Well, you're a determined little one. I'll give you that."
She nodded in agreement.

"Here's what I'm willing to do. You and I will talk to her together." He held up a finger. "But you have to feed it, take care of it, put it in the stable when it's cold, clean up after it and anything else that needs doing. And you'll have to help in the garden to pay me back for the feed. Agreed?"

She held out her hand to shake on it.

"Hold on there missy, there's no deal unless your mom says okay."

She grabbed his hand and rushed him up the back steps to the house. He stopped her on the porch and held up his finger.

"Hold on now, Nina. A man doesn't go barging into a lady's house without asking. It's not polite. She's not likely to be expecting company. I didn't think she was even home. Now, you go and see if she's willing to talk to us now. If not, find out when a good time is and I'll come back then."

She ran into the house without responding and then quickly returned, leading him into the kitchen. She motioned for him to sit and then disappeared. A moment later, she led Nora through the door and they both sat across from San. He looked at Nina, eyebrows raised and waited. After a long pause, she shrugged and turned to her mother, filling her in on the proposal. San was impressed by her boldness and competence. Now and then Nora cast a skeptical glance at San. Finally, she turned to him.

"Okay, it's your turn. At least that's what my sneaky daughter tells me. I have to tell you San, this feels like a set up."

"Well, join the club. There's no doubt both you and I have been set up like bowling pins. She knows what she wants and she knows how to go about getting it." He held up a hand. "But I was very clear with her that the decision is yours. If you say no then I'm with you all the way. She'll get over it."

"I don't know the first thing about goats." She rubbed her forehead.

"I'm no expert either but they're generally no trouble if you feed them regular. Like I said before, it can be a good thing for a child to raise and care for an animal. I told her she would have to do all the care-taking, and she can work in the garden to pay me back for the feed. It can add up and I know you don't need the extra expense.

"The stables were damaged by the fire and will take a little work. She'll have to help with that too. If she doesn't do her part, then you can always sell it."

"Are you sure you want the bother? You don't have to do any of this. You're not just feeling sorry for her because she's deaf, are you?"

"I don't believe it does a person, child or adult, any good for people to feel sorry for them. Understand them? Yes, when it's called for. But coddling a child only leaves them unable to take care of themselves. The same thing can happen to a grown person. Then where are you? If that's not harmful, I don't know what is."

"She has loved animals and growing things since I can remember, two things I could never give her. It would be wonderful if she had the chance to do both."

"Well, it's settled then." He looked at Nina. "That means you can have a goat."

She looked at her mother, who nodded, and then she ran from the kitchen without saying a thing.

"Does that mean she's happy?"

"She's thrilled. It's very generous of you, San."

"Not at all. The stables have always been a part of this house, and this is where you live. Maybe it will keep her away from the pasture. The bull up there is not one to bother, even if you're just a little girl."

"I hope you know what you're getting into. She can be a pest."

"I was resistant at first but now I don't mind. She's good company, mostly." He chuckled. "She has been

93

trying to teach me sign language but I reckon I'm not much of a student."

Nina walked back into the room holding a thin leather strap with a small turquoise bead tied to the middle. She looked at her mother for a moment and then handed it to San. She turned and ran from the room again.

"It's a friendship bracelet." She managed a crooked smile but looked as if she might cry.

"Is there something wrong? I can tell her that I can't accept it, if it's a problem." He wondered what would cause her mood to change so quickly.

"No, she wants you to have it. It just reminded me of something I'd rather forget." She rubbed her forehead. "Why does life have to be so complicated?"

"I wish I knew." He was embarrassed at seeing her in distress. "Has something happened? Is our friend Dewey back on the scene?"

She ignored his question. "Do I seem like a good mother?"

"I'm the last one you'd want to ask. But I can see you're devoted to Nina and provide for her the way a mother should."

"I want to be a good mother to her." She shifted awkwardly.

"What's worrying you, Nora?" He sensed she was holding back.

"I just want Nina to have a normal childhood. I want her to be safe. We've moved so much. I know it's hard for her." She hesitated. "And I've gotten myself mixed up with the wrong kind of men."

"She's a good kid. I think you're doing alright."

"No, I've made some bad decisions." She stood suddenly. "I'm sorry, I need to leave."

He stood, not knowing what to do. "I can pick out a goat for you, if you want me to. You can pay me back later."

"What? Oh sure, that would be fine. I'm sorry." She rushed out of the room.

San watched her leave and wondered at what had just happened. Something about the bracelet had disturbed her but he had no idea what or why. He put it in his shirt pocket and let himself out the back door.

Eighteen

San drove up the drive and through the gate, pausing at the road to check for on-coming traffic as always. A black pickup sat just off the shoulder a quarter of a mile down the highway. Ordinarily, he would have paid little notice to a car pulled off the blacktop, a common enough occurrence. But he had seen this same pickup before, twice loitering within a half mile of his house. A third time meant there could be no coincidence.

Changing his plans, he turned away from town, cruising down the otherwise unoccupied road and past the truck. The windows, tinted a deep black, made it impossible to see a driver or if anyone at all occupied the cab. Driving further down the road, he turned around in order to take a closer look, intending to jot down the license plate number but as he slowed the truck jumped onto the highway without warning, speeding past him, tires smoking, before disappearing around a curve. It made no difference. The license plates, covered in mud, were unreadable. Bothered by the incident nonetheless, he puzzled over possible explanations as he drove into town but little made sense and he soon forgot about it.

Linder's small frame house stood three blocks off the town square on a street lined with towering sycamore and live oak trees. Crimson and forest green trim complimented the otherwise drab coloring, giving the house a welcoming feel. San walked up the steps and rapped several times on the wooden screen door. The wide porch lay deep in shade. At intervals, carved porch columns framed the sun-drenched sidewalk and street beyond, where an elderly man in a large coat walked his small dog. Above the rooftops, a late autumn sky framed the courthouse clock tower in Cerulean blue. San breathed in the crystalline air and rapped on the door again, stamping his feet.

"Linder, open the door!" He yelled and knocked again. "Just because it's Saturday doesn't mean you can sleep all day. Besides, it's downright cold out here in case you didn't know."

The door of the house next door opened and a small woman stepped out, glaring at him through the screen door. A yapping Chihuahua circled her feet. She stared at San a moment longer, picked up the squirming dog and went back inside. He looked up and down the now quiet street for other annoyed neighbors and rapped lightly once more. The door opened slowly and Linder stood looking at him through the rusted screen. He wore a flannel robe and no shoes.

"What time is it?" He rubbed his eyes with a thumb and forefinger.

"I don't know but the sun is up. You've got to get going early if you want to find a good horse."

"A horse? What do you want with a horse?" Linder opened the door. "Come on in, it's cold out there."

"You're telling me. I woke up half the neighborhood trying to get you to answer the door before I got frostbite."

"Well, it's not all *that* cold." He held up his hand. "Don't tell me. Old Mrs. Kolcek and her obnoxious dog had to check you out. Am I right?"

"She gave me the evil eye, that's for sure."

"That's all she has to live for, I think. Nothing goes on around here without her knowing about it."

"How about I make the coffee while you get dressed? We need to get moving."

"I never said I was going."

"I'll put some whisky in it, just enough to warm you up." He held up two fingers.

"Alright. Fix us some coffee, *without* the booster, while I'm getting ready."

Within an hour, they were standing inside the livestock show barn three miles north of town, surrounded by the sights and smells of cattle, goats and horses. San led Linder up the stairs and onto a catwalk overlooking the stables. From there, they had a clear view of all the livestock available for purchase that day. Linder was surprised to see antelope, emu and other exotic game scattered about the barn in various pens and small corrals. He followed San until he stopped not far from the end.

"There's a nice looking mare." San pointed to the right. "What do you think?"

"You know I don't know anything about horses."

"You went out riding with me a time or two when we were kids."

"And that's all I know, not much."

"Come on Linder, you can't deny a horse is an impressive animal."

"I can't tell if a horse is a good buy or not but I can appreciate the beauty." He nodded toward a nearby pen. "What are those?"

Three miniature donkeys milled around a small corral below their feet. A fourth rolled in the soft dirt, it's lined, round belly squirming one way and then the other. Righting itself, the donkey stood, shook a cloud of dust into the still air and then commenced an energetic braying. The others immediately joined in.

"That's a good reason not to have one of those, if you ask me." San yelled above the noise.

"Are you really going to buy a horse?" Linder yelled back, scanning the stables.

"Not today." He motioned around the barn with one hand. "I'm trying to get a feel for the cost and what I want in an animal before I take the plunge."

"When's the last time you even rode a horse?" Linder looked at him skeptically. "You're not twenty anymore, in case you hadn't noticed."

"Every morning when I get out of bed. But being old and decrepit is not the problem. The problem is finding the right horse. That's why I intend to take my time."

"I bet you haven't climbed on a horse since you were eighteen."

"I was seventeen. I was too busy with sports and working to take proper care of my horses but I couldn't part with them either. I had college coming up so Gert and Mattie made the decision for me."

"Don't call me when you fall off."

"Linder, are you going to spend the rest of your life sitting around like an old man? Well, that's not for me." He waved off Linder's comments. "Besides, it'll come back to me as soon as I get in the saddle."

"Saddle sore is what you'll get."

"Come on, grandpa. Let me buy you a beer on our way to the sale."

"A beer? I haven't even had breakfast yet."

"Okay, I'll thrown in a couple of tacos."

They took seats midway up a semicircular gallery overlooking a round, glass-fronted arena. Red dirt marked with the overlapping imprints of horseshoes filled the arena floor. In one corner an auctioneer held a microphone and waited for the first horse to appear. He wore a long, tan coat and an enormous felt hat that cast his eyes in shadow. He put the microphone to his mouth as a very short, dark man led the first horse in on a red halter.

While they ate their tacos, San and Linder debated the pros and cons of each horse that paraded through the arena. San thought several were overpriced but was taken with a Palomino filly that couldn't have been more than three weeks old. The man leading her had looped the long halter behind her tail to keep her from bolting. Still, the filly nearly climbed over the mare as soon as the auctioneer began calling out bids. Shortly afterward, the auctioneer concluded the sale.

"San, isn't that Molly Christian?" Linder pointed a few rows down.

She stood talking with an older man and two women, holding a purse and looking as if she was about to leave. She wore a black shirt and jeans, and her hair, tied back in a thick braid fell just below her shoulders. By the look on her face, she seemed to be having a serious conversation. Just at that moment, she happened to look in their direction and her expression changed in an instant. She smiled, quickly making her way up the stairs, keeping her eyes on San.

"Well, I wouldn't have expected to see you again so soon. I knew there was a good reason to come here today. Oh, hello Linder." She sat next to San, placing a hand on his arm. "Is one of you in the market for a horse or do you just like looking at beautiful creatures?"

"Well, I know a good looking female when I see one, horse or human. But Linder here is the expert on beauty. He goes to museums and the like all the time."

"Museums? What museums? I can't remember the last time I stepped inside a museum, not that I wouldn't like to. I just never seem to have time for anything, even sleeping late on Saturdays." He glared at San.

"I enjoyed our lunch on Thursday, San. I was just telling my friends about it when I looked up and there you were."

"What brings you to the sale today, Molly? I didn't expect to see you here."

"Didn't I tell you? I have three horses and a mule at home. I've kept horses since I was a child. I don't know how I forgot to mention it, San. Now that I know you like horses too, will you come ride with me?"

"What on earth do you do with a mule?" Linder interrupted. "Are you a farmer as well as a banker?"

"Don't mind him, Molly. He didn't get his beauty sleep today because of me."

"Oh, it's alright. Socrates was going to be put down by the man who used him to pull a parade wagon advertising his barbeque restaurant. He's so sweet looking - Socrates not the man - and I couldn't stand the thought of them putting him down so I adopted him. It turns out he's as good-natured as he looks and I'm glad to have him. He's a calming influence on the mares too. They can all be a bit high-strung."

"The barbeque man named him Socrates?" Linder chuckled.

"Oh no, that was me. I wanted him to have a whole new life so I gave him a new name. He looks so wise, it just fit."

"Does he wear a toga?"

"Linder thinks he's the big scholar, Molly." San frowned at him. "But he can get out there with his egghead humor."

"There's nothing wrong with being well-read, San."

"I have to admit, Linder got me back to reading. I was never without a book when I was younger but somehow got away from it. He gave me *The Voyage of the H.M.S. Beagle* by Charles Darwin, and I haven't slowed down since.

"Did you know a tortoise that Darwin captured in the Galapagos Islands is still living in a London zoo? That was over a hundred and fifty years ago. Darwin sailed for five years and observed all kinds of places and things, recording it in a journal. He was even in an earthquake so he got an up-close look at the aftermath, including the results of a huge tidal wave."

"Get out while you can, Molly. It's hard to stop him when he gets to talking about Darwin. The next thing you know he'll start naming every living thing in sight by its Latin name."

"I do have to go." She stood. "I'm late, in fact, but I couldn't just leave after I saw you. Please come and ride with me, San. You don't even have to call. Just come anytime you can."

They watched her leave and then started down the stairs as well. The hall was beginning to fill again for a cattle sale. The forlorn wails of a calf echoed from behind the far wall as men in sweat-stained straw hats and dusty jeans filed past them. The acrid smell of overcooked popcorn mingled with stale coffee. San looked over at Linder and shook his head.

"You sure do know how to run a woman off, Linder."

"Lunch on Thursday, was it? You waste no time, Mr. Turner. I thought you were all business."

"As you know, the business with the blue car is over. Besides, she called me. I couldn't think of an excuse not to go so I went."

"That must have been a real sacrifice for you."

"She is a good-looking woman. I can't deny that, but..."

"But nothing." Linder interrupted. "I'm checking you in to the nut farm myself if you turn down her invitation."

"Only if they have pecans. I just can't get enough pecans."

"If it doesn't work out with Molly, there's always that good looking tenant living right next to you. What's her name? Nora? Now that I think about it, you're surrounded by attractive women."

San frowned. "Nora is renting my house, plain and simple. Don't start getting any hare-brained ideas about me and her. That sort of woman is trouble. You can see it from a mile off. The only reason, and I mean only reason I'm renting to her is because of that kid of hers."

"You're trying to tell me you don't think she's good looking and you're not interested, her all close by like that?"

"I'm telling you she's not my type and to get the cockamamie idea out of that peanut-sized brain of yours." He started walking toward the exit. "Just leave it alone."

"Me thinks thou doth protest too much." Linder followed. "I believe you *are* interested."

"Damn it Linder, I said leave it!"

"Alright, now don't get yourself all bent out of shape." Linder hurried to catch up.

On the way out, they walked through a smaller outbuilding filled with individual stables for the more expensive thoroughbreds and quarter horses. The aisles between the stalls, crowded with sacks of feed and ranching equipment, made for a slow exit. San rounded a corner as two men struggled to back a huge Palomino stallion into a narrow stall, its eyes white with fear. The horse repeatedly kicked the metal siding of the stall, each kick sending gunshot explosions echoing through the hall, contrasting eerily with the stallion's guttural screams.

San walked past as if strolling down a wide street but Linder stood frozen. He had never before seen an animal so intimidating, particularly a horse. All of his senses told him to move as far away as possible but he could see San a short distance beyond standing impatiently and his pride kept him from turning. He could feel the sweat trickle down the nape of his neck in spite of the cold. Finally he took a step, keeping his eyes focused on a spot beyond San, passing the stall after what seemed an eternity. He turned just as the horse jerked its head, bodily lifting one of the men off the ground, as another hoof on metal explosion echoed through the hall.

"Linder, you're looking a little pale in the gizzard. Need another beer?"

"That was one big horse." He took a deep breath.

"And ornery to boot. He knows there are mares around and he's all stirred up about it. He didn't even notice you."

"That's okay with me." He turned for one last look. "So, tell me San, what's the real reason you want a horse?"

"You're just full of questions today." He stopped. "It's like this. I have a place for a horse now and I have a little time on my hands. So, I thought it might be worth a try."

"There are lots of things you could do with your time other than own a horse."

"That's true. I have an orchard and garden now that takes my time." He was silent for a moment. "I reckon it brings me a little closer to Gert and Mattie. They gave me my first horse, you know."

"I remember."

"That's as good a reason as I can think of."

"I can't argue with that."

"Besides, I'm boarding a couple of horses for some folks in town that don't have a decent stable or place to ride. I figured I could use the income. You know we still lease out that property south of the house. It's a nice area to ride as long as you steer clear of the steers."

Nineteen

San walked out of the feed store with an assortment of lettuce, cabbage and broccoli seeds, as well as a fifty pound sack of feed pellets for the goat. He planned to start a winter garden as soon as he could clear the played-out tomato, green bean and okra plants. Nina had proved an able helper and a fast learner. Other than picking up feed as it was needed, San had little to do with the goat. Nina fed, washed and combed her as if she was a pet, which she had become to some degree. With Nora's help, Nina had even made goat cheese, although San had no taste for it. He was at a loss as to why anyone would eat it if given a choice.

He drove through the gate and down the drive, pausing to look for any sign of the black truck, and then parked near the stable. The goat Nina had named Rosie for its pink muzzle stood by calmly watching him unload the car. He stored the feed and had just tossed a forkful of hay into Rosie's pen when he noticed a strange noise coming from the house. He stopped and cocked his head, scanning the area and trying to identify the sound. He stood that way for a full minute.

Setting aside the pitchfork, San walked forward, carefully placing each foot in the soft dirt. He leaned towards the door, peering at the house with his body still hidden inside the stable. At first, he could see nothing unusual. Then he noticed one of Nina's shoes lying sideways next to and just under the back porch steps. It was not like her to leave her things lying around. As he stood looking at it and wondering why she might leave it there, something moved behind the stairs. For a moment, he thought his eyes were playing tricks on him. Then he realized that Nina was looking at him through the steps. Her eyes glistened between the openings.

She reached around the edge of the stairs and signed with one hand but he was unable to follow. He managed to remember the sign for "What?" and replied. She simply held up her hand, telling him to stay put. Then she pointed a finger up at the house and slowly spelled Nora's name, something San knew well. He silently cursed himself for not working harder to learn from her. Using a slim tree branch, Nina scratched at the ground to the left of the stairs, making the sound San had heard. She seemed to be trying to reach a small object in the dirt that he eventually recognized as a kitchen knife.

Stepping back from the doorway, he tried to clear his thoughts, deciding that he would first get to Nina. He jumped one of the stall gates, calming the small mare inside before climbing through the large window at the back of the stable. Crouching between the building and corral fence, he ran through the narrow walkway and across the yard to the far corner of the house. He knelt for a moment against the house, listening for any movement, and then rounded the corner closest to the stairs. Nina looked up at him, keeping perfectly still.

He motioned for her to come to him and she shook her head, pointing above her to the house again. He listened for a moment, hearing a man's voice, and wondered if it was Dewey's. Whoever it was would know San had unloaded his car and was now in the stable. He was likely watching, waiting for him to come out. He crouched low again and ran to the stairs, pulling Nina from her hiding place in one motion and running her back along the house and to the corral. He lifted her through the window and pointed to a small ladder leading to the hay loft. She climbed up it and vanished from sight in an instant.

Returning the way he came, San rounded the house, crawling past the stairs to a point just under the kitchen window. The voice clearly came from inside the kitchen. Unable to make out the words, San decided the man must be whispering. He thought he could hear Nora crying as well. He continued around to the front of the house, lifting a screen off Nina's open bedroom window and climbing in. He stepped forward and paused, the wooden floor creaking beneath his feet, before realizing he stood within range of Nora's voice.

"Please don't take her. I'm the only parent she's ever really known." She could barely speak.

"That don't matter. She needs to be at her home, not way down in Texas."

"But her home is here, with me."

"No, her home is with her people. Nina's grandmother wants her with family."

"Tell Mary that *I'm* Nina's people now." She pleaded.

"Look at yourself in the mirror, Nora. You're not our family. You're not even her mother. Now go find her and get her ready to go. We need to leave right away."

"She thinks of me as her mother."

"I'm her uncle and if it was up to me you could keep the little freak. But mother made me promise I'd bring her back to the family."

"I didn't want to take her away. I didn't want to leave, I had to. You know what her father would have done to me if I'd stayed."

"Jimmy's in prison. He's no good. Leave him out of this."

"He could get out at any time. What would he do to Nina?"

"If he ever gets out he better go far away. He makes trouble wherever he is and we don't need that. We can take care of Nina."

"But she needs a mother." She pleaded.

"Her mother is dead, remember?"

"Don't talk to me like that, Raymond. She was my sister." She sobbed.

San had stood frozen, not knowing what to do, not wanting to listen but unable to avoid it. He had thought Nora was in danger. Now it was clear she was facing a different sort of problem, but to her no less serious. He considered retreating the way he had come in. Instead, he calmly walked into the kitchen.

"I'm sorry to barge in on a family matter but I thought we had a burglar." His voice was matter of fact.

Nora and the man turned in surprise. He was no more than twenty San thought, probably younger, with dark hair pulled back into a ponytail. Nora's face was flushed and swollen. She looked away for a moment, wiping her eyes.

"You're the guy that lives out back." He eyed San warily.

"I'm the guy that owns this house."

"Oh." He raised his eyebrows. "I didn't know."

"And you are?"

"Um, I guess Nora and me are related. Her sister was married to one of my brothers."

"Do you have a name?"

"Oh, yeah, I'm Raymond Cloud."

San looked past him to Nora. "Are you alright?"

She nodded. He looked at them both for a moment, waiting for one or the other to say something, but neither would look at him. He started to leave, not knowing what else to do and then stopped.

"I know this is none of my business. But I found Nina under the back porch and I'm wondering what you want me to do with her."

The young man looked at Nora. "Go get the little retard so we can go."

"I said this was none of my business but I can't just let that go. Nina's a bright little girl, one of the quickest I've seen. You have no cause to talk about her like that." San stepped back into the room.

"You were right. It's none of your business." The man kept facing Nora. "Go get the brat."

"Nora, I have Nina somewhere safe and I'll bring her here if you want me to." San ignored the man and struggled to keep his temper in check.

"Look old dude, we'll take care of the freak." He grabbed Nora by the arm. "Do what I tell you."

San stepped forward and placed his hand across the man's wrist. "You don't want to touch her."

San held his gaze as he gradually loosened his grip on Nora. He stepped back and San stepped between them. San could tell he was trying to decide what to do. He finally looked away, walking across the room and pulling out a pack of cigarettes.

"Go outside if you want to smoke."

San watched him make his way to the front porch. He looked down at Nora. In spite of his reluctance to get involved, he felt compelled to help her. His main concern at the moment was Nina. He knew she was safe but he was unsure if she could count on Nora for protection. He decided he needed to better understand the situation.

"Nora, come with me."

She rose unsteadily, walking with him out the back door and down the steps. Her fragile state surprised him. She could take care of herself better than most and usually resented interference from him or anyone else. Yet she offered little resistance when he took her arm. As they walked away from the house she seemed to regain some of her composure.

"I'm not afraid of him." She shook her arm free. "I'm not afraid of any of them. Well, that's not entirely true. Jimmy would kill me if he had the chance. I turned him in for trafficking drugs. And now the family hates me. No surprise there. My life must sound pretty sad, huh?" She stopped and looked at him. "Why am I telling you all this?"

San motioned her into the stable, pulling a bottle of Scotch from behind the door. Unscrewing the top, he took a sip and then handed the bottle to her. She sniffed the top and quickly pulled back, looking at him.

"It gets cold out here. Go ahead, it'll do you good."

She put her lips to the bottle and took one long swig and then another.

"That'll do for now." He took the bottle from her hand, took another sip and replaced it.

"Thanks." She brushed back her hair. "I must look like a witch."

She sat on a narrow bench set close to the wall, staring out the open door. Anxious to get back to Nina, as she had been somewhat panicky when he pulled her from under the porch, San tried to relax, figuring it best to give Nora time to adjust. After a moment, she seemed to come out of her thoughts, turning to him.

"You're a strange one, San Turner. I can't figure you."

He looked down at her and rubbed his forehead. "Nora, what about Nina?"

"Nina? Where is she?"

"She's safe. What are you going to do?"

She stood and began pacing the floor, her eyes again glistening. Then she stopped and turned.

"The family wants Nina back with them. It's not fair. I took her when no one else wanted her. And I couldn't stand the thought of her growing up around them. I've had her since she was three and now they want her back."

"You have to send her back?"

"You heard what Raymond said. I'm only her aunt. I took Nina in but technically my ex-mother-in-law has custody thanks to the great state of Oklahoma. I took her because it's a bad situation and a bad family and there was nothing else I could do and still sleep at night. Two of the sons are in prison and you heard what Raymond thinks of Nina. The whole family is like that. They think that because she's deaf she can't be a normal, bright little girl."

"Why would they want her back then?"

"Raymond let it slip without meaning to. They think the state will pay them to keep her. They don't like to work so it's easy money."

"You don't get paid, do you?"

"No, I'm not supposed to have her. I don't want their damn money! I just want her to have a chance. I love her." She sat again and wept quietly.

San looked down at her and struggled with what he should do. He'd never been any good at knowing the right thing to say. That's Linder's department, he thought, but he's nowhere near. Finally, he sat down next to her. After a moment, she took his hand but continued crying. The she wiped her eyes and began speaking softly.

"My sister, Natalie, got mixed up with Raymond's family when we moved to Red Rock, where we had jobs. Our parents were not the greatest so she and I got away from home as soon as we could. At first, Raymond's brother Jimmy seemed nice enough. He and Natalie had Nina pretty quick. But after a year or two, she began acting strange. She would drop Nina off at my place with no warning, and then she wouldn't pick her up. I'd have to go find her the next day so I could go to work. I could tell Natalie wasn't taking care of Nina like a mother should. We fought about it all the time but it kept getting worse and worse. Finally, she confessed that Jimmy was dealing drugs and supplying her but said she promised to stop.

"She was starting to turn her life around too and then one day the law breaks down their door and arrests Jimmy and some other guy. They found Natalie in the bedroom overdosed on heroin. Supposedly, her death was an accident but I never believed that for a minute. I knew Jimmy had been messing around with another woman and wanted to be rid of her. I was so angry I testified against him about the drugs - maybe not one of my smartest moves. And just like that, Nina had no parents.

"I felt responsible for her, partly because I helped put her father away but mostly because they didn't want her and said so to my face. I couldn't leave her in a place like that. So we left and eventually ended up here."

"She's lucky she has you."

"No, I'm the lucky one."

111

"So, what do we do now? I should go check on Nina. She was fairly upset when I found her."

"Where is she?"

"She's in a special hiding place I used when I was her age."

San walked between the stalls to the back of the stable and up the narrow ladder, reaching into the loft to get Nina's attention. After a moment, she followed him down, running past him to Nora before he was halfway back down the walkway. After hugging Nora, she stepped back, signing frantically to her. San stood by waiting.

"She's saying she knows why Raymond has come. She read his lips when I first opened the door. That's when she ran off. She's afraid of him."

"I could see that when I found her."

Nora stepped back. "Lord, she has a knife. Nina, why do you have a knife?"

"She told you, she's scared of the guy."

Nora looked up at him. "She wants to stay here, San."

"You have to tell her the truth, Nora."

"I'll speak to her so you can hear." She turned to Nina. "Your grandmother Mary has custody of you, sweetheart. I'm sorry Nina but they want you back with them." She wiped her eyes. "The law says you have to go."

Nina shook her head and responded, looking at San and then back to Nora.

"She says we can all run away where they can't find us."

"No, sweetie, San lives here. This is his home. The law says you have to live with Raymond's family if they want you to."

She shook her head and again responded.

"She says they don't really want her." She looked at San. "What do I say?"

"Tell her the truth, Nora."

She stared at her hands for a moment and then turned to Nina. "I don't know if they want you or not Nina but your grandmother was given legal custody of you after your mother died. I've told you this before, sweetheart." She held her by the shoulders. "You know I love you and would do anything for you, but you have to understand."

Nina shook her head and signed a response.

"What did she say?" San sat across from them.

Nora slumped against the wall. "She said 'Not anything.'"

"Then tell her the truth."

"Why do you keep saying that? I've told her the way it is."

"That's not what I meant. She wants to know where you stand. Tell her what you're going to do."

"Oh San, what can I do? It's all of them and just me. I have no family."

"She still wants to know what you'll do. You should tell her."

"But what can I do?"

"Only you can answer that. What do you want to do?"

"I want to keep her here. I want her to grow up safe and happy. I want to protect her from the bad in the world. Isn't that what any mother would want?"

"It is. So what will you tell her?"

She sat looking at the floor, slowly rubbing her hands as if they ached. Nina looked from her to San and back, waiting for an answer.

"I'll take her back myself." She said to herself and then faced Nina. "We'll go back together. I'll tell them I'll apply for custody and send them the checks. I'll tell them you want to stay with me where you have a goat and a garden. You can tell them yourself."

Nina nodded and sat next to her, taking her arm.

"That sounds like the truth." San chuckled. "I'm not sure I'd offer them money right off the bat."

She faced him squarely, pausing a moment to gather her thoughts. "I have an idea but it's an awful lot to ask. Just a minute."

She turned to Nina. "I want you to go take Rosie for a walk. I'll be along in just a minute."

She waited until Nina had left the building. "It will be just me and Nina against them. They're a big family that's used to pushing people around and getting their way, doing whatever it takes, legal or not. I could use some help."

San stood and took a step back. "You're not asking me to go with you?"

"You don't know what difference it would make. They have no respect for women but they'll listen to a man, even Jimmy's mother will. She's a tough old witch but that's how she was raised. A man speaks and she'll listen."

"Nora, I'm glad to do whatever I can to help out but I have responsibilities here. I have to take care of these horses." He motioned across the room. "And I have someone coming tomorrow who wants to board a pregnant mare. I'll lose that business if I just leave."

"Please, just take a moment to think it over. I know it's asking a lot, but I have nowhere else to turn. I'm sorry to be asking, San but I feel like I have to do everything I can. It's Nina's life we're talking about." She pleaded.

"I know what we're talking about." He barked. "Don't talk to me like I don't know this is important."

"I know you care for Nina. It's so obvious. I'm sorry." Her voice was just above a whisper. "Forget I asked. It was unfair of me."

San started to speak when Rosie wandered just past the corner of the house. He watched the goat, waiting for Nina to follow.

"That's odd. I've never known Nina to let Rosie take the lead. We'd better check on her."

Rounding the house, followed by Nora, San could find no sign of Nina. Nora turned back toward the kitchen, disappearing through the door as San hurried to the front of the house, hoping Nina would be waiting, distracted by some new interest. But the porch stood empty. He called to Nora.

"How did Raymond get here?"

She stepped out the door. "He said he and a friend drove down in his pickup."

"Was he inside?" He opened the screen door.

"Oh my god, I thought he was still out here smoking." She put her hands to her mouth.

"He's got her." San slammed the door. "Son of a bitch just took her! With two of them, it wouldn't have been hard to do. How could I not see it?" He paced the floor.

"Oh god, we have to go after them." She ran to her car.

"Slow down, Nora. They're long gone. This was their plan all along. I'll call the sheriff."

"No, don't do that. It won't do any good. I don't have custody, remember?"

"Damn. That's the first thing they'll ask. Then they won't do a thing except maybe arrest you."

"I should have known. Why did I let her out of my sight?"

"We both should've known."

"I have to do something. I can't just stand here." She climbed in the car, started it and then shut it off, laying her head on the steering wheel.

San walked to the car, opening the door and taking her by the arm as she sobbed quietly. Handing her his handkerchief, he led her back to the porch, settling her on a slatted wooden bench before stepping to the stairway where two massive columns framed the broad opening. Looking down the hill to the rooftops and church steeples marking the town, and on to the distant line of hills now reddish in the fading light, he recalled the view as one of his favorite memories, one he often returned to when something weighed on him.

"How long will it take you to pack?"

She looked over at him. "No time at all."

"You know where they live, right?"

"Of course I do." She stood.

"If we hurry, we can make the state line by midnight."

Twenty

San

I wasn't more than seven or eight when Gert and Mattie gave me a puppy, a brown and white mix with one black paw. I named her Jet because she was the fastest dog I'd ever seen - maybe a little too fast for her own good. She would run down jackrabbits and cottontails regularly. She even ran down a roadrunner once. She never killed a one that I know of. She just subdued them for a moment and then let them go. They would jump up, running off in a flash as if they had escaped on their own while she calmly watched them.

I finally decided that she had some greyhound somewhere in her past. It wasn't just that she was fast, it was the way she tackled whatever she was after with one of her front feet. She would be running full tilt and reach out, sending the critter into a tumble, then hold it on the ground for a moment with a paw. She was strange that way. Any other dog would never let a caught animal free, the instinct for blood too strong. But she had somehow overcome her nature and it to her was all just a game.

Her evenness of temper came through in other ways too. I once took a bone right out of her mouth to impress a friend who had bet she wouldn't allow it. She didn't even let out a growl. She only looked at me with a hurt expression, like she was being punished for some unknown offense. After I gave back the bone, she trotted off with it, eyeing me warily for a while, as if to say there were limits to her patience.

Anytime Gert or Mattie was sick in bed she parked herself next to the door, leaving only if one or the other of us was in the room. Normally consigned to stay outdoors, she'd find a way to the sick room and ignore any attempts to move her back outside until Gert or Mattie was again up and about. During those times her manner was almost human.

One crisp fall day, after I'd had her six or seven years, she came up missing. I looked everywhere with no success. It was so unlike her that Gert and Mattie went into a panic, calling the sheriff's office to help with a search. Anyone else would have been told the sheriff has more important business than looking for lost dogs, but they had taught most of the people in that office in one or other of their classes and commanded a certain respect. A deputy arrived within the hour and we spent the rest of the day driving the back roads, calling out the window and scanning back lots and pastures for any sign of her.

It was strange and disorienting for her to go missing on such a beautiful day. A cold front had come through the night before, and the sky appeared scrubbed clean, almost crystalline. It spread out above us as if it had a physical presence separate from and superior to the lowly earth. The sky seemed to fill the very air we breathed, every molecule pressing itself on the land below. In the distance, the horizon had gained a life of its own, changing moment to moment as the ever-present streaks of cirrus clouds wove their way overhead in an endless tapestry of shape and hue. The beauty of it only served to worsen an already sad day.

As the time passed, my worst fears began to become reality. It's a hard time when a young person first encounters the idea of death up close. I tried to escape the thought that I might never again see Jet. Only just that morning she had run off with one of my shoes just for the sport of watching me chase her. But I knew the chances that we'd find her running up the road were fading. I reckon Gert finally spotted my sad face in the rear view mirror.

"San, you know what a good dog Jet has been for this family, don't you son?"

I nodded.

"And we want what is best for her. I know you're a strong boy, San. You can face whatever we may find today."

I nodded again and looked at her in the mirror, hoping she was right.

The sun had set, but light still spilled across the green-tinted horizon when I spotted her. Gert was driving. Mattie grabbed her arm, pointing her to the small form laying several yards off the road. My heart sank as we approached and could see little in the way of movement. We sat, silent and unmoving, none of us wanting to face what we had feared. The deputy drove up behind us before we had even opened a door, walking past the car and on to where she lay. He had brought Dan McCullough, the local veterinarian. The vet knelt for a moment, and then turned and shook his head. I managed to open the door and walk unsteadily to where he stood.

"It's no good, San. She'll have to be put down."

He walked back to the car and spoke quietly with Gert. I made myself look at Jet for a brief moment. She was all twisted up but I could see she was still breathing. I knelt, laying my palm against her head, and then felt the deputy's hand on my shoulder. The vet was with him.

"I'm sorry, San. I don't have what I need to put her down. In the rush to get here I didn't check my bag to be sure I had enough serum. I had to use more than the usual amount on a big Mastiff last week, and it just slipped my mind.

"It'll be a half hour before I can get back." He paused and took a breath. "She's suffering, San. The deputy here has a rifle he uses for this sort of thing. She won't feel it. I think we ought to put her out of her pain as soon as we can."

118

"I spoke with your aunts and they agree. You can wait back at the car, son, if you want to." The deputy spoke softly.

The deputy was back before I fully understood what was about to happen. My mind seemed to jump from one thought to the other, unable to make any sense. I looked back at the car and saw Gert and Mattie standing by, waiting for me to join them. The sky above them captured the last light of day in a deep, rose-colored glow, casting the broken horizon in featureless shadows. The deputy's rifle stock reflected the light and glistened a glassy reddish-brown and everything around me appeared unusually clear and detailed, as if made of some fragile substance. I reached out and held the gun barrel.

"I'll do it."

The deputy stared at me. "Your aunts are waiting back there for you, son. I can take care of this."

"I want to do it. It's only right. She's my dog and she knows me, so I should be the one."

The deputy looked back at the vet and my aunts, and then stepped away, handing me the rifle. I bent once more to touch her ear and she lifted her head briefly. Then I aimed, blinked the water from my eyes, and pulled the trigger.

Twenty-one

Linder walked through the stables behind San's house, looking for the oats he would scoop into the plastic buckets hanging from each stall gate. San had called the night before saying he was on his way out of town and asking that Linder care for the boarded horses, as well as Nina's goat, while he was away. He told Linder he would explain later but it was clear from the sound of his voice that there had been some sort of trouble.

He stood for a moment, trying to familiarize himself with the stable. Keenly aware that he was out of his element, he was determined to do his best to help his friend. To his right, six individual stalls occupied one end of the building, three on each side facing each other with a wide walkway between. Bales of hay, tin buckets, three-legged stools, unopened bags of feed and low wooden benches crowded the open area. Leather halters and ropes draped across benches and hung loosely from the gate posts as if thrown there in afterthought. A hand painted sign of each horse's name hung at the top of all but one gate, and over the wide stable doors was written the Latin "Equus caballus". San has been reading Darwin again, Linder thought. As if on cue the horses whinnied one after the other and stretched their necks over the stall gates.

Linder had given San a stack of paperbacks a few months ago, Darwin among them, in hope that they would take his mind off all that had happened during the past year. Once an avid reader, San had all but given up books. He said he had no patience for reading and instead preferred hunting, fishing or other such activities. But Linder managed to convince him active men could also have an intellectual life, appealing to San's love of history and using figures like Jefferson, Franklin and Darwin as examples. He complained initially but the plan eventually paid off, as evidenced by his Latin scrawl overhead. Linder turned, looking back into the stable.

On his left, the building rose to a loft where stacked bales of hay leaned unevenly. Sparrows flitted between the rafters, chirping frantically among themselves as if carrying on an endless argument. Beneath the loft, a line of pitchforks, hoes and shovels hung on twelve-penny nails next to a workbench covered with bottles, cans and jars. In one corner, Nina's goat, Rosie, stood in a separate stall that opened onto the small corral. He spotted a scoop lying on the bench behind a large plastic jug half-filled with an opaque brown liquid.

As he walked to the table, Linder noticed the sound of an approaching car through the open doors. It circled between the house and stable, coming into view for an instant and then stopping abruptly. Between the bird, horse and goat noises, it was no surprise he had failed to hear it earlier. He wondered why any car that ventured down the long drive would come all the way to the back of the house. No one other than San knew he was there. He stood still, listening. The car door closed and footsteps moved back and forth along the building, the coarse gravel sounding like wet snow underfoot. He felt the hair rise on the back of his neck.

"Linder, are you in there?" Jules' voice echoed through the doorway.

Sighing with relief, he stepped through the door into the bright sunlight. "You had me worried for a second, Jules. I couldn't imagine who might come all the way back here."

"I thought that was your car." She holstered her pistol. "But then again, I wanted to be sure."

"What are you doing here?"

"I was about to ask you the same question. Although that doesn't mean I'm not glad to see you." She smiled at him and then peered into the building. "I'm guessing San asked you to take care of his critters for him."

"Good detective work, deputy. Unfortunately, I have no idea what I'm doing."

"I had horses when I was growing up. I'll give you a hand." She walked up next to him. "I'll bet they have some hay in there, Linder. We could go for a roll before San gets back."

"Jules, is that anyway to talk to a man of the cloth?"

"You must mean bed sheets, sir." She smiled. "I'm sure glad you're not one of those Catholic priests. Or those preachy Puritan types either."

He had never known a woman to be so frank. "Do you talk this way to all your men?"

"I'm picky. I'm only interested in one man."

"Anyone I know?"

"Oh, come on Linder, play along."

"Don't we have another archery lesson this afternoon, Jules?"

She smiled. "Archery? Is that what you call it? Your place at four on the dot, sir."

"We'll take up this conversation again then. In the mean time, I have a job to do."

"Alright, but you could try to have some fun sometime without scheduling it."

"By the way, what is it San asked you to do?" He decided to change the subject.

"He asked me to keep an eye on the place while he's gone. He's still worried about someone prowling around."

"Did he tell you why he had to leave all of a sudden?"

"Nothing specific, but I can't recall ever hearing him sounding so worried. He just said he might need my help later." She turned to look at him. "I'm afraid it has something to do with that little girl. Just my woman's intuition."

She walked into the building, greeting each horse in turn. Linder studied her. Her deep-set, hazel eyes reflected her no-nonsense but fun-loving demeanor, one of her many contradictions. She could turn cold and distant in an instant if offended or the situation required it. Then again, something about her voice made her seem vulnerable. She was an attractive woman, he knew, but she remained a mystery to him. He couldn't seem to reconcile the hard and soft of her, the deputy and the woman.

She looked up. "What are you gawking at, Linder? You have a job to do, remember?"

He walked to the workbench, grabbing the scoop, and returned. "Where do we start?"

"Each of these hay bales will break into cubes." She broke off the section of hay. "Give each horse one. They'll also need water and some oats, if you've got them."

"That's what this is for." He held up the scoop.

She scanned the walkway and reached behind a bench. "Here's a bag of oats. I'll handle this if you'll take care of the hay and water."

They worked through the stalls together while Jules spoke softly to each horse as if she'd known the animal for years. While she commented on the qualities of a horse, she pointed out commonly-used names for horse color, tools and care. They came to the last stall and she stopped for a moment, peering over the gate and studying the occupant. She stepped back, looking up and down the walkway outside the stalls.

"Linder, this horse has a limp. See if you can find a cleaning tool for the hoof. It's a short, big-handled knife with a curved blade. I don't see one around here. Try that workbench over there." She pointed across the room.

Linder rummaged through the crowded workbench, overturning empty boxes and opening half-full cans of nails. He had a vague idea of the general shape, but worried he would look right at the small tool without knowing it. He studied each area of the bench carefully. Jules had just asked what was taking so long when he saw it, partially hidden by an empty cardboard box. He moved the box and as he did so the tool fell behind the bench, completely out of view. Crawling beneath the table, he probed the space between the thick supports and the stable wall. After a moment, he located the tool and as he lifted it out, the edge caught on a folded piece of paper wedged in a narrow opening behind one of the table legs. He pulled the paper out along with the knife.

Handing the tool to Jules, he studied the paper while she cleaned the horse's hoof. It was a two page computer print-out detailing the amount and dosage for poisoning by arsenic. The pages described where to purchase the arsenic, how to add it to food without notice and what symptoms to expect. Other than the grim subject, the excerpt might have been a recipe from a poorly written cookbook. He stared at it in disbelief as Jules emerged from the stall, dusting off her knees with her hat.

"You look like you've seen a ghost, Linder. I wasn't doing surgery. She only needed her nails done. No blood."

"Take a look at this." He handed her the paper.

She read it quickly. "That San Turner, he does have a sixth sense for crime. Now do you really think it's a coincidence that this just happens to be hidden here in this building? Even still, it's circumstantial and probably wouldn't make a bit of difference to the sheriff." She shook her head. "Those poor old ladies, Linder, they didn't deserve to go that way."

"It does cast their deaths in a different light."

"There's one thing I've never understood about this." She handed him the pages. "If the young guy poisoned them, what was his motive?"

"My initial guess was that he had convinced the aunts to put him in their will but that wasn't the case." He leaned against a gate. "What's your theory, deputy?"

"The usual reasons are either love or money, or both. I think we can rule out love. They didn't put him in their will but that doesn't mean money isn't a possibility. He could have stolen from them and then they found out about it. Or he might have found out where they kept their cash - San said they didn't trust banks - and then gotten them out of the way so he could steal it. Although I doubt retired teachers their age would have had much in the way of savings."

"I see Holmes, so does that make it 'elementary'?"

"You think you're funny but there's a problem with this line of thought. He could have easily taken their money without killing them, especially as old as they were. That makes it a weak motive. The sheriff would see that right away and say the idea of poison is fantasy, regardless of the paper."

"It's back to square one then."

"What are you going to do with the paper?" She picked up her hat and put it on.

"I think we should tell San but not until he gets back. It sounds like he has a lot on his mind." He folded the pages and stuffed them into his shirt pocket.

"You're probably right. I wouldn't want to do anything without asking him first."

They walked to the small orchard and sat under a gnarled pear tree. San had bought a hardwood bench, placing it near his grandmother's favorite spot in the garden. As the autumn sun warmed their backs, the cracked and bent tree creaked in the light wind, its bare branches casting a filigree of shadows at their feet. Jules looked at Linder for a moment.

"It's nice here."

"The aunts loved this garden. It's good to see it back in shape." Linder motioned with his hand.

"You and San have known each other a long time, haven't you?"

"We grew up together. This was a second home to me, sometimes more like a home than my own house."

"Do you see much of your parents?"

"My mother died years ago. I never knew my father."

"What family do you have left, Linder?"

"I have a brother I haven't talked to in years." He stared into the distance.

"Why not?"

"I finally got tired of doing all the work to keep in touch with him. He never called. He never came to see me. I've lived in my house for over fifteen years and he visited once for maybe a total of twenty minutes. The last time was ten years ago."

"Did you invite him?"

"Yes but I got tired of asking." He picked up a twig and tossed it across the fence. "I don't much like talking about it."

"Okay, I'll talk instead. I'm from a big family; three brothers and a sister and I'm somewhere in the middle. It's a problem trying to get together anymore because they're married and have kids. They can really get on my nerves but we find a way to see or talk to each other without too much time going by. Everyone does their part." She paused and turned to him. "I can't imagine how frustrating it would be if they didn't."

"I've gotten used to it."

"That's not something a person should have to get used to."

"It must be nice having a big family to turn to if something goes wrong."

"I'd be lying if I said it wasn't. But then again, there are times when I dream of moving to Australia so I wouldn't have to see them. Especially when they think they can run my life."

He studied her. "You're the holdout in your family. Why don't you have kids?"

"I'm in no hurry and I'm not sure having kids is right for me." She took his hand. "Besides, I'd have to meet the right person."

Linder glanced at his watch. "I didn't realize we'd been here so long. Are we finished? I need to get back to work."

"I didn't scare you off, did I?"

He laughed. "I'm not that easy to get rid of. I have an appointment that I'm going to be late for."

"I'll feed the goat. You go on." She patted the pocket holding the paper. "Put that somewhere safe."

"Don't worry."

She leaned and kissed him lightly. "I'll see you at your place this afternoon. Tell that old lady next door to stop staring at me or I'll get the law after her."

"She doesn't approve of you being at my house at all hours."

"Tell her you're under investigation for unseemly behavior. Or you hope to be soon, anyway." She smiled at him from under her hat.

Twenty-two

They drove north through the night, passing in and out of dying towns marked only by faded road signs and the occasional flashing yellow light. Shuttered buildings appeared briefly in the amber glow and then vanished as if a dream. Nora watched them recede and felt the emptiness of the dense night close in around her. She imagined herself falling down a deep well, the light rapidly fading, the air passing through her lips thin and cold. They had driven in silence for over an hour and every time she thought of Nina she felt as though she could not breathe. She wished San would talk to her.

She wondered at how she had changed since taking in Nina. Before that time, she had been tough and independent, able to handle whoever or whatever came her way. She counted on no one and needed no one. Boyfriends came and went like new addresses and meant as little. Jobs were just a paycheck.

But Nina had altered her in ways she scarcely understood, the difference so slow and subtle it passed without notice until now. The thought of life without her seemed incomprehensible and terrifying. She felt alone and exposed in a way she could never have imagined.

A ghostlike form appeared out of the darkness, passing through the headlight's outer glow in a slow glide. For a moment, it seemed to float before the car like a mirage. Nora sat still, saying nothing as she watched it disappear into the night. She glanced at San and wondered what she had seen or whether she had actually seen anything at all.

"Bubo virginiannus." He murmured.

"Are you speaking English?" She thought she must be hallucinating.

"That's the Latin for a species of bird, the great horned owl. Didn't you see him just now?"

"Is that what that was? I thought I was starting to see things."

"It can have a wing span of up to five feet and go after animals much larger, even porcupines. The wings are designed so they make almost no noise and they hunt mostly at night, so the unsuspecting critter never sees them coming."

"What a lovely thought on a dark and cold night."

"It is getting colder. We may run into trouble if it starts to snow. When we stopped for gas, the lady at the counter said there's a chance tonight and tomorrow. These little back roads can't handle much of anything frozen. I don't want to worry you, but we should talk about what we'll do if the weather gets bad."

"I can't stop thinking about Nina. I feel so responsible. If anything should happen to her, I don't know how I'd go on."

"Nora, we need to focus on finding her. Try not to worry."

"She must be so scared."

"Nina's a smart girl. She knows you're not going to let her go without doing something about it. Besides, they want to return with her safely so they can collect the payments."

"I hope you're right. If they hurt her, they'll never have a moment's peace. I'll kill the bastards. I'll do it slow and enjoy it."

"Remind me never to cross you."

"She must be lonely. None of them knows sign language. They never bothered to learn."

He realized she needed to talk about Nina. "She does alright with ignorant types like yours truly. If you don't mind my asking, was she born deaf or did something happen?"

"She could hear fine when she was born but she has a condition that causes her to gradually lose her hearing. She even learned to talk some before it started to get worse."

"So she could hear when she was little. Can she hear much now?"

"That's what the hearing aids are supposed to help. She does better up close but she usually needs to read lips as well unless the person can sign. She's still sort of new to sign language herself."

"I admire you for taking her in."

"I didn't do it because she's deaf. I don't pity Nina. I love her just as she is."

"I wasn't thinking of her deafness. It takes a brave woman to take in a child on her own."

"I never felt brave. I knew what her life would be like growing up with people that didn't want her. I knew that someone had to take her out of there and I had to be the one to do it. There was no one else."

"It sounds like you know what you're talking about."

"My parents weren't much good at being parents. They had their own problems and split up when my sister and I were young. They probably should never have had kids. We shuttled back and forth between them but they always seemed caught up in their own lives. We were pretty much on our own."

"That can be hard on a child."

"You heard what it did to my sister. She was older and remembered when things were better at home. She resented the change."

"She was all the family you had?"

"Except for Nina."

"You never had kids of your own?"

"No, never. I just turned forty so it's not likely I ever will."

"Having kids is not in the cards for some people, no matter how much they want them." A lump caught in his throat and he was angered that people who should never have children so often have them, while people who want them are unable to.

"Well, you've seen what a great judge of men I am." She paused, looking out the window. "You said Nina's better off with me but I'm not so sure. I brought her around the likes of Dewey, didn't I?"

"You shouldn't have brought someone like that around her."

"I didn't mean to."

"You should have known better."

"You don't understand." Her voice broke.

"I know that a child shouldn't have to be around a lowlife like Dewey."

"He was so charming at first. That's what hooks me every time. They come across all fun and exciting in the beginning. And then everything changes and they think they own you, like you're a piece of property and they can do whatever they want to you. Because of Nina, I had sworn off men but I thought Dewey was different. I was a fool.

"As soon as he said a mean word to her, I knew I had to get out. I was so ashamed that I had exposed her to that kind of treatment. Of course, I should've known leaving him wasn't going to be that easy. It never is. So there he was in Curley's Cue knocking me around."

"Why did you take Nina into a place like that?"

"You make me sound like a monster."

"I don't tolerate the mistreatment of children."

"You're quick to judge people, San."

"I know what I see."

"You do, do you?" She glared at him. "I do book-keeping on the side and Curley owed me for work I had done. I never intended to go in, but he had left out an important account and asked me to make the correction right there, as a favor. It took five minutes to correct. Curley gave Nina some ice cream and I was just waiting

131

for her to finish up when Dewey walked in. Just my bad luck, I guess."

"I think he was following you and saw his chance."

"That's a scary thought. I figured him as a lightweight."

"Those can sometimes be your most dangerous types. They're unpredictable."

"Well, I'm done with him and he knows it."

"That's best for Nina and probably for you. So, eventually Nina won't hear anything, only silence? It's hard to imagine what that would be like."

"I try to think of all that she *will* be able to do."

"That's a good way for a mother to think."

Nora noticed a light clicking on the windshield. "Speaking of hearing things, what's that sound?"

"It must be sleet. Although it's so small I'm having trouble seeing it."

Within minutes the roadside began to lighten as snow blew perpendicular to the blacktop like a fine, white sand. Snowflakes trailed across the hood in swirling eddies before vanishing. A line of trees beyond the headlights took on a ghostly blue-white hue against the darkness beyond. In the distance, a yellow glow appeared above the road, filling the horizon with light.

"We'd better stop in up here to see what this weather is doing. That is, if there's anything open. My concern is black ice. It can be hard to see on these small roads." San slowed the car.

"It must be nearly midnight. I could stand some coffee."

"You and me both."

He pulled into a near-empty parking lot fronting a low wooden building. The roof carried a light dusting of snow. Windows on either side of the wide entrance cast long shadows into the street, illuminating a closed storefront on the opposite side of the road. Blurred figures moved behind the fogged glass, disfigured by the spreading frost. He and Nora sat for a moment and then went in through a glass door plastered with fliers for wild game dinners, domino tournaments and church bake sales.

San followed Nora to a booth under the row of windows. Sitting across from him in the overstuffed blue seat, she brushed back her thick tangle of amber hair and unzipped her coat. Figuring she must look particularly haggard in the harsh fluorescent light, especially as tired as she felt, she peered at a small clock over the counter, surprised to find it past two in the morning. She glanced across the table at San, who sat staring at a menu as if hypnotized, and realized her appearance is the last he would notice.

After a moment, a waitress approached from the far end of the room. Humming softly to herself through smacks of chewing gum, she pulled a pen from behind her ear and a small pad of paper from her apron pocket. Her left hand, covered with turquoise and silver rings, one for every finger including her thumb, held a slight tremor. Her plum-colored lipstick clashed with the pink cloth hat she used to keep her hair back.

"What can I get for you folks tonight? Or is it this morning? I guess you can take your pick, honey."

"Coffee for me." Nora tried to muster a smile.

"Another cup of coffee and two slices of your apple pie." San handed her his menu. "We're headed north and could use some help with road conditions. Is there anyone around who knows if they're passable?"

"Our cook would know. He drove an eighteen wheeler for a hundred years and still checks in with every trucker who stops by. I'll ask him to come talk to you, darlin'. He should be able to help."

"Thanks."

"Anything for a good-looking man," She turned to Nora. "No offense, hon'."

As they sipped their coffee, a man pushed through the kitchen door. He stared at them for a moment from behind the low counter and then walked around one end, adjusting his stained apron and muttering to himself. He stopped at their table and stood, holding a stack of menus to his chest and saying nothing. The deeply furrowed lines around his eyes sagged like dikes about to break. Pulling at his gray beard, he eyed Nora before turning to San.

"Ben Fiddlin." The man nodded.

San wondered what in the world he meant. "With what?" He finally said.

"No, that's my name."

San nodded toward Nora. "Mr. Noe, this here's Nora O'Quinn."

"Ben Fiddlin!" He yelled back.

San glanced at Nora and frowned. "And just what exactly have you been fiddling with, Mr. Noe?"

Nora put her hand to her mouth, suppressing a laugh.

"Are ya'll from Austin or what?" The man pulled at his bulbous nose.

"Why no, Mr. Noe, we're not from Austin." San rubbed his forehead and stole another glance at Nora, who stifled a grin but appeared every bit as perplexed as he felt.

"There's no 'No' to it, it's Fiddlin!"

"Fiddlin, it is." San guessed, having no idea what the man meant.

"Alright then." He slapped the table with his thick fingers.

"Alright then, Mr. Noe."

The man turned bright red and spoke very slowly. "My name is Benjamin Franklin Fiddlin. That's the name I was born with and that's the name I'll die with. Now if you snooty-minded Austin folks want to make fun of it, I don't know why you expect my help."

Nora jumped up, no longer able to contain herself. "I have to go to the ladies room!"

"My apologies, Mr. Fiddlin, but there's no need for insults. It was just a misunderstanding." San held up his hands.

"What's wrong with her?" The man watched her go.

"Female problems, I expect." San hoped to steer the conversation away from Nora and back to the weather. "Now, I understand you may know about the road conditions north of here."

"Where are you all headed?" He sat across from San.

"North into Oklahoma, to a place called Red Rock."

"How soon do you need to get there?"

"It's real important that we get there soon, right away in fact, so we can't waste any time. The only reason I stopped is to find out about the weather."

"I figured it had to be important for you to travel this time of night in such conditions. A friend was in here a while ago and said the snow and ice is pretty thick in spots up that way. I wouldn't advise that you attempt it alone." He nodded across the room "Now, there are two fellers who are going that way in a rig and if you was to follow right behind them, you'd be alright. If it got too bad, they could help out. That's your best bet other than waiting it out here. I'll ask them, if you like."

"I'd appreciate it."

"There's one thing I didn't mention. Them two are a little funny, if you know what I mean."

San shook is head. "I don't think I follow you."

"They don't care for women like you and me do. They're real nice, mind you, but some folks get nervous around them that's a little light in the step. I'm not bothered. I say live and let live. Is that going to be a problem?"

"Not if they can help us get to where we're going."

"I need to get back to the kitchen but I'll ask them to come over and visit with you and the missus."

He walked to the far end of the counter where two young men sat talking and spoke to them briefly. They looked toward San's table and one of them waved. San was trying to decide if he should wave back when Nora reappeared.

"Did that man just wave at you?"

"Not only that, he's going to come talk to me about helping us out if it's alright with you."

"Help with what?"

"Getting through this stretch of bad weather without losing too much time."

"How are they going to do that?"

"Why don't we let them tell us? Here they come."

The two men approached the table, one fair with short blond hair, the other dark. Both were clean-shaven, with a gold stud in one ear. Tall and thin, they looked as if they could be brothers.

"Hello." The blond man held out a hand to Nora.

"I'm Sydney. This is Arthur. Everyone but me calls him Art." They all shook hands.

"Please sit down." Nora moved across the table and sat beside San.

"We understand you are trying to go north on important business." Sydney began.

"It's very important." Nora interrupted.

"Well, you're welcome to follow us. The truck will leave a track that should make driving easier for you. If it gets bad, we'll be close by." He reached out and put his hand on Nora's. "We'll take care of you sweetie. Try not to worry. You're going to have that pretty face all wrinkled if you keep it up."

Art pulled a phone from his pocket and looked at San. "Now, just keep your phone on and call if you have any trouble. A macho man like you can still ask for help if you need it. You do have a phone, don't you?"

"Sure." San touched his coat pocket.

"Vibrate or music?"

"Uh, I use the ring tone."

"Oh, I prefer to vibrate. It gives me a thrill when someone calls."

"Arthur likes his toys." Sydney smiled. "San, do you like to travel?"

136

"I haven't had much chance." He shifted uncomfortably.

"Arthur and I love it. We're from Austin, which we love, but driving lets us get away as much as we like. And, we get paid to do it. Can you believe that?" He nudged Art. "We were in New Orleans last year for Mardi Gras. Arthur went as Carmen Miranda, complete with spike heels, and I was Liberace. I strapped on a friend's portable keyboard and even had tiny plastic candelabras glued on each end.

"We like to spend time in Galveston but it's so sad after the hurricane. Arthur and I lived there when we were first together, only a few blocks off the sea wall. We could watch the surfers walking to the beach in their tight wet suits from our balcony. I must say, they do take good care of their bodies."

"Sydney, you don't have to do all the talking." Art turned to Nora. "Where in Oklahoma are you going and more important, why there of all places? It's barely civilized."

"My sister died and her little girl is there. Her father's family has taken her from me and I'm going to try to get her back."

"They took your child? How can they do that? Oh, sweetie that's terrible." Sydney took Nora's hand. "I'm so ashamed. Here I am talking nonsense when you have a child to find. Arthur, you can't waste any more of their time gossiping. We must get them going right away."

"Me waste time? Who's the big talker in this family, huh? We all know the answer to that now don't we?"

They got up at once and turned for the door. "Come with us, companeros! Vaya con Dios!"

San and Nora followed at a distance.

"I hope you know what you're doing." Nora whispered.

"I have no idea what I'm doing but I'm determined to find Nina. If following them is what it takes then that's what I aim to do." He stopped and looked at her. "Are you with me on this?"

"If you weren't willing to keep on, I'd be taking my chances with Art and Syd."

"That's what I wanted to hear."

Twenty-three

San and Nora followed the eighteen-wheeler through the night, the pale red form disappearing and reappearing behind sheets of snow like some wayward barn. San concentrated on following the dark tracks left by the truck's huge wheels, struggling to keep the surreal scene from putting him to sleep. Nora leaned against the passenger-side window dozing fitfully.

As they came over a low rise the snow lightened and then stopped altogether. Roadside drifts still exploded into swirling clouds as they passed, the snow pelting the windshield like fine sand. To the east, the horizon emerged in an unbroken line beneath the silver glow of an immense sky. They had reached the high plains.

A brightly painted truck stop appeared out of the darkness and Art leaned out of the window, waving them to a stop. Figures bustled in and out of the building in the early morning half-light. Icicles hanging from the undersides of cattle trucks and cars looked like dirty teeth slowly melting into oil-like pools. Art hopped out of the cab, closely followed by Sydney, and tapped on Nora's window. She awoke with a start. Still half-asleep, she watched for a moment as the two men jumped in place to warm themselves before she rolled down her window, wiping the sleep from her eyes with the back of her hand.

"This is where we have to turn east on the Interstate. The word is that the roads are fine from here on to where you're going." Sydney reached in and took Nora's hand. "I wish we could do more. We talked about it the whole way. We'll be thinking good thoughts and hoping you have your little girl back soon."

"Here's our address and phone. Please let us know how you are." Art leaned in and smiled at San. "Come for a visit any time. It isn't far."

Nora turned to San, smiling, and then turned back to the window. "You're both so very kind."

"I want to thank you for running interference for us." San leaned toward the open window. "I believe we might've run into trouble without your help."

Sydney rubbed his hands together. "It's a little nippy out to do much socializing."

"You must be freezing. Get back in your truck."

They each leaned through the window, kissing Nora on the cheek before hurrying back to the truck. Sydney waved as they pulled through the parking lot, soon disappearing into the distance. Nora sat back, staring out the windshield after them, her hand to her cheek.

"There are still a few decent people left in the world." She sighed.

"I'm not sure I'm ready for a visit but there's no denying they went out of their way to help us. Did you know they left the diner without even drinking their coffee?"

She turned to look at him, eyebrows raised. "I thought they were ready to go."

"They were after they heard the reason we needed to keep moving. But they came in after us and left two pieces of untouched pie on the counter."

"Oh San, I think I'm going to cry."

"Alright, that'll get me back to driving. We've lost time but should reach the border soon. Raymond Cloud will have lost time too." He turned the ignition. "Are you ready?"

She looked out the window. "I thought the landscape was starting to look familiar. My home town is not far from here."

San pulled onto the road, now clear of snow. "Bring back memories, does it?"

"Unfortunately."

They lapsed into silence as the low sky turned a gunmetal gray, the horizon flattening to a sharp edge in the morning light. Trees became fewer by the mile and eventually seemed to vanish altogether except for the occasional cottonwood or willow along the edge of a shallow draw or canyon. Oil rigs and pumps dotted the broad pastures lining the road. Hereford and Black Angus cattle, scattered like confetti against the snow-covered fields, grazed sparse grass behind endless miles of barbed wire fence.

They entered a small town along a wide, curving boulevard flanked by low yellow brick buildings and asphalt parking lots. Storefronts sporting windows painted in the maroon and gold of the local high school slid by. Massive Live oaks lining side streets stretched their tangled forms into a green tunnel over the narrow roads. San turned onto a small driveway leading up to a pink cinderblock building adjacent to the county courthouse. The sign over the door read *La Casita* in red, orange and blue lettering. Nora sank into her seat as San set the brake.

"Okay with you if we have migas for breakfast? I have a hankering for some salsa." He studied her for a moment. "You don't look so good."

"It's just strange being back here." She had a sense of being watched.

"We can keep moving, if you'd rather." He could see the worry in her face. "I'd have to check how far to the next town."

"I'm just tired." She sat up. "We need to eat and you need a break. You should've let me drive after our last stop."

"I'm more hungry than tired."

"Let's go eat then. I hope you like eggs."

"I'll take them any way they have them." San pushed open the restaurant door. "I like jalapenos with my eggs. They're guaranteed to wake you up."

They ordered at the small counter and took a booth in the corner at Nora's request. She couldn't shake a vague feeling of apprehension, as if something important lurked nearby, something she was unable to see, something obvious yet hidden. While San picked up their coffees she peered out the window, eventually focusing on the building directly across the street before recognizing it as at the county jail. No surprise she felt uneasy, she thought. She relaxed into the vinyl seatback.

"That's the county jail." She nodded toward the window. "I was a little too familiar with that place as a teenager. I didn't realize we were right across the street from it. I guess I had put it out of my memory."

"Memory can be funny that way." San sipped his coffee.

"I do have gaps in my memory. I used to worry it had to do with knocked around by my ex but I finally decided my memory's better than most. It's just the bad I can't remember so well."

"Forgetting the rough times may not be so bad. There's plenty I wish I could forget."

"You don't strike me as the type who is bothered by much, especially something as flimsy as a memory."

"You'll decide a good memory is over-rated if it keeps you awake at night."

"But aren't there things other than your car keys you want to remember? Like the people you love. People like your aunts?"

"I could never forget Gert and Mattie."

"But sometimes you want to?"

"Only the ways I let them down."

"We all let down people we love at one time or the other. It's part of being human."

"Being human is no excuse."

"You're too hard on yourself, San."

"There are things I should've done better."

"There are things I never should have done."

"That too."

"I'm a fine one to talk. I've been beating myself up over Nina all night."

San just looked at her.

"I know, you think I should feel guilty."

"Only if it helps you do better next time."

"Who else could you never forget? Your aunts can't be the only ones."

"It's not something I dwell on."

"Were you ever married?"

"I was."

"And?"

"And what?"

"Are you always so talkative or is it just me?"

"And now I'm not."

"I get it. You were married and now you're not married." She knitted her brow. "You don't strike me as the divorcing type."

San looked at her for a moment trying to decide what to say. "She passed away about a year ago."

Nora's face fell. "Oh San, I'm so sorry. I didn't…"

"It's not something I talk about." He looked away.

"It was thoughtless of me."

"There was nothing wrong with asking."

"But you don't want to talk about it."

"That's right."

Nora looked at him for a moment. "If you ever do, I'd like to listen."

They were interrupted by a slim waitress with dark eyes and hair, looking fifteen at most. She set two steaming plates on the table and left. San pulled his plate closer and stared at it, trying to remember how long it had been since he had thought of Janie. He looked up and realized Nora had yet to touch her plate.

"Nora, don't mind me. I've never been much of a talker under the best of situations. Linder's the one who can talk.

143

Now, you've had a long night, and we still have a way to go. You need to eat."

He picked up his fork and waited. Nora looked at him as if to say something, and then pulled over her plate and started eating. San did the same. As they ate, San wondered whether he could ever tell Nora or anyone else about Janie. Where would he start? What would he say? The closest he had come was with Gert and Mattie shortly after Janie died. Even then, it was little more than a review of who they had seen at the funeral and what he should do with her things. Given time he might have approached them to talk about her. But they were gone now.

Nora gasped and San looked up at her, wondering what was wrong. All color had left her face. She sat perfectly still, staring into her plate as if in a trance. He thought she must be sick.

"Is there something wrong with your breakfast? You're looking a little pale."

"Can we go now? I'm not feeling so good." She continued facing the table.

"Maybe you're tired out. Do you want to take a moment and see if you get to feeling better?"

"I just want to go." She glanced up quickly and again lowered her head.

"Alright, whatever you say."

She seemed to be acting strangely, sick or not. As he reached for his wallet, a pair of silver-toed cowboy boots approached, stopping slightly behind him. He turned up to see a stocky man in black jeans and t-shirt, his dark hair pulled back into a tight ponytail. From his angle, San could see that the man had two black eyes behind his wrap-around sunglasses. The man whistled through his teeth.

"Geez, look what the cat dragged in, Eddie." The man chuckled. "Nora, you decide to come home or something?"

She stared into her plate, making no effort to answer.

"Cat must have got your tongue when he left you here. You got nothing to say to your old friends? " He tapped his foot. "You're probably wondering how I knew you were here, huh? Well, my cousin is in that damn jail over there and he got word to me. We got connections all over this town, and even some outside. You know, places like prisons."

"I can't talk now. We stopped here for breakfast but are on our way someplace else, someplace important. We're in a hurry so let us finish our meal, please." She glanced at him for a moment and then looked away.

"That ain't too friendly is it, Eddie? All this time away from here and she doesn't want to talk to us? Well, I feel like talking so I guess you're going to have to listen, woman."

"You heard what she said." San looked at Nora as he spoke. "She has someplace to go."

"San, leave this to me." Nora faced him and shook her head.

"Yeah, leave it to her. She still remembers how to please a man, I bet."

"You don't have to put up with this, Nora."

San started to stand and felt the man's hand on his shoulder. The other man stood beyond his field of vision and San wondered whether he would be a problem.

"Where're you going old man?" The man squeezed San's shoulder.

"Take your hand off my shoulder if you want to keep using it." San faced Nora.

"That ain't so friendly either, is it Eddie?" He laughed again.

San grabbed the man's hand, twisting it to his left and standing in one motion, forcing his face to the table. He managed to miss both plates. San held him there while the other man backed away, his oily hair falling across his wide eyes and a field of purplish acne scattered along his cheeks.

"What's your name, junior?" San stood over the man.

145

"Let me up, man. I didn't mean nothing. I was just funning Nora."

"I'm waiting for a name."

"Ronnie Fox. Okay man, let me up. You're hurting my arm."

"Now, Ronnie Fox, you're going to walk to that table over there where your friend is standing and sit down without saying a word, understand?"

"I understand."

"And you're going to stay there and order your breakfast while we go on our way."

"I promise, just let me go."

A large man appeared at San's side wearing a white apron smeared with stains and a white paper chef's hat. His beefy arms stretched beneath a white undershirt. San released his grip.

"What is the problema here? Ronnie Fox, are you giving these good people trouble in my place? Tell me you're not doing that."

"It was just a misunderstanding, Mr. Garcia. I didn't mean nothing." He rubbed his arm as he walked away.

"Hello, Mr. Garcia." Nora managed a smile.

"Why, it's Nora O'Quinn. I didn't recognize you. Please forgive me."

"It has been a while."

"Que pasa? What brings you back?"

"We were just passing through and needed breakfast. This is San Turner."

"I'm glad to meet you and honored that you came here." He looked over at Ronnie and Eddie. "Those two are trouble but mostly harmless. I'll be sure they don't bother you anymore."

"It's okay, Mr. Garcia, we were just leaving. We still have a ways to go."

"Take some coffee with you. I'm going to have a talk with those two." He nodded toward Ronnie's table.

San poured two cups of coffee, pressing the white plastic lids in place while Nora waited by the door. She watched Mr. Garcia shaking a thick finger at Eddie. Ronnie turned and stared at her, raising his chin slightly. She saw only malice in his crooked smile. Mr. Garcia snapped his fingers in Ronnie's face as she turned and stepped out the door.

"Do you always have to act like a lawman?" Nora stood, looking over the hood of the car.

"I can't tolerate impoliteness."

"I could have handled Ronnie. I just didn't want to have to."

"So, I saved you the trouble."

"He and Eddie are more dangerous than Mr. Garcia realizes. I hope he didn't get on their bad side. Like Ronnie said, they have connections."

Twenty-four

They crossed the border into Oklahoma under a slate-gray sky. The undulating clouds seemed to change constantly, morphing into surreal forms of inverted caves, hills and valleys. Nora gripped the steering wheel with both hands, peering over the dashboard, her knuckles white against the dark vinyl. The road had become a patchwork of potholes and long-ago resurfaced asphalt. Gravel clattered beneath the wheels as the washboard blacktop rattled the car to a deafening roar. Dilapidated shacks and mobile homes appeared in the distance, flanked by gutted cars and overfull barrels of trash. A lone tree stood against the horizon.

Each mile they traveled seemed to increase Nora's worry. The incident at breakfast had temporarily occupied her mind with a past she had almost forgotten, but as they passed into the familiar look of the reservation Nina again haunted her thoughts. What if they could not find her? What if she had been harmed in some way? Nora gripped the wheel even tighter.

"So, this is beautiful Oklahoma." San yelled over the din.

She glanced at him. "This is a poor area. We're on the reservation now."

"You'd better slow down before the road takes this car apart."

"Okay, but I hate to lose more time." She squinted through the windshield as if trying to spot something in the distance.

"Better to get there late than not at all."

Just as he finished speaking, the car lurched and then sputtered fitfully. Nora looked at San and then into the rear view mirror. She twisted around, craning her neck to see out the back as the car continued to slow.

"We're smoking."

San turned to look. A large cloud of white smoke briefly obscured the road behind them and then vanished in the stiff breeze. The car lurched again and another cloud of smoke vanished behind them. Nora slowed and the car rolled to a stop.

"What did you do?" San opened the door and got out.

"I didn't do anything." Nora slapped the wheel.

San knelt, peered under the car and then released the latch, lifting the hood. White steam engulfed the front of the car. He stepped back as the engine hissed and crackled, eventually emerging from the steam. Nora stood to the side surveying the horizon. After poking around the engine for a moment, San stepped back, turning to her.

"The damn radiator hose is busted." He paced beside the car. "That chaps my hide. I just had the car checked out a month ago."

"Can we drive it?" Nora kept scanning the distance.

"The engine overheated but should be okay with a new hose." He slammed the hood. "And no, I don't carry a spare. We're stuck here until I can find a replacement."

"There's a house over that way." She pointed across the barbed wire fence to an empty plain.

"I don't see any such house." He squinted at the horizon and pulled a phone out of his pocket.

"Your phone won't work out here."

"Great. So, we hitchhike. That is, if anyone ever drives this road." He turned his back to the raw wind.

"See those telephone poles? They lead to the house of an old woman I know. That's if she's still alive."

"One old telephone pole isn't going to be much help." He eyed her skeptically. "Are you sure there's a house over that ridge?"

"Trust me. Just because I'm a woman, doesn't mean I can't do anything right." She wondered if it was true.

"I knew I shouldn't let you drive my car." San paced along the highway.

"I didn't break your radiator hose."

"You were driving too fast."

"You should've taken better care of your car."

"I always take care of my vehicles."

"Come on, let's go." She started walking.

"There's nothing out here." He gestured in a circle.

"What's the matter? You can walk, can't you?"

"Only when I have to."

"Don't like to walk, then?"

"We have cars so we don't have to walk."

"Except when they break down. Then we walk." She called over her shoulder.

"I'll walk, but that doesn't mean I have to like it." He started after her.

They followed the road for half a mile before coming to a battered metal gate spanning a rutted track. The gate stood half open. Tufts of blonde grass bordered an overgrown drive that curved around a cement stock tank before disappearing over a low hill. Passing through the gate, they followed the road through stands of cactus and by a rusted windmill rattling before the steady breeze.

As they neared the top of the rise, a small house and out-building came into view. Beyond, the sharp horizon cut between land and sky. A mottled blue pickup squatted beside a low shed serving as one side of a broken down corral. In front of the house, a single red metal chair sat beneath a bent mesquite tree. Wisps of smoke trailed off the chimney, vanishing in the wind.

"Well, it looks like someone's at home." Nora quickened her pace. "Let's hope they're in the mood for visitors."

"I just hope they have a phone that works. They're not likely to have a radiator hose."

Nora stopped a short distance from the house. San passed her and then turned, waiting for her to follow. She kept her eyes on the front door.

"Are you coming or what?" San turned his collar to the wind.

Nora shook her head.

"I thought you were in a hurry."

"It's polite to wait a minute before you knock on the door. It's best if she opens the door before we knock."

San surveyed the area. "That truck's seen better days. I doubt it'd make it to the gate without falling apart."

"Try to be nice. We need help, remember?"

The door opened and a small, bent figure appeared, dressed in a faded blue cotton dress and red shawl. Her clay-colored face peered from beneath an orange scarf. She held the door open and motioned toward the gate with the back of her hand. San and Nora looked at each other. She again motioned toward the road without a word. From where she stood, Nora was unable to see any expression on her weathered face. She took a step forward and the woman withdrew, closing the door. San stood behind her, squinting into the sun.

"So, what happens now?"

"We wait."

The door opened again and the woman again gestured toward the road with her hand. "You go." Her voice was a hoarse monotone.

"Mrs. Cortez it's Nora O'Quinn. Do you remember me?"

"You go." She pointed behind them.

"I'm looking for little Nina. Do you remember her?"

The woman studied Nora for a moment as if trying to recall her face and then waved her forward. They approached the house, stopping at the front step. Nora thought she saw a figure pass behind the nearest curtained window but the image vanished so quickly she decided it could have been the wind swirling through the open door.

She glanced at San as the woman opened the door wide, motioning with her head to enter. As Nora approached, she held up her hand.

"Who is he?" She frowned at San.

Nora turned. "This is my good friend, San Turner."

"He must stay outside."

"Can't he come in?"

"I don't like the look of him, like trouble."

"Mrs. Cortez, he's helping me find Nina. Please let him come in and listen. He won't be any trouble, I promise."

The woman glared at San. "You must be silent and no trouble."

"No trouble." San repeated.

They passed through the door into a dimly lighted room. The house consisted of two large rooms, one a combined living room and kitchen, the other bare except for a small bed. The unpainted walls held a crudely carved crucifix and a sepia print of two hands clasped in prayer above half a dozen partially burned candles, a cloth doll and a painted statue of an angel kneeling before Mother Mary. In one corner, a thick-shouldered man with a black cap on backwards slouched in a narrow kitchen chair, eyeing them. A curved scar crossed his bloated face from forehead to cheek, white against his purplish nose. His long hair dangled loosely about his neck.

San and Nora sat at a wooden table in what appeared to be homemade chairs painted bright red and green. Mrs. Cortez moved from counter to counter without speaking. While spare and worn from years of use, the house appeared clean and well kept, the faded linoleum of the kitchen floor spotless. A pile of neatly folded blankets, topped by a small pillow sat next to the sofa, which leaned slightly to one side. After several minutes of silence, Mrs. Cortez set two cups of coffee on the table and sat.

"This is my grand-nephew, Gilbert. He stays with me sometimes when his mother kicks him out of the house." She nodded to the man in the corner, who made no response. "He has to go now." She turned to face him. "Go wait for your brother up at the gate, Gilbert, eh?"

"It's cold up there, grandmother." He frowned and glared at San.

"Do as I ask you, Gilbert."

He got up with a start and grabbed a coat before slamming the door on his way out.

"Gilbert has much anger in him. It keeps him from understanding the balance of the world and the spirit." She faced Nora and tapped her chest. "Do you understand such anger?"

"I think I've seen it."

"Yes, you have seen it."

"Mrs. Cortez, we need your help."

She held up a hand. "I remember your mother; that she died long ago."

"Yes."

"And your sister."

"Yes." Nora whispered and seemed to sink into her chair.

"You are of the Cloud family, eh?"

"My sister married one of the brothers."

"And your sister's daughter, Nina is of the Cloud family."

"I'm trying to find her." Nora's voice broke.

"What of your father?"

"I don't know." She stared at the table.

"He is still living."

"I don't know."

"You have not seen him, eh?"

"Not in years."

"Ah, I see."

"I'm here to find Nina. The Cloud family has taken her. Will you help me?" Nora pleaded.

"Patience, mija. You must say you will go to see your father. Then I will help you."

"What?" Nora stood.

153

"He is still with us. He stays in a nursing home in Wilton."

"He's still alive?"

"You must go see him."

"He told me to never come back. He doesn't want to see me." She stood and began pacing.

"You must promise to go see him."

"Will you help us then?"

"This man is helping you?" She nodded toward San. "Yes."

"Why, what does he want?"

San frowned. "I can speak for myself."

"No." She held up a finger.

"He doesn't want anything, Mrs. Cortez."

"A man, he always wants something. You know this thing."

"No, he's a good man." Nora sat and faced her. "I have no one, Mrs. Cortez, no family, no one to help me. I had no right to ask him but he agreed to come with me, to help me, anyway."

"You have no one."

Nora looked around the room as if looking for an escape and then replied. "I have no one."

"You still have a father. As bad as he was, he is still your father. You promise me you will go to see him?"

"Yes." Her voice was a whisper.

"I will help you." She reached across the table and took Nora's hand in hers. "I see you are in pain, mija. Your spirit is in pain, is it not?"

"I'm afraid for Nina. I tried to be a good mother…" She stopped, unable to finish the thought.

"It is not too late." She put a hand on Nora's shoulder and stood. "You can still be a good mother. Maybe have more ninos and ninas."

"Oh no, I'm too old."

"How many years are you?"

"I'm forty, too old."

"No, not too old. Don't worry." She patted Nora's arm. "Nina could still have a sister."

"I have to find her. I don't know what they'll do to her."

"Sit back in your chair, daughter."

She lifted her shawl, draping it over her head before reaching into a basket and removing an egg. She then took a lime from a bowl sitting next to it. Standing behind Nora, she ran the egg along her neck and shoulders, and then down each arm, saying nothing. She did the same with the lime. Finally, she placed the palms of her hands on Nora's head and held them there. After a moment she spoke.

"Your pain will be less now, mija. You must go to your father. He knows where they keep your Nina." She gently lifted Nora from the chair. "You must go now."

"He knows?" She stared in disbelief. "Thank you, Mrs. Cortez."

She turned to San and held out a set of keys. "You can drive a truck?"

He stared at the keys. "Our car is broken down about a half mile from your gate."

"This is something I know. My son will be here later. He will fix it for you."

"I'm grateful to you, Mrs. Cortez so don't take this the wrong way. Will that truck make it to wherever we're going? It looks like it's been a mile or two."

"The truck is like me, old and ugly but tough. It can take you."

"Alright then, we appreciate your help."

"Do not be like most men and mistreat her." She walked them to the door.

"I'm here to help." San stepped through the door. "I'll take good care."

"She can care for herself. She is strong. I said do not mistreat her only."

"I'll take care of your truck then."

Just as they were leaving, she took Nora by the arm. "There is much bad with the Cloud family. Your friend, he will keep you from harm?"

"Yes."

"Then travel with God, mija."

Twenty-five

San circled the truck, occasionally kneeling to have a closer look at one of the tires and mumbling to himself. He lightly pounded the rear fender with the palm of his hand. A cloud of rust littered the gravel below in a low hiss, quickly vanishing in the stiff wind. He pulled his collar up and studied the sky, which had darkened to gunmetal gray above the blonde horizon, wondering if they would have to contend with more snow. He looked up as Nora climbed into the driver's seat and closed the door. She held out her hand out the window.

"You're in the wrong seat." He stood by the window.

"I know where we're going. I can drive."

"Mrs. Cortez gave the keys to me, remember?"

"She didn't want you to feel useless and left out." She looked out the windshield.

"Useless and left out?"

"I admit you did a fair job of not being any trouble. But she knew your male ego needed a boost."

"My what?"

"Hand over the keys so we can go."

"Move yourself over so I can drive."

Nora turned to look at him. "San, I need to drive. I need to feel like I'm doing something for Nina. Please, let me have the keys."

San could see the determination in her eyes. Under the autumn, cloud-strewn sky they seemed deep green rather than hazel, like artesian pool scattered with flecks of blue. He realized that before today he had always avoided looking directly at her. He had no reason as to why. It was as if she could see something in him he could not see for himself, something he wanted to avoid. Looking into her eyes, she appeared both vulnerable and strong, having bared herself to Mrs. Cortez as he sat watching yet seeming the better for it. He suddenly knew he wanted nothing more than to look at her, to study her face. Instead he handed her the keys, looking away.

"San, you look terrified. I'm not that bad of a driver." She laughed.

"I'm just hoping the weather will hold." He walked around the back of the truck and climbed into the passenger seat.

Nora drove back up the rutted road past the windmill and stock tank, and over the small rise separating the house from the highway. The gate and cattle guard lay a short distance ahead. San leaned forward, pulling his pistol from his beneath his coat and setting it on the seat between them. Nora slammed on the breaks.

"That's a gun!"

"That's right."

"What's it doing there?"

"As much as I appreciate a good firearm, and this is a good one, it is a bad practice to sit on your pistol."

"You had it with you when we spoke to Mrs. Cortez?"

"I did."

"But why?"

"I like to be prepared when I'm walking into an unknown situation."

"We were asking for her help."

"You never know what an individual might do."

"Are you always so distrustful of people?"

"You're starting to sound like Linder." He frowned and looked out the window. "Let's go."

"But not everyone is out to do you harm."

"I wish I could believe that."

"That must be a lonely view of the world. Don't you trust anyone?"

He turned to her. "If I know them well enough."

"You trust Linder."

"Most of the time."

"And your aunts, you trusted them."

"Completely."

"But they're gone now. Don't you trust anyone else?"

"I've seen too much of the dark side of people."

"That just sounds like an excuse to avoid trying."

"What did you think of Mrs. Cortez's grand-nephew?"

"What does that have to do with anything?"

"It's just a question."

"He gave me the creeps and didn't seem to like us being there."

"I've seen plenty of angry young men. He wasn't a problem but he could have been."

"I suppose. Still, I believe that most people are good."

"Take a look around. Most people just look out for themselves. Sooner or later, they'll let you down."

"Oh, is that why you're sitting in a broken down pick-up five hundred miles from home?"

"It's different when there's a child involved."

"But it still seems a lonely way to live." She looked at him for a moment. "I trust you, San. I hope you'll be able to do the same for me some day."

She turned onto the highway without giving him a chance to answer. On the horizon, giant wind turbines as tall as sky scrapers danced a silent ballet as they slowly turned in unison. Rusted oil pumps stood behind barbed-wire fences like long-forgotten hobby horses frozen in mid-stride. San cursed himself silently for his cool response to Nora. What made him say those things? Did he even believe what he'd said? He had no answer.

As they came over a rise, the grain silos of Wilton came into view above the level plain. Soon, lines of tin-roofed houses and cottonwood trees emerged from beneath the silos. Nora crossed the ever-present railroad tracks and passed the county courthouse, its sandstone and granite archway stretching nearly two stories above the street. She turned onto a gravel side street. To the left, a white shiplap church with a narrow red roof sat next to a low brick building surrounded by thick-trunked pine trees. An empty wheelchair sat next to the front door as she turned into the parking lot and set the brake.

"You don't have to come in if you don't want to. It could get ugly."

"Sounds like you could use some help." He wanted to apologize but was at a loss for words. "I'll come along, but only if it's what you want."

"Let's go, then."

They walked through two sets of glass doors, stopping before a large wooden desk. The chair behind it was empty. Light reflected off the polished tile floor in narrow bands the greenish color of shaved ice. As San and Nora stood looking at one another wondering what to do, a voice echoed from down the hall.

"Elton, honey, now you know you can't be getting around without your walker. You don't want another broken hip, do you? Alright darlin', alright now."

A large woman wearing a white dress and shoes backed out of a doorway carrying a tray of bottles, all in shades of amber. Her hair, streaked with gray and pulled into a tight knot, contrasted sharply with her dark skin. She turned and began walking towards them. When she finally looked up, her broad face broke into an equally broad smile.

"I'm so sorry there was nobody to greet you, honey but our Mable is out with a sick child today. I'm Bertha Cole, the day nurse. I surely do hope you didn't have to wait none too long out here, darlin'." She set the tray down and looked at Nora. "Now aren't you a pretty one. You related to somebody here, child?"

"I'm here to see Delbert O'Quinn."

"Why sure you are hon'. I can see the resemblance. Oh, 'cept you're way prettier." She laughed deeply.

"Do you think he'll see me?"

She frowned. "Well, old Del, he doesn't have visitors but just once in a while. It makes me sad but I don't tell him. I tell him he's so ornery he run peoples off *all* the

160

time. Now I'm not joshing you, darlin' but Bertha will see what she can do."

She disappeared down the hall, emerging from a doorway after a moment and waving them to follow. Nora looked at San, her face clouded with emotion, before walking toward the doorway while Bertha stood aside and waited. Once they approached, she placed her thick fingers on Nora's shoulder.

"He won't let me open up the curtains so it's a little dark in there. You just call on Bertha if you should need any little thing, hon'."

"I will." Nora reached up to squeeze her hand and then walked through the door.

As her eyes adjusted to the dim light, she could make out a figure in the far corner of the room slouching to one side in a wheel chair. She tried to recall how long it had been since she had seen her father and decided it had been ten years or more. She scarcely recognized him. A tall man, his body seemed to have fallen in upon itself, like a long-neglected house. His face sloped to one side, forcing his mouth into a permanent scowl. He raised his bald head and squinted.

"It's you." His speech was slightly slurred.

"Hello daddy."

"What are you doing here?"

"This is San Turner." She gestured to San.

"Good to meet you, sir." San nodded.

"I asked you a question." He ignored San. "You show up out of the blue after all this time. What do you want? I don't have any money. You want money for that druggie sister of yours? Tell her I'm broke and she'll have to find someone else to buy her drugs."

"She's dead, daddy." She sat. "Don't you remember?"

His eyes widened for a moment and he ran his hand over his face. "Hell yes, I remember."

"I don't mean to bother you, papa." She leaned forward.

His face seemed to drop. "It's been a long time since anyone called me that. I don't mean to snap at you. It's just that I haven't been feeling too well."

"I'm sorry to hear that. Is there anything I can do?"

"Now don't start feeling sorry for me, damn it!" He tried to get up out of his chair and then fell back. "I don't want anyone's pity."

"Alright." She shifted in her chair, trying to find her words. "I'm trying to find Nina, daddy."

"So, that's why you're here?"

"That's why I'm here."

"Not to see me, then."

"I didn't know you were here. Mrs. Cortez just told me."

"That old busy-body meddles in everyone's business."

"I thought you must be dead by now."

"You'd have liked that wouldn't you?" He smirked. "Why didn't you try to find me?"

"You told me you never wanted to see me again, daddy. Don't you remember?"

"I never said that."

"You told both Natalie and me to never come back and that we weren't part of the family anymore."

"You probably think I beat you too."

"You did beat us." Her voice was almost a whisper.

"Your sister always did have a problem with the truth, the ungrateful bitch."

"Don't talk about her like that." Her voice trembled. "Natalie tried to protect me and so you beat her worse. You beat mama too."

"You must think I'm some kind of idiot, coming here and telling all kinds of lies and expecting me to believe you."

"No daddy, I don't think that." She stood.

"Why did you come here?"

"I told you. I'm trying to find Nina. Please tell me where she is."

"Why should I tell you anything? You're no better than your sister."

"Because Nina is your granddaughter, daddy."

"If I tell you, will you stop spying on me and leave me alone?"

"If that's what you want." She said quietly.

"I'm not sure I remember."

"Please try."

He ran his hand over his face. "I believe Nina is somewhere over by Black Mesa, near Red Rock. The night nurse told me. A friend of hers works at Red Rock Bank and knows everything that goes on around there. You'll have to ask her. The name's Knudsen, Olga Knudsen."

"Thank you, papa." She leaned and kissed him lightly on the forehead. "Is there anything you need?"

"Don't pity me."

"I don't mean to."

He ran his hand over his face again, resting it on his scalp. "Your mother put you up to this, didn't she? She wants to make me suffer."

"Mama's been gone a long time."

"Gone where?"

"Goodbye, daddy." She turned and walked out.

San walked beside her, searching in vain for the right words to say. As they neared the exit, a voice called to them.

"Just a moment, child." Bertha walked to where they stood, taking Nora's hand in hers. "Bertha has been around these old folks here for a long time so you listen to me. Don't you let yourself be upset the way your daddy talks to you. He talks that way to everybody, including me. It's not you personal like, you hear?"

Tears filled Nora's eyes. "You're very kind, Mrs. Cole."

"I'm just Bertha. You come and visit us any time and Bertha will take good care of you. I'll watch out for your daddy too."

She took San by the arm and led him a short distance away. "Now you got to care for this child, you hear?' She whispered. "Her daddy can say some hard things, I know. She needs some care right now and you got to do what you can to soothe her mind. You know what it is to need to be cared for?"

"I think so." He lied.

"She needs some care." She let go of his arm.

San turned, walking to where Nora stood beneath the foyer lights and taking her by the arm. A dry snow swirled beneath their feet as they pushed through the door.

Twenty-six

Linder drove away from San's house, turning left onto the highway and passing a small Lutheran church before noticing a brown, low-slung sedan in his rear-view mirror. The driver seemed to be following him. He had seen the car in the church parking lot across from San's gate and given it little thought, but he now realized he'd had a vague feeling for days that someone was watching him. He decided to take a detour rather than going straight to his office, turning off the main road and winding through a wooded residential area. The car eventually turned, vanishing from view. He pulled into his office parking space, watching the street in both directions for several minutes before taking a deep breath and laughing silently at himself.

His final appointment having cancelled at the last minute, he left for home earlier than usual, stopping on the way for a bottle of wine to share with Jules later in the afternoon. The fading autumn light scattered through the trees as he pulled into his driveway. The local free clinic must be open in the basement of the First Baptist church, he thought as he scanned the area. The street had more than the usual number of cars crowding the curb, and the closed in feeling it gave added to the sense of unease that had returned as soon as he stepped out of his office. He climbed the porch stairs, nodding to his next door neighbor, Mrs. Kolcek. She frowned and turned in her blue porch chair, the Chihuahua in her lap growling like an electric motor. Linder opened the door, stepping through.

He set down his brief case and carried the wine to the kitchen, placing it in the refrigerator. As closed the door, a sound came from behind him and for a moment he thought that Jules had arrived early to surprise him. He turned just as the black barrel of a pistol flashed before him in a blur and then a white veil spread across his vision. His feet and then his legs went numb, and he seemed to float above the floor as the face of a young man, his head shaved and tattooed, momentarily passed beneath the curtain of white. Then there was nothing.

Linder awoke with a start. His cheek throbbed mechanically as he peered about the kitchen, his right eye swollen to a squint. He sat upright, leaning against the wall and pulling at the tape binding his hands behind his back. Struggling to stand, he fell back in a wave of nausea. He looked up, trying to focus as the man walked through the kitchen door.

"You better stay where you are unless you want to be out for good." He gestured with a broad-barreled pistol.

"What do you want?"

"You know what I want." He smirked. "You don't remember me?"

Linder studied him through the fog that seemed to cover his mind. "You were at Curley's. Your name is Dewey."

"That's right, professor. You and your friend the cop decided to mess with my personal business. That was not smart."

"That's why you're here? You want revenge?"

"No, I don't care about that. I'm looking for Nora."

"Why look here?"

"I know all about you and her. I know she sees you at your office. And you were at her place today."

"You've been stalking her."

"I've been keeping an eye on what's mine, professor. She's not yours. She belongs to me." He laughed. "You think I'm just going to stand by and let a wimp like you move in on my woman?"

"You think I've been seeing Nora?"

"I would've bust in on the two of you at her house today but that damn woman sheriff showed up."

"The only relationship I have with Nora is professional."

"You think you're real smart, professor but I know what I see."

"You think she'd come here?"

"I don't know, maybe. But I want you out of the picture when I talk to her. I'm going to take her away from this dump. I have it all figured out. All I need now is Nora."

"She's gone. She left sometime last night."

"She's gone? Why should I believe you?"

"I went to her house to take care of the animals for my friend, the cop."

"He's with her?" His forehead contorted. "Where did they go?"

"I don't know."

"You don't know or you won't tell me? I put a bullet in your knee, you'll talk." He scratched his jaw with the gun.

"It was some sort of emergency. They left in the middle of the night."

"You're lying. I put a pillow over this thing and no one will hear it." He held up the pistol.

A car door slammed nearby. Dewey bent, grabbing Linder by the arm and dragging him around the corner into the utility room.

"Make noise if you want someone to get hurt." He left Linder leaning against the washing machine.

Linder looked around the room for something to cut the tape binding his wrists and his eyes settled on his composite bow leaning in a corner, the steel-tipped arrows attached to one side. A spare arrow stood next to it. He kicked off his shoes, pulled his knees close to his chest and slipped his arms beneath his feet in one motion. His mother had always said he must have inherited a double-jointed back from her aunt Ida to have such flexibility. He was grateful for it now, whatever the reason. He slid over to the corner. Just as he took the spare arrow in his hand, he heard

Jules' voice. From where he sat with his back against the wall, he had a clear view of the front door.

"Linder?" She called and knocked lightly. "I got to leave work early."

Linder could see Dewey moving between the windows, trying to get a clear view of the car or Jules. He held the pistol in both hands. It was clear he would have no hesitation in using it.

Linder's mind raced with what to do. In a moment Jules would walk through the door. He had left the bolt unlocked, knowing she would be along eventually and he would only need to tell her to come in. He had done it often enough. Even with no response, had no doubt she would open the door on her own at any moment. Scraping his wrists against the arrow point, it became clear cutting free would take far too long, and if Dewey caught him he would dispatch him without hesitation. Jules called his name again as Dewey moved into position before the door.

Linder's instinct took over. He grabbed the bow, turning it sideways and placing his feet on either side of his hands. Holding the bow steady, he bent and took the feathered end of the arrow in his mouth, maneuvering it to his fingers and placing the notch squarely between his hands. He leaned back, pulling the arrow along the guide with all his strength until the steel tip rested squarely between his feet. Dewey stood, gun in hand, two yards from the door as the knob turned. Linder heard the cock of the pistol's heavy firing pin. He knew Jules would have heard it too but the door was already beginning to open and she would have no time. She would just be reaching for her gun.

The door swung open and Linder caught sight of Jules, their eyes locking for an instant. He knew in her determined look she would die to protect him. He nodded sideways and she stepped back just as he released the arrow. For a moment, he thought he had missed completely. There was nothing to suggest anything had happened except for a slight jerk of Dewey's shoulder.

Then he reached with one hand to his right side, turning to look at Linder. He raised the gun and fired, the wall just above Linder's head exploding before the house erupted with the deafening roar of gunfire. By the time Linder had wiped the drywall from his eyes Jules stood over him, squinting as she shoved the pistol back into the holster.

"Oh my, Linder, you're a sight. Stay where you are until I get some ice. I doubt you can stand. I've already called for an ambulance."

"Is he dead?" He was having trouble thinking.

"Oh, yeah." She returned with the ice. "I think he was done for when he fired at you but I took no chances. He only got off the one shot."

"You mean I didn't miss?"

She looked at him and for a moment her eyes lost the hard look of the deputy. She reached down and brushed the hair from his forehead.

"I wouldn't be standing here now if you had missed."

She knelt, holding a towel wrapped around a handful of ice to his cheek as sirens echoed off the houses across the street. Linder reached up, putting his hand, still taped to the other at the wrist, to her face.

Twenty-seven

The road to Black Mesa was lightly dusted with snow but the sun shafted through the broken clouds, sending cream-colored columns of light careening to the south. San and Nora drove the narrow highway west through uninterrupted stretches of board-level plain, crossed now and then by shallow, rock-strewn arroyos. The road abruptly descended into a broad valley dotted with Cottonwood trees and long-neglected wire fences. Weathered clapboard shacks and mobile homes, some listing to one side, stood beneath the gnarled trees. Beyond, a ragged line of dirty rooftops and narrow steeples broke the valley floor, marking the town of Red Rock.

Nora turned on Main Street and parked outside a shop selling custom-made quilts, its shop window consumed by a large quilting machine containing a half-finished quilt that appeared to be made of a shredded American flag. The headquarters of the county Republican Party, the door covered with months-old fliers for a wild game dinner, stood next door. Red Rock bank occupied the corner.

As San followed Nora through the bank doors, he was bothered by a feeling that he had forgotten something important, as if he had misplaced his keys. He instinctively reached for his keys and remembered he had left them with Mrs. Cortez. He scanned the interior of the bank, wondering if he had been there before, although he knew he had never set foot in Red Rock or any other part of western Oklahoma. A sign under a mural of two cowboys team-roping a steer read "Welcome to Red Rock, Oklahoma, Home of the West". Nora turned and looked at him.

"Is something wrong?"

"You mean other than the fact that I was up all night?"

"You just had that far off stare."

"I have the feeling I'm missing something."

"That's right. We're missing our chance to find Nina unless we can talk to Olga Knudsen soon."

"You're right. There's the receptionist." He pointed to a desk in the middle of the room.

The bank was free of customers except for a razor-thin man in a denim jacket and felt hat. He wore his boots outside his jeans and appeared to be covered in a light coat of yellow dust. The two tellers before him stood beneath a limestone wall that rose to meet a pressed tin ceiling embossed with stars and crossed arrows. San and Nora stood waiting while the receptionist, who had yet to notice them, engaged in a heated discussion over the phone with her boyfriend. Just as they were about to try something else, heavy footsteps sounded on the marble floor behind them. They turned to find a large-boned woman, her hair tied in a crown of braids, facing them with her hands clasped together as if in prayer. She wore no makeup but her rosy cheeks contrasted sharply with her light skin.

"May I please be of help?" She spoke through a thick accent.

"We are hoping to talk with Olga Knudsen."

The woman looked past Nora, frowning at the receptionist and then straightened. "I am Olga Knudsen."

"Is there somewhere we can talk?"

"May I kindly ask your name?"

"Please forgive me. I'm Nora O'Quinn. This is my friend, San Turner."

"You are Delbert's daughter?"

"Yes."

"Oh, my goodness. Come this way, if you would. Please call me Olga."

They walked into a wide office filled by an oval mahogany conference table surrounded by black leather chairs and a broad oak desk. They sat and Olga studied Nora for a moment before smiling.

171

"I knew your sister, you know. She was dark-haired, so different from you. When I first came here from Sweden, I taught piano out of my house. She was my favorite student. She often stayed over when, how should I say, things were rocky at home. Is that okay for me to say, Nora?" She reached across the wide table as if to take Nora's hand.

Nora's eyes grew wide in recognition. "You're Mrs. Schwettman. I remember now. You seem so young."

"Yes, well, I got married when I was only sixteen. I was from a small town and a very traditional family that believed in marrying their daughters young. But I got rid of that old German. He was no better than your father and finally I had enough. That's when I changed back to my family name and started working for the bank. I still miss the teaching though."

"Natalie loved going to her lessons so much. I have to confess I was jealous."

"I loved her like a daughter." She put her hands over her mouth. "I was from a big family but had no children of my own. My students were like my children. But Natalie was so unlike any of them."

"In what way?" Nora was intrigued.

"She was like a little mayfly when she first started with me, so delicate and vulnerable. I wanted to protect her. But there was only so much a piano teacher with no money and a bad husband could do and, little by little, she became hard - like my grandfather's leather strap – at least on the outside. It hurt my heart to see it. I understood it was the way she survived your father and I tried to provide a safe place for her. Only when she played the piano did she seem like the old Natalie."

"She loved her music. It was always her favorite subject in school. And since we didn't have a piano, it got her away from daddy."

"He must have been hard on you as well, Nora."

"He was hardest on her."

"Yes, I know. Then she met up with the Cloud boys and I lost her. She had outgrown her lessons and only came to my house to use the piano, or just to visit. But then she stopped coming at all."

Nora started, as if she had woken from a dream. "Ms. Knudson...Olga, can you help us find Nina?"

"I had heard you had taken her in after Natalie died. I was so pleased she would be away from that family. Living with the Cloud family would only mean trouble for a young girl. How old must she be by now?"

"She's ten. I've had her since she was three. I couldn't bear to see the way they treated her and knew I had to get her away from there."

"But they want her back."

"Raymond Cloud and a friend of his took her. I was right there and should have never let it happen." She stared at the table. "I'm so afraid for her."

"Yes dear, I know. But since you're here now, let me tell you what I know." She smiled. "You'd be surprised how much you hear when you work at the only bank in town. Raymond and his friend were caught in a snow storm and only just arrived, although I had already heard they were going to bring Nina back up here. They have her over at the Beaver place because old Mr. Cloud is very sick with cancer. Do you know where that is?"

"Yes, I remember."

"They don't think you're brave enough to come after her."

"I'd do anything to keep Nina safe."

"I can see you would. But it may be harder than you think. Mrs. Cloud is a formidable woman."

"I'll pay them to let me keep her. The only reason they want her is for the child support money they'd get."

"I heard that story too, so I checked. There is no child-support money."

"But then why would they take her? They were glad to be rid of her when I took her in."

"They don't know yet. They probably got bad advice from an attorney hoping to make some easy money off of their stupidity and greed."

"So, once they find out there's no money they'll let me take her back won't they?"

"I hope so, sweetheart. But they have a mean streak and are hard to predict." She paused and looked at Nora for a moment. "There's something else you should know. The sheriff says her father may be paroled soon."

"Jimmy Cloud is getting out?" Nora turned to San, her eyes wide. "Oh God, San, we have to get Nina out of here soon. I don't want him having anything to do with her."

San looked across the table at Olga. "I know a little something about law enforcement. How sure is the sheriff about that?"

"He thinks it's just hearsay put out by the Cloud family to intimidate the community but he said he can't be sure."

He nodded. "Thank you for the warning but we need to stay focused on what's real, not what might be."

"I think that's wise, Mr. Turner." Olga studied him for a moment. "May I ask you a question?"

"A quick one. We'll want to get moving."

"You have an unusual name. What is it short for?"

"Santana is my given name. My father was born in Mexico."

"Your family is from Mexico?"

"My grandfather was with the American Consulate and eventually married into a wealthy Mexican family. My father came to Texas as a young man. That's where he met my mother."

"What town in Texas did you say you are from?"

"I didn't say, but it's Lander. Why do you ask?"

"Nora's sister, Natalie, was very dear to me. I'd like to know what I can about those who have a connection to her." She turned to Nora. "You will need a place to stay while you're sorting out this business with Nina. Would you both do me the honor of staying at my house? It's a large house and it seems even larger now that my mother has passed on. Please let me help you. It would mean a great deal."

Nora looked at San. "You do need to sleep at some point."

"Sleep? I don't believe in it."

"I think that means we'll kindly accept your offer, Olga."

"It's good of you to be so hospitable." San stood. "Now, we'd better get moving."

"Yes, I understand." She scribbled something on a business card and handed it to Nora. "Here's my address and phone number. Ask anyone in town if you can't find it."

As they stepped through the door, a loud voice echoed through the lobby. Across the room, a man dressed in jeans and a pearl-buttoned, long-sleeve shirt gestured wildly with one arm as he argued with one of the tellers. His closely cropped hair glowed silver against his clay-colored skin. He turned as the teller spotted Olga, and she stopped, looking at them for a moment as if waiting for the man to do or say something. He raised his arm and waved, the other arm hanging limply at his side, and then began walking toward them. He appeared to be drunk.

"Victor has decided to pay me a visit. He rarely leaves his home anymore." Olga whispered.

"Where does he live, the drunk tank?" San snorted.

"His house is on the reservation, like most of the county residents."

"What's wrong with these people?"

"What people do you mean, San?" Olga turned to him.

"I'm talking about the Indians up here. They don't take care of their homes, they let their cars fall apart and they can't hold their liquor."

"Persons of Native American descent make up eighty-seven percent of our county population."

"They have no self respect, just like the wetbacks back home."

"We are a poor county and people do the best they can. I prefer to look at each person as a unique individual, not a race or ethnicity. I hope they would do the same for me."

"He's uniquely drunk." San scoffed.

Nora frowned at him. "I'm surprised at you, San. You're usually fair-minded and sensible. How can you use names like wet back when your father was born in Mexico?"

"That's different. They were hardworking people not illegal aliens."

"Most of the people you call names are decent and work hard for little pay. You can't just lump them all together and say they're no good."

The man drew closer and his face contorted as if he was in pain. Raising his good arm, he placed his hand on Olga's shoulder without a word, staring at her for a moment. Then without warning, he collapsed. San grabbed him under the arms, easing him into a nearby chair as the teller he had yelled at earlier appeared and handed him a glass of water. He sat with his head down while Olga whispered to the side of his face. He nodded his head lightly as she spoke.

After a moment, she stood and escorted Nora and San across the lobby and through the door. They stood together on the sidewalk.

"Victor's grandson was killed in Iraq two months ago. He had raised him since he was a baby because his parents were teenagers and not up to the responsibility. Victor was a decorated soldier in Viet Nam and lost the use of his arm, as you could see, but I've never known anyone as hardworking. Yesterday he finally received his grandson's personal effects and, evidently it was too much for him."

"I reckon he has a right to tie one on." San looked into the distance.

"Please be careful, both of you. If you need anything, call me."

"Thank you Olga." Nora took her hand. "You're too kind."

"Goodbye, then."

San turned without a word and walked to the car.

Twenty-eight

San

Janie and I had a fight the day of the accident. I don't recall the point of the argument but it had no real importance, I'm sure of that. It was the rare case we would argue over a thing that had any real meaning. We could talk over serious concerns as if they were a leak that needed fixing but it was the minor, everyday differences that would send us into a tailspin and before I knew what had happened, I had already said half a dozen things I didn't intend. That didn't mean I wasn't too stubborn to take any of them back. I was as mule-headed as always and ended up walking away without a word instead of setting things right again. I don't know if I was trying to punish her or myself but it accomplished both as often as not and there we'd be, miserable until we sorted it out. It was impractical to the nth degree and that irritated me as much as anything. So, as predictable as the August heat, I'd stew over our fight until I was cooked.

We were on our way back from seeing her younger sister, Georgia, who was recovering from a ruptured appendix. They're poor people and Georgia resisted going to the doctor because she said they couldn't afford another medical bill, what with a child born premature and needing expensive care. That decision nearly killed her. Janie had been staying with Georgia for a time, taking care of her and the children. I made the trip back over to east Texas, where the family lived, to bring Janie home.

I find it puzzling the way we remember some things and forget others. Except for the particulars of our fight, I remember every detail of that day and the next, right up to the accident. The road east out of Lander wound through grass-covered rolling hills and farms dotted with dairy cows the black and white pattern of Oreo cookies. Sycamore trees, bright yellow in the autumn sun eventually gave way to thick stands of Pine trees interrupted here and there by cleared fields and unpainted shacks the color of dried mud. Old black men sat on porches littered with cast off furniture, the stuffing escaped like errant handfuls of cotton.

Georgia's trailer house stood on the edge of town among hundred foot tall Pine trees and engineless cars suspended on cinder blocks above the patchy lawn. A long wooden ramp angled away from the front door, ending at the gravel driveway. Bicycles lay about as if no longer wanted. Adjacent to the house, the orange metal front of an auto shop owned by Georgia's ex-husband cast an unnatural light into the underbrush. Chickens scattered as I pulled into the drive. I sat in the car, not wanting to go in and wishing Janie had no family she felt obliged to help. The last thing I felt like doing right then was being nice to people.

Now that I think back on it, I reckon I had been out of sorts for a while. I'd been working a case that I couldn't get off my mind, no matter what I tried. Unlike some in law enforcement, I was never bothered by any feelings for the perpetrator or the victim. A case was a problem to be solved. In my view, any personal thoughts only interfered with finding answers and had no place in the investigation. But this case was different.

I first heard about it when a sheriff in the area contacted our office with an urgent request for assistance. A man had broken into a luxury lakefront house located in a remote portion of a well-known resort without the owner's knowledge and had lived in the attic for some time before he was discovered. He had repeatedly abused one of the young girls living in the house. He had then taken the family hostage, demanding that they provide him with a

179

large sum of cash and their private jet, which was located at the resort's small airport, in order to make his escape. The family would drive him. The mother had managed to alert the sheriff's office of the plan, and the sheriff then contacted us. The remote location on the end of a narrow peninsula presented a challenge to the law enforcement's plan.

A decision was made to hide two Rangers in back of the family car and apprehend the suspect while protecting the children. The Rangers took their positions in the back of the car without detection, and were poised to take control of the situation when something went badly wrong. The gunman somehow discovered the officers just as the family pulled out of the driveway. In the ensuing gunfire, one officer was killed instantly and the other wounded, along with the mother of the children. Her ten year old daughter died at the scene. I was there and watched her take her last breath. That was the image I could not shake. Even though I was there only as back-up, as a senior officer I felt responsible.

I finally pulled myself out of the car and walked up the long ramp fronting Georgia's trailer, every other board warped and creaking from the heat and humidity of the past summer. Inside, Damien Thibodaux, Georgia's ex-husband, sat cleaning his greasy finger nails with a rusty Buck knife. Damien had never quite moved out, in spite of their divorce. His oily hair stuck out from beneath a grimy Quaker State cap. He looked up and scratched his thin beard without as much as a nod of his head. Everything about him seemed coated in grease.

Janie and her sister walked into the room, each carrying a small child. I had long before stopped trying to keep track of the children, so they could have belonged to neighbors for all I knew except that their dirty faces looked like small versions of Damien, grime and all. The living room floor, a gauntlet of bedclothes and toys, was crowded with overstuffed furniture. The paneled walls held children's drawings taped at odd angles between beer posters and a gun-rack shouldering two small-caliber rifles. I said my hellos, opting to stand rather than sit in the hope we would leave soon. I could see in Janie's eyes that she knew I had no intention of staying any longer than necessary, so she handed off the child and went to get her bag. Before she left, a flash of anger crossed her face. I could see that she didn't appreciate my attitude toward her flesh and blood. She was no doubt tired yet still concerned for her sister's welfare so I reckon we were both spoiling for a fight in our way.

We started arguing before we even reached the car. I believe it started with my complaint that I spent half my life waiting because she was never ready to leave on time and went from there. In my anger, I walked half a mile down the road before realizing how ridiculous I looked stumbling along a ragged highway in the middle of nowhere. When I returned Janie wouldn't even look at me.

We drove for over an hour without saying any more than was necessary. It started to rain. After that, my memory seems to fade. All I know for sure is that I lost her on that day. The doctors said some memory loss is common when a person sustains a concussion, especially the period just before and after the injury. As much as I'd like to believe a merciful god would arrange for our bad memories to go away, I see no mercy in the events of that day.

Twenty-nine

San pulled up to the home of Johnson Beaver, a squat house of cinder block painted sky blue. The red trim and doorway seemed to vibrate in the mid-afternoon sun. A nearby stand of Scotch pines, meant to cut the ever-present wind, cast a grid of shadow across the metal roof. The surrounding lawn stood trimmed and immaculate. The door to the house opened before San had a chance to cut the engine and a short, lean man stepped to the threshold wearing jeans and a red plaid shirt, his silver hair framing a deeply-furrowed, coffee-colored face. The man raised a thin arm, waving toward them. Nora opened her door and waved back.

"I'm Nora O'Quinn, Mr. Beaver." She called as she approached the front steps.

"You are Nina's mother." He took her hand. "I was hoping you would come for her."

Nora took a breath and stepped back. "Do you have her here?"

"No, Raymond Cloud was here with her but he has taken her to be with the Cloud family." He turned to San. "You are helping Nina's mother?"

"I'm San Turner. We're here to take Nina home, Mr. Beaver but it sounds like we've come to the wrong house."

"Please call me Johnson." His voice was a hoarse monotone. "Maybe the wind has brought you here for a reason. I can help."

He waved them through the door into a simply furnished living room. Unpainted wooden shelves filled to overflowing with books covered an entire wall. He motioned them into the kitchen where sunlight streamed in through curtain-less windows. Compact bunches of dried plants hanging from the back porch rafters filled the room with a chorus of fragrance. Jars and tins lay scattered over the counters, some half-filled. Johnson motioned for San and Nora to sit while he poured three cups of coffee into thick-lipped mugs. He sat across the table from them and gestured around the room with his hand.

"I make teas and preparations from local plants and herbs when people ask me to. Some of them I grow and some I find driving the back roads around Lake Meredith, where the land breaks into many canyons."

Nora surveyed the room. "It looks like you have quite a selection."

"It is good to have something to do when you're old. I live here alone. My family is all gone now." He stared at his hands.

Nora shifted in her chair anxiously. "You were saying you can help us."

He looked at her. "I know the Cloud family. They are my wife's cousins but I have no use for the way they choose to live. Still, they will listen to me."

"Let's go while it's still light out." She grabbed her purse.

"Nina will not be there. They had to take old Mr. Cloud back to the hospital. Raymond brought Nina here because having her around the house upset the old man. His mind has gone away and he doesn't understand many things." He touched Nora's arm lightly. "We will leave soon."

"I just want to see Nina."

"I remember your sister, Natalie. She came here once or twice to see my wife about making a dress for Nina. It was for a wedding where Nina was the flower girl. She must have been about two. Your sister was very proud."

"I had forgotten she could be a good mother when she wanted to. Mostly, I remember her neglect."

"That Jimmie Cloud was bad for her. My wife would try to tell Natalie but she would not listen." He stared at his hands again. "My wife was a good woman. She tried to take care of people when they were lost."

"I don't want Jimmie having anything to do with Nina."

"He is her father and may want to see her if he ever gets out of prison. I think they should keep him a long time but they let them go early these days. You should have a friend like Buffalo Kick, in case Jimmie decides to come see you." He smiled.

"Buffalo Kick?"

He pointed to the corner where a tarnished, double-barrel shotgun leaned against the wall. "My old friend has stopped many fights when people were acting like animals instead of human beings. She can yell louder than any man."

"That's a sizeable rifle, Johnson. I'd guess she packs a wallop." San picked up the shotgun.

"That's why I named her Buffalo Kick. I keep her close by because the coyotes will sometimes kill a lamb or try to steal my chickens. But I haven't had to shoot her in a long time. The coyotes are smart and know what she looks like so all I have to do is show her to them. It saves me from wasting shells too." He chuckled.

"You take care of this place by yourself, Johnson?"

"My wife died about a year ago, and my two sons live in Oklahoma City. They say they are busy and have no use for life on the reservation so I don't see them much."

"Don't they call?" Nora leaned on the table.

"They are busy and I am old. I understand."

"It must get lonely."

"Let me show you something." He stood.

He led them though the back porch and down a short set of stairs to a wooden gate marking the entrance to a large garden. Rectangular beds, edged in stone, stood in neatly arranged rows between gravel walkways. Black and white speckled chickens patrolled the fence like guard dogs while sparrows flitted beneath the plants. A small grove of fruit trees lining one side of the garden shuddered before the breeze. Extending off the nearby stable, a covered porch containing a wooden bench and two rusted metal chairs sat opposite. Beyond the fence, the wind hissed through a thick row of Pine trees.

"Those are my herbs." Johnson pointed. "And I have lettuce, spinach and cabbage, most all the autumn vegetables. I have peaches and apples in the summer, and I even grow enough grapes to make a little wine."

"This is quite a garden, Johnson." San bent, plucking a sprig of rosemary.

Johnson walked to the porch. "My wife loved being out here."

"It's very peaceful." Nora sat on the bench.

"She would sit where you are sitting and watch me work, telling me what she wanted planted and which bed to put it in." He gestured across the area. "She said that this was her church."

"You must miss her."

"I feel close to her here, and close to the land. It is a spiritual place, not a lonely place."

"Everyone should have a place like that." She looked at San. "San and Nina have made a nice garden. She loves being out there."

"She's a big help. I've never known a child to work so hard."

"Do you have children, Mr. Turner?"

"Call me San. My wife and I tried but never did have any kids. It was a disappointment to her."

"Your wife may be too old to have a child but you are not. Old Sam Rains had a son when he was sixty, the old bull." He chuckled.

"My wife died." It was all San could say.

"I am sorry to hear of it."

They sat for a moment in silence, listening to the wind whistle through the power lines overhead. A dark line of clouds crowded the horizon to the north.

"Those clouds could mean snow." Johnson motioned with his head. "We had better go."

They walked around the house and crowded into the cab of Mrs. Cortez's truck as San turned the engine. Johnson closed the passenger-side door and then opened it again immediately.

"I forgot something."

He hurried into the house and returned a moment later with the shotgun under his arm. He patted the barrel like a favorite dog.

"We may need my friend to yell a little." He placed the rifle in the truck bed and got in. "You never can tell how the Cloud family will be, peaceful like the summer sky or angry like a storm."

"I'm glad to have her company." San put the truck into gear.

Thirty

Nora sat between San and Johnson as they drove south and the road began to descend into the Canadian River watershed, its steep valleys carved like layer cake into the soft red and yellow soil lying beneath the limestone cap rock. Mesquite crowding the broken highway vibrated in the wind. Partially hidden shacks and rusted mobile homes emerged briefly from the thicket and then vanished. A nice spot for illegal activity, San thought as he negotiated the sharp turns that wound toward the river.

They came over a slight rise and Johnson pointed down the hill and to the right, where an unpainted frame house sat in a low meadow flanked by two mobile homes and several out buildings. San slowed the truck. Fifty gallon drums over-flowing with garbage sat scattered among rusted out cars and piles of trash. Two pit bulls strained against chains staked to the ground, their cryptic movements etched into the ground like a warning. Weeds choked the rutted drive.

As San turned onto the dirt and gravel path, descending slowly toward the house, a black pick-up came into view parked between a battered sedan and a late model flat-bed truck. Long-forgotten bags of trash languished next to the mobile home, their contents scattered over the lawn. He saw no sign of movement in or out of the buildings. Johnson held up his hand, stepping out as San cut the engine.

"You can get out now but stay close. If they are at home, we will know soon."

Johnson walked to the side of the truck and leaned against the bed while San and Nora stood together watching the house. Curtains moved behind a nearby window as the dogs barked and rattled their thick chains.

The door opened slightly and then closed. After a moment, it opened again. A short, dark woman stood in the doorway, glaring at them.

"Johnson Beaver, why you bring these people here?" She gestured with one hand.

Johnson stood and looked to his right and left. "You used to take better care of your land, cousin. You had pride in your home, like our grandfather taught us. What happened?"

"You should not bring them. They have no business here."

"Where is Nina? This is her mother and she has come for her."

"She is not her mother."

Nora took a step. "I've been more of a mother to her than anyone."

"Who is this man?" She pointed to San.

"He is a friend of mine and of Nina's. Isn't she here?" Nora walked toward the house. "I see the truck Raymond was in when he took her. Please let me see her."

"Raymond says this man, he looks like the law." She turned back into the house. "Raymond, come here."

The door opened as Raymond and another man stepped through, walking down the short set of stairs and into the yard, the old woman following behind. Raymond's long hair, no longer held back in a ponytail, hung below his shoulders, drifting before the constant breeze. His companion's thick shoulders, covered by a light jacket, hunched beneath a wide head marked with tattoos. The men glared at San.

"You were not exactly friendly to me when I was at your house, now were you?" Raymond approached San.

"I didn't like the way you talked about Nina."

Raymond turned to Nora. "Why are you here? I thought you were afraid of us Clouds."

"I'm not afraid." She locked eyes with him. "I don't hold anything against you or Jimmie or any of your family. I just want to take Nina home."

"Maybe we hold something against you and your worthless sister for leaving us with the little freak." He took a step toward her.

San stepped in between them. "You need to show some respect for other people, son."

Nora shoved San aside. "Let her come with us."

"Why should I let you have her?" Raymond scowled.

"She belongs with me. I love her. Can any of you even talk to her, sign to her?" She took a breath. "Please let me take her home."

"How much is it worth to you?" He reached out to stroke her arm.

"Get your hands off me." She slapped his hand away.

Raymond reached out again and San grabbed his wrist, twisting it to the left and behind his back in one motion. Just as San reached for his pistol, the tattooed man grabbed him from behind, sending the gun careening into the dirt. Nora stood looking at the pistol, unable to move as Mary Cloud bent to pick up the gun. Coming to her senses, Nora shoved her aside, grabbing the gun and waving it in the direction of the three struggling men.

An instant later a deafening roar echoed over their heads as Johnson stumbled backwards, slamming against the side of the truck, the big shotgun in his hands, smoke drifting from the muzzle in a swirl. He snapped the barrel open and replaced the two shells, stepping away from the truck and slapping the gun together again.

"I must have hit both triggers at the same time." He chuckled. "I told you it's been a long time since I shot old Buffalo Kick. Don't worry, my eyes are not so good any more but she can still see well enough."

He leveled the gun at the group. The tattooed man released his grip and the three men separated, quickly stepping away from each other. Mary Cloud eyed Johnson.

189

"So what you going to do now, cousin?"

"Nora is waiting for an answer to her question. Where is Nina? She wants to take her home."

Mary turned to Nora, her black eyes narrow. "Raymond was wrong in what he did but right about it costing you. How much are you willing to pay?"

"I'm a secretary. I don't have any money."

She smacked her thin lips. "You will need to pay five hundred dollars if you want Nina."

"Five hundred dollars?"

"Don't you think the little freak is worth it?" Raymond smiled.

San took a step toward him and then stopped himself. He had never wanted to hit anyone more than he did at that moment. Turning away, he walked across the drive toward the nearest mobile home and began pacing next to a torn bag of garbage, its contents spread across the gravel. The smell of solvents wafted past. Lost in his anger, he thought little of it. The odor surrounded him again for a moment, burning in his nostrils, and then vanished in the shifting breeze. His mind seemed to pull in all directions at once until his a pile of empty packages caught his eyes. He stared at the trash, only half-listening to the conversation behind him.

"The Cloud family once acted with honor. There is no honor in what you do now." Johnson gestured with the shotgun barrel. "I am ashamed to be related to this family."

"You want Nina, you pay five hundred dollars." Mary's mouth broke into a crooked smile.

"Let me see her." Nora still held the pistol.

"She is not here. She is with Uncle Lester."

"She is with Lester?" Johnson frowned. "He cannot care for a child, especially a child that is deaf."

"We were sick of trying to talk to the little retard." Raymond turned to Nora. "Pay us and you can go get her."

Nora looked at each of them. "I told you I don't have that kind of money."

"We'll sell her to somebody else then." Raymond spit. "You and your lawman can go home."

"We can't just leave."

"This is business. If you're not going to pay us our money then we're done talking." Mary waved her hand dismissively.

San turned and stepped forward. "What sort of business do you have going in that trailer, Ray?"

"I don't know what you're talking about." Ray glanced at his mother.

"You should take better care of the place, like Johnson said, so you don't have varmints scattering your trash around. Especially the sort of trash used to make speed."

"You're hallucinating, man." Raymond danced in place.

"Raymond, you bring a child into a place where you make drugs?"

"Stay out of this, Johnson!"

"Your eyes are looking a little funny, Ray." San stepped closer.

"You're psychotic." Raymond paced.

"I tell you what we'll do. We'll call Children's Services and let them sort out where Nina should be. Now, you should know that it's likely they'll bring the sheriff to someplace this out of the way."

"You don't need to bring no state workers out here." Mary took Raymond's arm. "Stop jumping around like a little boy, Raymond!"

San turned to Mary. "I guess you don't want the sheriff getting too close to your business here, now do you?"

"We have no business. This is where we live."

Raymond pulled away from his mother. "Let them have the freak. She broke my damn cell phone. What do we care what happens to her?"

Mary Cloud looked at each of them and spit. "Go ahead and take her. She's been too much trouble for this family already."

"Where do we find her?" Nora barked.

"Lester lives in Borger, across the State line."

"I know his house." Johnson opened the truck door. "We will leave this place. We are not welcome."

San stepped to within inches of Raymond's face. "If I ever see you anywhere near my house again, or if you do anything to Nina, I will hunt you down."

Thirty-one

Nora drove the featureless highway to Borger, rounding a wide curve and entering the grass-covered circular turnabout on the edge of town. In the center, dozens of prairie dogs stood motionless next to their dirt-covered mounds while cars and trucks sped past seemingly without notice. The pointed mounds cast long shadows in the late afternoon light. Johnson directed Nora through the middle of the former oil boomtown, past the turn to the nearby refinery and into an older neighborhood of modest frame houses. Most were fronted by broad, covered porches overlooking small yards. Faded children's toys cluttered the walkways.

They pulled up to a two-story house surrounded by thick pines, the yard a carpet of needles and scattered sprigs of grass. Ivy covered the brick wall left of the front door, including all of one window and part of another. A weathered porch swing moved slowly in the breeze. The house, grand as compared to the other houses on the street, also seemed humble and unassuming in its wild and unkempt state. A lamp glowed in one window.

"I hope Lester will let us have Nina without any trouble." Nora cut the engine.

"Lester has lived here by himself for many years. He will want to talk." Johnson stepped out of the truck.

"He lives alone in this big house?" Nora stood at the curb.

"Our grandmother was not of the reservation. My grandfather met her when he was working the refinery here in Borger. Her father owned land outside of town where they found oil and he built this house for his family. When the well went dry, they lost everything but the house. She passed it on to Lester because she knew he would need a place to live. Come in and you will see."

He led them up the steps and onto the porch. Small brightly-painted figures, unseen from the street, sat on window sills, hung from eves and stood in corners. A turquoise cat with red eyes stared at them from the porch rail. A purple toad, its lime-green tongue extended, guarded the door. Paper strips, littered with words, dangled from the ceiling, drifting in the light wind. Johnson knocked on the door frame and stepped back.

After a moment, the door opened and a small, roundish man opened the door. He stared at them for what seemed a long time, his eyes large behind rimless glasses, and then a look of recognition slowly crossed his face. The fingers of one hand danced frantically but he said nothing. Johnson finally spoke.

"Uncle, it is Johnson Beaver here to see you."

"Johnson Beaver, Johnson Beaver, come in, come in, come in." He spoke in a rapid twang.

"Uncle, these are my friends, San Turner and Nora O'Quinn."

"O'Quinn, O'Quinn, O'Quinn. Yes, I have been waiting, waiting." He hurried across the room, turned and quickly shuffled back.

Statues and partially carved wooden figures in various states of completion leaned in corners and covered two long tables stretching across the wide room. Oversized sheets of newsprint marked with charcoal sketches littered the floor and several chairs. Small ink drawings of what appeared to be religious figures and saints dotted the far wall. Jars of paint lined a makeshift shelf.

"I see you are still busy, uncle." Johnson fingered a drawing.

"Yes, still busy, still busy, still busy." He paced, his right hand fluttering against his chest. "Let me show you, Johnson Beaver."

Nora turned to Johnson. "Is Nina here?"

"Uncle, we are here for the girl, Nina." Johnson placed a hand on Lester's shoulder, interrupting his rapid pacing.

He stopped, looking at Johnson. "Yes, she is in the back making a statue. Come with me."

He led them into the kitchen. Clay figurines and jars stuffed with sculpting tools and brushes jammed the counters. Dirty dishes filled the sink next to a forgotten quart of ice cream, slowly melting into a thick pool. Two sets of breakfast dishes occupied a small space on the kitchen table that had been cleared of statues. Beyond the table, several broad windows overlooked the back yard, where Nina sat at a wooden table intently molding a clay horse. Nora stood at the window watching her.

"Please let her finish." Lester faced Johnson. "Soon, soon, soon."

Johnson stepped next to Nora. "It is safe here. Can you wait?"

Nora sat at the kitchen table, facing the windows. "She looks so happy."

"So, uncle, tell us what you are working on now."

"Working, yes, working. When Saint Julia's burned, all the old wooden saints burned too. I am replacing all the statues for them."

"That sounds like a big job, Mr. Cloud." San stood next to Nora.

"Big job, big job, yes. Let me show you."

He led them back into the front room and nodded toward the floor. "First, I sketch the saint in different ways. From the sketches, I pick one or two, one or two, one or two. Then I paint the final pose, to make sure it will be what I want. Those are on the wall, there, there, there." He pointed.

"My mother said uncle was an artist even as a young boy."

A young boy, yes, a young boy." He repeated and walked to the table, wood chips cracking beneath his feet.

"Then I turn the drawing into a statue, like the old statues that were burned, very sad, very sad."

"The entire church was destroyed, Mr. Cloud?" San studied a painted figure.

"Destroyed, yes, destroyed. The inside and the roof were gone, gone, gone but the stone walls were left with porticos where the statues had been before they burned. There is Saint Peter, the one with the beard, and Saint Teresa over there, there. The apostles are the large wooden figures and the other saints are the smaller clay figurines."

"And you paint them also?"

"Painted, yes, painted, all painted."

"Here she comes." Nora stood.

The back door opened and Nina walked through and then stopped, staring at Nora and San as if unsure what to do. After a moment, she walked to Lester, handing him the clay horse and turning to face Nora, her eyes full of tears. Nora held out her hand and called her name. Nina stepped back.

"Nina, we're here now. You're safe." Nora knelt. "We're going home."

"They took me." Nina signed emphatically. "You let them take me."

"We didn't know that's what they would do. Did they hurt you?" Nora signed.

"No, they didn't hurt me." Nina shook her head and signed to Nora. "Tell them. I want everyone to hear."

"She wants you all to hear."

"How could you let them take me?" She looked from Nora to San and back. "They hate me."

"We found you as quick as we could."

"They put me in a closet because I broke something. I kept waiting for you and San but you didn't come."

"Oh Nina, sweetheart, we drove all night and all day to find you."

She looked up at Nora. "They had guns. I was scared."

"I know. We were scared too, honey."

"What if they come back? Don't let them take me again."

"They won't take you again."

"How do you know?"

"We came here from your grandmother's house. They won't bother us anymore, Nina. Please believe me." Nora wiped her eyes.

"But you let them take me once. How could you let them?"

San knelt beside Nina. "Nina, it's not your mother's fault, it's mine. I should have known what they'd do. All the signs were there and you did your best to tell me but I just didn't see it. I let you down and I'm sorry for it. I give you my word I'll do everything I can to never let it happen again. If anything had happened to you, I…" His voice trailed off.

Nina reached out, taking his hand in hers. "I knew you would find me."

Thirty-two

Nora pulled up to Olga Knudson's house in Red Rock a little past seven o'clock. The sun had already set by the time they left Lester's house, making the difficult drive to Red Rock even more so. Johnson had decided to stay and get reacquainted with his uncle, so after Nina agreed to trade her clay horse for one of Lester's miniature porcelain horses they bid Johnson and Lester good night. Nina gazed at the sculpture in the dashboard light until falling asleep against San's shoulder. Exhausted by the previous forty-eight hours, San and Nora drove the dark road, talking little so Nina would sleep. Every light in Olga's house appeared to be on as Nora nudged the truck against the curb. She set the brake and leaned her head against the steering wheel. San stared at the house in a daze.

"I guess I'm not used to staying up all night and driving across half the state anymore." He rubbed his eyes. "There was a time when I wouldn't have noticed."

"There was a time when you didn't have to worry with a single mom and her ten year old daughter." She smiled. "I bet you wish those days were back."

"No, I don't wish that." San whispered.

Nina stirred against him and opened her eyes, looking from him to Nora. She craned her neck to get a look at the house.

"I guess we ought to go in." Nora prodded Nina with her hand and opened the truck door.

The red brick house sat on a corner lot filled with trees and closely cropped hedges flanking the front door. The house appeared to have been built within the last ten years and had a neat, well-tended look about it, as if the owner was unusually organized. Even the walkway seemed scrubbed clean. San stopped and looked at Nora.

"Are you sure this is what you want to do? We don't know much about this lady and this town is bound to have a hotel or two."

"Oh, it's 'lady' is it? I bet you'd never talk about me like that." She smiled. "Besides, I'm not about to get back in that truck."

"She could be some sort of nut case or axe murderer."

"Are you suspicious of everyone?"

"Mostly, I guess."

Before they had a chance to ring the bell, the door opened and Olga stood smiling at them.

"I thought I heard that old truck rumbling out here. Please come in." She stepped aside. "You must be exhausted."

"A little tired, yes, but Nina slept most of the way." Nora walked into the house.

Olga turned to face Nina. "Hello, Nina. My name is Olga. I was a friend of your mother's."

Nina turned to Nora with a questioning look.

"She thinks you mean me."

"I'm sorry, sweetheart. I meant your mother, Natalie, your biological mother. I gave her piano lessons when she was about your age." Olga studied her for a moment. "Are you hungry?"

Nina nodded.

"I have a casserole in the oven. It was all I could think of, not knowing when you might get here." She pointed to a doorway across the room. "The kitchen is just this way."

The living room was sparsely furnished with dark, angular furniture, giving the room a clean, logical feel, as if each piece would fit only in its current location and no other. Books and magazines, some lying open, covered the coffee and end tables. Large monochrome paintings filled each of the four walls, the muted colors giving the room a quiet, introspective feel.

The brightly painted kitchen contrasted sharply with the adjoining room. Blue and yellow Mexican tile shimmered beneath darkly stained cabinets and crimson wall paper. An oval Maple table surrounded by chairs stood beneath a stained glass chandelier. The table was set for four.

"It's good of you, Mrs. Knudsen but please don't feel obligated to feed us. We can order a pizza delivered or something." San rubbed his forehead.

"Yes, it's enough you are putting us up for the night. To tell the truth, I'm so tired that dinner never even crossed my mind." Nora sat at the kitchen table.

Olga motioned for San and Nina to sit and within moments she had filled their plates with steaming casserole and thickly sliced bread. She placed a glass of milk in front of Nina and set cans of beer on the table. San quickly grabbed one and popped it open. Olga sat picking at her plate and watching them eat.

"This tastes amazing, Olga. Do you mind if I ask what it is?" Nora took another bite.

"It's a Swedish recipe my mother gave me before I left home."

"Does she still live in Sweden?"

"She died some years ago, a short time after my father."

"They must have been good people to raise such a kind person."

"I was fortunate when it came to parents." She smiled sadly. "Nora, there is something I must tell you. I received a phone call from the nursing home this evening. Your father died just after noon. He was due to go to lunch when they found him. I am sorry."

"I am sorry to hear it also, Nora. That was not long after we saw him, wasn't it?"

"Yes. He seemed to be alright, didn't he, San?"

"About as ornery as Bertha said he could be." San looked at Olga. "He said some things that a daughter ought not to hear."

"I don't know what to feel." Nora stared at her plate.

"There's something else, Nora." Olga put her hand on Nora's arm. "Bertha said there is a letter addressed to you."

200

"I should go over there."

"They have sent his body for cremation, following his instructions. There's nothing you can do tonight."

"We'll go tomorrow." San nodded at Nora's plate. "You should eat more, even if you don't feel like it."

"My appetite seems to have left."

"Have a beer then." San popped open another can, handing it to her. "He seemed a difficult man but he was your father."

"He liked it when I called him papa. He could be sweet and charming one minute and then outright mean the next."

"It's difficult to lose a parent, even if they were not quite the parent we had hoped for." Olga patted her arm.

They lapsed into an awkward silence. Nina lay hear head on the table and closed her eyes.

"San, what of your parents, are they still living?" Olga cleared the dishes.

"They were killed in a motor vehicle accident when I was very young. My two aunts raised me."

"Did your two aunts live in Lander, Texas?"

"Right up until the day they died."

San reached across the table to hand Olga a plate but lost his grip, sending the plate crashing to the floor.

"Damn it!" He bent down and gathered the broken pieces. "That's a fine way to thank you for a good meal. My apologies, Olga. I believe I'm too tired to see straight."

"No apology necessary. It's no wonder." She walked to the door. "Leave the kitchen to me. Let me show you where you'll sleep and you can get some rest right away. San, you're on the couch in the study and Nora and Nina get to share the guest room bed."

Olga pointed out the rooms, which were already prepared for them. San and Nora said their good nights and were half asleep by the time they climbed in bed.

The next morning they sat at the kitchen table drinking coffee. Nina was still asleep. Olga began clearing the breakfast dishes.

"I've been thinking about my father." Nora handed her a coffee cup. "I had seen so little of him in the last twenty years, I hardly felt like I knew him. But talking with him yesterday made me realize that he was not always so hard to get along with. He tried to pass on to me what he thought would help me make it in life. I know I didn't make it easy on him. In spite of our differences, I want to pay my respects now that he's gone."

"That sounds like a good idea, Nora. It's a way for you to make peace. It is possible to take from our parents what is good, in spite of their limitations."

Nora turned to San. "Will you go with me to the cemetery? I'd like you to be there."

"Sure I will."

Nora noticed that Olga seemed preoccupied as she moved about the kitchen, wiping the same counter repeatedly and saying little. Turning to San, she finally spoke.

"San, last night you said you were raised by your aunts."

"That's right, Olga."

"And they had no children of their own?"

"Neither of them ever married."

"What sort of work did they do?"

"They were both teachers. Mattie taught math and Gert was the English teacher in the town school."

"Oh, my." She sat down, facing him. "San, I believe I knew your aunts."

"Pardon?" He stared at her.

"She said she knew your aunts." Nora repeated.

"But their last name wasn't Turner." Olga frowned.

"No, that was my father's name. They were my mother's sisters and went by McGee."

"Gert and Mattie McGee?"

"Those were my aunts."

"I managed their account for years."

Suddenly, the significance of the name Red Rock became clear to him. Molly Christopher at the bank in Lander had told him about a transfer of funds to a bank in Oklahoma. He had been too tired to make the connection until now.

"They had an account here in Red Rock?"

"They had been sending money up here for years. The account was set up in another name and they acted as trustees. You didn't know?"

"I know they transferred a thousand dollars from their account back home to a bank in Red Rock not long before they died, but I had no idea why."

"You don't know what the money was for?" She sat across from him.

"No idea. I'm hoping you're about to tell me."

"Oh my, San, I don't know where to begin." She ran a hand across her mouth. "You do know your mother was adopted, don't you?"

"Adopted?" He sat back. "Are you sure we're talking about the same family?"

"Oh, dear." She rubbed her hands together. "I'm not sure if I should be telling you this but what else can I do? Your mother was adopted by your aunt's family when she was a baby. After your mother died, your aunts found and contacted her biological family. At that time the family was living near here, on the reservation."

"You mean my mother was Indian?"

Olga nodded slowly. "Your mother's biological mother was quite young when she became pregnant with your mother but she already had another child, a boy, who had been born with a severe disability requiring medical attention at great expense. She lived with her parents but was still unable to properly care for both children, so she put your mother up for adoption.

203

"When your mother died, your aunts set up a trust fund in her memory to help the family care for her brother. The family accessed the funds for many years through the account, as they needed. The brother became very ill and eventually died. The money you mentioned was for the extra medical expenses and his funeral."

"Why didn't your aunts tell you?" Nora shook her head. "It doesn't make any sense."

"I'm sorry to have to tell you this. It must be a shock."

San mulled over the story, having trouble taking it all in. What had seemed a mystery surrounding Gert's and Mattie's death had turned into a completely different sort of puzzle. He tried to imagine what they might have been thinking.

"My aunts went out of their way to create a normal home life for me. My guess is that they didn't want anything to keep me from feeling a part of their family." He thought out loud. "Gert, in particular, was practical that way and she could bend Mattie to her way of thinking when there was a need to. I already had some likelihood of feeling an outsider, considering they were not my real parents. Then, there was the fact that my father was from Mexico. If they had added to the mix that my mother was adopted straight off the reservation, it's likely I would have been cast adrift. A boy with no moorings can become a real problem."

"So, Olga, does the family still live here?"

"Well Nora, yes and no. The boy's mother, San's grandmother, left the boy with her parents one day and was never heard from again. She was too young to have a child with a severe disability to care for. Her older brother, who never married, agreed to take in the child. The grandparents died some time ago but the brother is still living across the border in Texas. He's about ninety years old by now, I think."

"That would make him your great uncle, San. Think of it. You have an uncle."

"I don't know what to think." He stared at the table.

"Don't you want to meet him? He's family."

"I have no family. Gert and Mattie were my family and they're gone."

"You're not the only one who has no family left." Nora placed her hand on his arm.

"And, my aunts weren't even blood-related. How do you like that?" He shook off her hand. "I'm a damn mongrel."

"I know it's a lot to take in all at once but this man was your mother's uncle. You should at least meet him."

"All I know of my mother is what my aunts told me, and now I know what they left out."

"That's why you should go talk to him."

"We have somewhere else to go now." He looked at her. "You should get Nina."

San stood, nodded to Olga and walked out the door. Nora sat looking after him, wondering at the strange turns a life could take. Olga sat next to her and handed her a business card.

"On the back is the address for William Rivers, San's uncle." She pressed the card into her hand. "San is a good man but he is confused. He is lucky to have someone like you love him so."

"I don't know what you mean. He's just a friend. He helped me find Nina."

"I'm not young anymore but I can see the way you look at him."

"I just feel bad for him. He's been through a lot." Nora interrupted.

"And the way he tries not to look at you." She finished her thought.

"Olga, you're imagining things. Please stop." Nora blushed. "But thank you for being so good to us."

"Alright sweetheart, I'll stop." She took Nora's hand again. "Thank you for allowing me some time with you and with Nina. It has meant much to me. You are welcome here again any time."

"I'd like that, Olga."

"I will miss you, but I'll say one more thing and then you can leave." She squeezed Nora's hand. "Please think about what I said. There I've said it, now go."

Thirty-three

Jules opened the door, stepping into Linder's house as she balanced a bag of groceries in one arm and waved to someone outside. As he rose from the couch, a white veil passed across his vision and he bent for a moment to avoid passing out before walking to where she stood. She studied his face.

"Oh, darlin', you look like you went one too many rounds with the champ. You need to get back on that couch." She stroked his cheek with her free hand.

"I'm fine. Let me take those groceries for you." He reached out.

"You men always want to be tough when you need to take it easy. You just follow me to the kitchen and sit down."

"I'm alright."

He sat at the table, watching her as she moved about the kitchen unloading the groceries. He liked the way her hips moved under her tight uniform. Beyond her, through the door, the living room looked as it always had, as if the events of the previous day had never occurred. Using her connections, she had called in a favor and arranged for a crime scene clean-up crew to clean the house while they were at the hospital. The only evidence left of the shooting was a hole in the wall next to the utility room door. Linder turned and stared at it.

"Old Mrs. Kolcek actually waved at me just now. She must think I'm some kind of hero, cleaning the town of riffraff and hooligans." She chuckled. "Her Chihuahua still hates me."

"He hates everyone. Don't take it personally."

"I just left San a message on his cell…"

"I don't think there's a signal wherever he is. Why were you trying to reach him?" He interrupted.

"I was about to tell you."

"Sorry, not hearing from him worries me."

"After you found those print-outs on arsenic poisoning, I decided to do a search for suspected poisonings in a five state region surrounding Texas. I figured someone had already done one but I couldn't find a record of it and thought it was worth a try. I didn't really expect to find anything but to my surprise, I did."

"You found someone that was arrested for poisoning people?"

"A suspect that's still at large, but it gets better. The victim is an elderly woman in Oklahoma. They confirmed she was poisoned with arsenic." She sat, smiling. "Not only that, but the suspect is a young man believed to have come to Oklahoma from Texas."

"That's some news."

"They even have a name, although it turned out to be bogus. No surprise there."

"How do they know so much?"

"That's the best part. The old lady survived."

"San will want to go after him. I should go up there."

She took his hand. "You're a good friend, Linder, but you're in no shape to travel."

"He wouldn't let that stand in his way if he was in my place."

"He doesn't have me around to make sure he behaves. You had a concussion, remember? The doctor said no driving for a week."

"I can drive." He stood and his vision blurred.

"Look at yourself now. You're white as a sheet. You'd better sit back down before you pass out." She took his arm. "Besides, San is up there to find the girl. He won't give up on that."

He sat. "I know him. He'll want to do both."

"The authorities will have the suspect in no time. They have a photo."

"They have a picture of the guy?"

"They put it in the papers and on the news. Trust me. It's only a matter of time."

"You're probably right."

She reached across the table and touched his cheek. "I'm glad you weren't hurt any worse, Linder."

"It was a close call." He turned to the utility room door. "I owe you."

"No, you don't." He slowly shook his head. "I killed a man, Jules. I still can't believe it and I don't know how I'll live with it. Pastors are not supposed to kill their fellow man. I've always been against violence yet look what I was capable of."

"You did what you had to. He would've done worse to you."

"How does a person become evil like that? How does God let that happen?"

"God wasn't in this house yesterday."

"Where is God, then?"

"I wonder that every day. It comes with the job."

"I've been giving it a lot of thought, Jules. Not just since yesterday, but for a long time." He looked at her for a moment. "I'm going to leave the church. I can open up a part-time private counseling practice and do alright."

"That's a big decision. I've always thought a pastor's job is more than just a job, more like a way of life, a big commitment."

"It's just that I don't know what I believe anymore. How can I talk to people about belief when I'm unsure myself? I've gotten to where I leave God out of the conversation if I can. And, I feel like an imposter when I do have to talk about faith."

"I would never want to tell you what to do with your life but it sounds like it would be an impossible situation for you to continue very long."

"That's just it. I can't continue when I feel like I'm being dishonest with people who come to me for help. I'm supposed to help them and instead I feel like I'm deceiving them."

"I know you'll do what's right. You do have integrity, Linder." She took his hand.

"Well, that's something."

"I'd tell you more but I'm afraid you'll start thinking you're God's gift to women." She stood. "You should eat something. How about an omelet?"

"I'm not used to having someone cook for me. I think I'm going to like it."

"Enjoy it while you can. I've never been one for hanging around the kitchen."

"I know something you're good at." He grabbed her as she walked by.

"Down boy, you're supposed to be taking it easy." She set a frying pan on the stove.

"I'll take it anyway you want it."

"Hush now, I need to concentrate."

Thirty-four

Nora held Nina's hand as she followed a gravel path winding through the cemetery. San followed, carrying a small box. The funeral home director had shown Nora the location of the gravestone on a color-coded map inside the cemetery office. She had asked San to carry her father's ashes for them as she couldn't bring herself to carry them herself. Nina turned occasionally, trying to get a better look at the box.

They had to walk through the oldest part of the grounds to get to the plot, passing gravestones set for young children, some dating to the eighteen-thirties. One stone held the names of a husband and wife who had died on the same day, only weeks after their three children. Nora found it impossible to imagine losing one child, much less three. She turned to face the flat horizon, low clouds torn by the cold wind racing just above the land.

They stopped before a granite marker set flush with the neatly-trimmed lawn, a precise, rectangular hole fronting the base of the stone, a small mound of soil waiting nearby. Nora stared at the marker. Surveying the area, San noticed a large headstone several yards away with the name O'Quinn carved across the top, Natalie's name listed along with her mother's. Past gravesites passed through his mind, filling him with an empty longing he could put no words to. Nora turned to him.

"I had forgotten my sister's grave was here until last night. I haven't been back since she died and I guess I just put it completely out of my mind. So, I told Nina all about it. Shameful how I could forget my sister so completely, isn't it?"

"There are plenty of things I'd like to forget."

"That's my mother." Nina pointed to the marker, signing to San.

He had picked up enough sign language to understand a few words but little more. He faced her so she could read his lips.

"Did you know that I was raised by my two aunts after my parents died? I never thought about it until now but I was the only kid in town with two mothers." He stepped closer to her. "I was too young to remember my mother. What I know about her I learned from my aunts. Nina, you ask Nora to tell you what your mom was like, how she played the piano, what color she liked, everything she can remember. You do that, you hear?"

"I have two mothers too." She signed.

Turning from him, she walked to Natalie's gravestone. Nora studied San for a moment.

"You have a friend there." She nodded toward Nina.

"She's a good kid." He held up the ashes. "Are you ready to do this?"

"In a minute. Do you mind if I ask you something?"

"Go ahead." He set the box on the brown grass.

"As we were standing here, I realized that you've spent a lot of time in cemeteries saying goodbye to people you loved."

"I was thinking the same thing."

"It must have been so hard to lose your wife and then your aunts, the only parents you ever knew, in such a short time. How did you manage?"

"I'm not sure if I managed anything. I just got up every day and got on with life."

"What was your wife like?"

He shifted uncomfortably. "She was a good person, better than me by a long shot."

"What happened to her?"

"She was badly injured in an accident."

"What sort of accident?"

San looked to the horizon, seeing nothing. He had never talked with anyone about that night. He wanted to avoid it now but felt compelled to speak. He turned to her.

"The car hit a slick patch of road at the wrong time, left the pavement and collided with a tree."

"And she was killed?"

"She survived several months but never regained consciousness."

"Was anyone else hurt?"

"No."

"She was alone?"

"No."

He turned away. Nora waited. She finally spoke.

"San? What happened?"

"I was with her. I was behind the wheel." He stared at his hands. "I walked away with a few bruises and a mild concussion."

"Oh San, I'm so sorry." She reached for him and then stopped herself.

"I should've watched the road. I knew better."

"It was an accident."

"The world would've been better off if I had been the one that died."

"Don't say that, San."

"I'm just taking up space."

"That's not true. You're a good man." She touched his arm.

"I wouldn't be missed like she is."

"You mean a lot to Nina. Don't you know that?"

He stopped pacing and turned to her, the lines on his face easing slightly. Nora looked at him steadily.

"I've never talked to anyone about that night."

"It must be hard to think about. What a nightmare."

"A nightmare." He repeated. "I dream about it all the time. I've been over it a million times in my head. The rain was heavy and the highway was a mess of reflections and splashing water. A truck passed, covering the windshield with spray. I never saw the water pooled in the center of the road. Everything happened at once. The car seemed to float for a second, then we veered off into the dark, then nothing."

"That's so horrible, San. It was a coincidence it happened all at once, just chance."

"Isn't that all there is, chance?"

She stared at him. "I don't believe that."

"Chance is the one thing I do believe."

"There's more, there has to be. Look at the stars on a clear night and tell me it's all just chance. Look at a young child and tell me that's not a miracle. I don't understand it but I feel it."

Just then Nina walked up, her hands filled with small flat stones. She nodded to Natalie's gravestone, walking to the gravesite and kneeling before placing the stones atop one another in a small cairn. She turned to face them.

"It's a marker so she can find her way." She pointed. "I have some for my grandfather too."

Nora nodded at San, facing the marker as he placed the box into the small grave. She picked up a handful of dirt, sprinkling it over the grave, followed by Nina. Then she handed San a handful of dirt.

"You're part of the family too."

As San pulled up to the nursing home Nora and Nina hopped out of the truck, rushing toward the entrance. San hurried after them. The air had turned decidedly colder and a few dry snowflakes swirled at their feet as they stepped through the door, the too warm air inside smelling faintly of scrambled eggs and urine. The hallway now seemed alien and unwelcoming, as if no longer having someone to visit let them see the place with stark clarity. A voice echoed from down the hall.

"Hola! I am there quick. Un momento."

A short woman dressed in white waved from the end of the building and began hurrying toward them. Her rust-colored skin shone in the fluorescent light, framed by dark hair flaked with gray, poking from beneath her nurse's cap. On the counter before them a plastic crucifix stood by as if blessing all who passed, faded plastic flowers and a small lighted candle surrounding the base. The woman approached with a broad smile, slightly out of breath.

"That's my little alter, to keep me company. It gets lonely here and a little sad sometimes." She crossed herself. "You don't mind, no?"

"No, not at all." Nora glanced at the statue.

"Oh, my, but you must be Nora. I am sorry but Bertha had to leave. I am Rosa." She nodded, still trying to catch her breath. "Bertha told me you would be here for your father's things. I will get them for you."

After a moment, she returned with a small paper bag and a letter, handing them to Nora.

"There is very little. He had gotten rid of most everything. I don't know why. He was not a happy man."

"No, he was not a happy man."

Nora glanced in the bag, which contained a worn leather wallet, embroidered handkerchief and set of keys. Handing the bag to San, she opened the letter, reading the shaky scrawl aloud.

"Nora, I spent all my money on this damn nursing home. It's a hell of a thing. The government pays for it now. They own me, the bastards. What little I have left is in the wallet – a couple hundred I think. The car is yours. It was the only thing I owned I ever really cared about. If she were still alive, your sister would say it was the only thing at all I ever cared about. You'd probably say the same, but neither of you were ever much on gratitude." Nora looked up from the letter. "That's all there is. No good luck, good-bye or have a nice life, nothing but his signature."

"Ornery until the end." San held out the bag. "Congratulations, 'mam, let's see what sort of vehicle you now own."

She took the bag and fished out the keys, holding them at eye level.

"A Cadillac? Well, that explains it." San smiled at her. "Who needs a daughter when you have a Caddy?"

Nora frowned at him for a moment before breaking into a smile, trying to stifle a laugh. An instant later she doubled over, laughing hard and stumbling around the lobby. San and Nina looked on in wonder. Heads appeared in several doorways down the hall and San put a hand on her shoulder.

"Get a hold of yourself, Nora, you're scaring the residents."

Nora raised upright, her face contorted, and then leaned into San, sobbing.

Thirty-five

"I had a voicemail from Jules just now when I turned on my cell phone." San ran his hand across the Cadillac's hood. "A woman in her seventies was poisoned and the authorities in this part of the state are looking for the suspect."

He and Nora stood in the parking lot behind the nursing home, next to the shining metallic-blue car. Nina climbed through the interior, inspecting the smooth seats and tinted windows as if searching for clues. The bare limbs of pecan trees rattled overhead like bones. Nora's eyes were lined with concern.

"You're going to go looking for him, aren't you?"

"They even have a photo of the guy."

"And you think it has something to do with your aunts?"

"There's no telling, but I couldn't live with myself if I left here without trying to find out. Jules gave me the name of a sheriff I can talk to." He patted the car fender. "I don't know that I've ever seen an older vehicle in such good condition. She should see you home safely. I'd better say goodbye so you and Nina can get moving, it's a long drive."

She studied him. "Tell me you won't do anything foolish with that big pistol of yours. Nina and I want to see you back in Lander soon."

"I need to do whatever it takes to know what happened to my aunts, but I won't be reckless about it. I plan to ask Johnson to lend a hand." He watched as Nina toyed with the dashboard knobs. "Tell Nina I'll see her at the house."

"Think about going to see your uncle while you still can." She handed him the address. "Thank you, San for helping find Nina."

"There's no need to thank me. You did it yourself. I was just along for the ride."

She reached out, briefly touching his arm, and they stood in an awkward silence.

"I'm no good at saying goodbye so I'll just go. Be sure to let Linder know when you get back in town." He turned and walked to the truck.

The sky had cleared and a shifting wind vibrated against the windows of the sandstone courthouse as San walked through the doors and into the sheriff's office, shaking off the cold as he stood before the front desk. The high ceilings creaked as if preparing for the next gust before a young officer with a shaved head showed up and led San into the sheriff's office. The young man disappeared down the hallway.

"What can I do for you, Mr. Turner?" The man gave San a quick glance and returned to a thin file lying open on his desk.

"A friend in the Lander County sheriff's office said you have a photo of the suspect in a recent poisoning case. I'd appreciate it if you'd allow me to have a look."

"And why would I want to do that?"

"I have a personal interest."

"And that would be what exactly?"

"I don't make a habit of talking to people who won't look me in the face."

The man looked up from his desk and eyed San, a tinge of annoyance on his broad, dough-colored face. On the wall behind him a dust-covered stuffed pheasant hung between a framed college diploma and a family photo. In front of him a broad-brimmed Stetson sat perched on the edge of the desk next to a name plate reading "Sheriff Dan Dodgen".

"Alright Mr. Turner, what's your interest?"

"I'm an ex-Texas Ranger from central Texas. Not long ago, my two elderly aunts died under suspicious circumstances. At the time, they had a young man living out back and helping them around the place. I believe he had something to do with their deaths. Detailed information off the internet about poisoning with arsenic was found hidden in the building where he stayed. I want to know what happened to my aunts."

"That sounds to me like the business of the local authorities. What do they have to say?"

"They ruled the deaths as due to natural causes."

"And you think there's more to it?"

"You have the attempted poisoning of an old woman near here. Arsenic was the poison."

"You came all the way to Oklahoma because of that?"

"I was here on personal business when I heard."

"We've had more than one poisoning case around here. I take it you mean the woman that survived."

"You've had more than one case?"

"I would call them suspected poisonings. The old folks were cremated and thrown to the four winds before we had any suspicions. But the suspicions are still there regardless."

The young officer knocked crisply on the door frame and entered the office. He showed little emotion but his voice held a trace of concern. He stood at attention.

"Excuse me for interrupting, sir but Judge Nelson just called and asked that you come to his office right away. He said it was urgent."

"Thanks Earl. No need to be so formal, son. You can go now."

The officer turned and left. The sheriff stood and looked over his desk.

"Earl's a bit too serious about his work but he's a hard worker and means well."

"I've known the sort."

"As an ex-lawman, you know that when the County Judge calls we generally try to accommodate. I'll leave you then, Mr. Turner. Now, you might just happen to see that photo in a file that was accidentally left open." He tapped his thick finger on the open file. "I don't expect that you'll be here when I get back."

He walked to the door, stopped and turned.

"One more thing. I won't have you harassing the good people of Oklahoma with questions or anything of the sort, especially a sick old lady. We take a dim view of ex-lawmen forgetting they're not in the business anymore and stepping over the line. We call it interfering with an investigation. I'll bring you in if you try it." He nodded. "You have a good day."

San stepped around the corner of the desk and looked at the open file. The candid photo was taken from the edge of a dinner or party of some kind, apparently without the suspect's knowledge. He was young, with a thin, innocent-looking face and dark hair. He seemed to have the same features as the man San had chased at the bank. Looking at the photo, San could see nothing to indicate the person behind that face was capable of the poisonings but he knew from experience that meant nothing. There was also a description of a car.

He committed the description and image to memory, coming back around the desk just as the young officer walked in. San bent and picked up a ballpoint pen.

"Here it is." He held up the pen. "I thought I'd lost it. I appreciate your help."

He walked past the officer and through the outer door.

Thirty-six

San eased the truck over a barely visible rutted track, stopping just below the edge of the rise. Knee-high grass vibrated in the gusting wind. High clouds, lit by the mid-morning sun, streaked the sky in brush strokes of brilliant white that disappeared into the southwest horizon. He turned to Johnson Beaver.

"So, Johnson, the route number I found at my aunts' house is the address just over this ridge?"

"It's the old Coleman place. Mrs. Coleman's son, Rivers, rented it out after she died. He lives in Montana now and has no use for it, except for the money he gets off oil and rent. You can see he isn't taking care of the place." He pointed to the right. "The property goes for a mile in that direction. Mrs. Coleman's father ran cattle on the ranch until he died. The family found oil not long after and gave up ranching some years back."

"Which way is the main road into the ranch?"

Johnson pointed to the left. "The main road leads to the house and is over there. We're on a road they used to check on the cattle back in the old days. I hunted antelope and bobcat out here when I was a boy. Back then I was the best tracker in the county. I tracked and found a mountain lion once but I didn't shoot it, I just looked at it. That cougar was the only one I ever saw and I wanted to see if I could track it again, so I watched it for a while and then let it go on to wherever it was going. I tried to track it many times after that but never found it again. The tracks would just disappear. Most cougars are careful and smart but that one was a ghost."

"Let's hope my guess is right and the man we're looking for is not as smart as that cougar."

"You asked me to help you find this place and a man who might be here. What do you hope to find?"

"Justice for my aunts."

"What did this man do?"

"He conned my aunts into trusting him and then poisoned them to get at their savings."

"What will you do if you find this man?"

"I'd like to pistol whip him and haul him in at gunpoint, or worse." San grumbled. "But I promised Nora I wouldn't be reckless about it."

"You have much anger."

"I have anger." He opened the door and stepped out. "Don't worry, Johnson. I'll let the sheriff do his job."

Johnson walked around the front of the truck and took several steps up the side of the ridge. He stopped, holding his hand out with the palm down, and then kneeled, falling forward and inching his way to the crest. San followed and peered over the edge. In the broad swale below a low ranch house stood between two huge Cottonwood trees and a weathered barn. Dust swirled though the broken down corral. A faded red sedan, parked near the front steps reflected sunlight into the house through a porch window. Johnson studied the house through binoculars.

"There's only one car in sight." San spoke in low tones. "Any guess on how many people are at home?"

"There is no grass around the house, so the tire tracks are easy to see. Only one car has come in. It is a long way down there but I can see one set of footprints going in the house. Soon, they will be lost to the wind."

"So, now we wait."

"You will know this man if you see him?"

"Yes, I'll know him."

"You hope to find justice."

"I owe it to my aunts. I should've protected them from people like him."

Johnson rolled onto his back and stared into the clear sky. "I once had three sons. Now I have two. My youngest son drowned in Lake Meredith when he was ten. "

"I'm sorry to hear that, Johnson."

"I told him many times to never go on the lake alone but he was stubborn like me and did what he liked anyway. That day he was angry with his brothers for teasing him about not catching any fish, so he took the canoe out alone. A big storm came up with no warning and the canoe was lost, him with it.

"For a long time I had shame that I had not been able to keep my son safe. I was angry and hard to live with. But one winter day something made me go back to Lake Meredith. Standing on a cliff above the lake, I realized my only thoughts of my son were of that one day, the day he died. In my shame I had forgotten to remember all the good days we had together. I was thinking only of myself. I thought he would want me to think of him doing the things that we liked instead of only that one day. So I stood on that cliff and made peace with him."

"It's hard to imagine losing a child."

"You hope to find justice. Hope also to find peace."

Johnson raised a hand, holding it slightly above his chest and cocking his head as if listening before he turned over, again raising the binoculars. San listened but heard only the wind whipping across the ridge. In the distance, a faint line of dust appeared briefly and then vanished in the stiff breeze. Johnson lowered the binoculars. He turned to San, a scowl on his deeply lined face.

"A truck is coming. It belongs to Raymond Cloud."

"All I hear is the wind. You can hear a truck and tell who it belongs to?"

"My eyesight is not so good but I can still hear, and the wind I know well."

They watched the flat bed truck roll up to the house. Raymond Cloud and another man got out and stood waiting, their arms folded. After a moment, the front door of the house opened and a thin man with dark hair walked out. Johnson handed San the binoculars. San studied the young man's face, surprisingly clear in the dry air as Raymond handed him an envelope and nodded to his partner. He pulled two boxes from the bed of the truck, taking them into the house while Raymond talked with the man. After another trip involving the exchange of more packages, Raymond and his partner climbed into the truck and left, sending a cloud of dust over the house. San reached into his pocket and fished out his cell phone.

"He's the one we're looking for. I'm going to call the sheriff's office." He handed Johnson the binoculars. "Keep an eye on him."

"I wonder what he and Raymond are up to."

"It's about to be over, whatever it is." San held up a finger. "Hello, deputy, this is San Turner. I was just there to speak with Sheriff Dodgen. Tell him that I've found the poisoning suspect at the old Coleman ranch. You can pick him up here real easy, if you'll send someone right away."

"He went back inside the house." Johnson lowered the binoculars.

"There's a deputy not far from here. They said they'd call on him." San studied the house. "What's on the other side of the corral and barn?"

"There used to be a horse trail leading to a box canyon. You can see the top of it over there." He pointed to the right. "If you follow this ridge, it will take you there."

"He might run that way when the patrol car gets here. Is there a way out of that canyon?"

"If you had a horse or a four-wheeler you could make to the highway in less than twenty minutes. It would take an hour for a deputy to drive over there."

"Is there anything other than the highway over there?"

"There is a small town that is slowly dying. It has many old houses."

"Houses where a person could hide out or steal a car?"

"Mostly old people live there now."

Johnson pointed over San's shoulder, where the flashing lights of a patrol car slid across the horizon. The car turned toward them and disappeared below a rise, leaving a momentary trail of dust. San turned to Johnson.

"I'm going to keep an eye on the canyon in case he tries to run." He motioned with his hand. "Signal me with a wave if you see him heading out the back. When the deputy arrives, go on down and let them know we're here. I'll meet you there."

San crouched low and made his way along the ridge, occasionally peering over the top to maintain his bearings. Flint and limestone clattered beneath his boots. Below the top of the cliff, thick brush trailed down into the swale and would make progress difficult if he had to venture into the canyon. Just as the ridgeline curved to his left, a path emerged in the undergrowth, surprisingly clear and well-marked. He looked across the canyon and could make out Johnson peering at the house through the binoculars.

At that moment, the patrol cruiser topped the hill and drove noisily into the low swale, its lights still flashing. San cursed under his breath at such carelessness. A deputy got out and stood by the car door, one hand to the radio microphone the other on his still-holstered pistol, before disappearing into the barn.

A moment later, something caught San's eye and he looked up to see Johnson waving wildly towards him. San could see nothing but then heard the high-pitched whine of an approaching four-wheeler. It sounded surprisingly close. He stood and hurriedly reached under his coat for his pistol but as he pulled the gun free the lining of his coat caught the hammer, wrenching it from his grip. He fumbled for the handle before it tumbled out of reach, skittering down the canyon slope. He knew he had no time to retrieve it.

He peered down the path for some means of stopping the man, the sound of the four-wheeler increasing by the second, but could see nothing. The vehicle sounded large enough to run him down should he foolishly try to block the path. Then, at his feet he caught sight of a weathered, half-buried fence post, the goat wire still attached. He pried it from the earth. The post was one end of a make-shift wood and wire gate still attached to an ancient cedar on the other side of the trail. He pulled the post across the path and into the brush, wedging it against a stout limb. He could only hope the man would be moving too fast to notice the rusted wire. San turned, scrambling through the brush to retrieve his pistol, reaching the gun as the four-wheeler passed and then suddenly stopped with a loud crack. The engine went silent.

San slowly approached the over-turned four-wheeler but the man was nowhere in view. He looked up the path and back down the hill, finally catching sight of him through the brush running down the trail, back towards the house. San followed cautiously, hiding his pistol in case he came across the deputy, determined to avoid another careless mistake. As he emerged from the brush he found the area empty, silent except for a strange whimpering coming from inside the barn. He approached the barn and stepped through the open door, spotting the deputy face down in the dirt. San again pulled out his pistol, crept toward the deputy and squatted, finding a pulse. The deputy moaned as San turned him onto his back. San stood and moved toward the whimpering sound. Leaning against the edge of a nearby stall, he peered around the corner. Against the far wall, the young man stood on his toes, straining to keep his head still as the curved tines of a pitchfork pushed tight against his throat. Johnson spoke without turning.

"I have been waiting for you. My arms are getting tired of holding this old pitchfork and I'm afraid they might start twitching. I don't know which direction they will go if I have a cramp, down or up."

The man let out a squeal as the points of the pitchfork tightened beneath his jaw. San walked into the stall, stopping next to Johnson.

"I'd appreciate it if you'd hold him there for a minute longer, Johnson. I have a couple of questions." He drew within inches of the man's face. "You assaulted a deputy. You're going to jail. You also poisoned an old woman. Why?"

Johnson lowered the head of the pitchfork slightly so the man could speak.

"Go to hell."

Johnson pushed the tines tight again.

"Okay!" He hissed.

"So, why poison some poor old woman?"

"You can't prove I poisoned her." He smirked. "Why do you care? Old people just take up space and will die soon anyway."

"One didn't die and she told the Sheriff what you did. She even has a picture, a pretty good picture. The law has it now."

"I saw the ambulance take her. She wasn't breathing."

"She's breathing now. The lab results confirmed it was arsenic. They've tied you to other poisonings. You're going to jail. If you want to go in one piece, answer my question."

"I thought the law was here because I'm dealing drugs with Raymond Cloud."

"Nope. So, why poison grandma?"

"Money. I convinced her to give me access to her savings accounts to protect her from computer fraud, and then I transferred the funds to a bank in another town. It was so easy. You can get those dried up old widows to believe anything, especially if they have no family left." He squinted at San. "She's just some old lady. Why do you care?"

"You don't remember me, do you?"

A look of recognition slowly crossed his face.

"It's you, the guy from Texas who was after me. I knew you looked familiar. I can't believe you followed me all the way up here."

"You killed my aunts. Why?"

"I've answered enough questions."

San raised his pistol, the light from a nearby window glinting off the chrome, and pushed the muzzle against the man's forehead. Johnson lowered the pitchfork.

"A deputy over there has a concussion thanks to you. I could put a bullet through your head right now and no one would ask any questions. They would only thank me for protecting one of their own. You wouldn't care, would you Johnson?"

"I have shot many varmints that needed killing."

San lowered the pistol slightly. "Now, I just told you the truth. It's your turn."

"I went to work for them because I owed somebody money, someone that'll hurt you if you don't pay up. I was desperate. After a while, I got the idea about offering to protect their savings. They didn't trust banks so I convinced them to trust me, and I eventually withdrew the funds without them knowing at first. But they were more with it than I thought. I could tell they suspected something was wrong." He sounded as if he was reading a soup recipe. "I researched the poison on the internet. You know the rest."

San suddenly felt as if knees might give way. He could feel the blood leaving his face. He raised the pistol. Johnson stepped next to him.

"My friend, you have your justice. Now hope for peace."

"Not likely, Johnson but I appreciate the thought and the help."

The sound of voices came from the direction of the house. San lowered the pistol and stuffed it beneath his shirt just before the sheriff walked through the door.

"You don't waste any time, Mr. Turner. Hello, Johnson."

"Do you remember hunting this ranch together?"

"I do. You brought me and my brother out here more than once when we were teenagers. I always hoped to see that cougar."

"He was too smart for us."

"That he was." He pushed back his Stetson. "So, I saw my deputy. He was wandering around outside a little confused, with a big knot on his head. And now I see you have our suspect cornered."

"I'd appreciate it if you'd take him off our hands. Johnson and I have another stop to make before it gets too late."

"You found what you came for then, Mr. Turner?"

San glanced at Johnson. "I believe I did."

Thirty-seven

San and Johnson hiked back to the truck and climbed in, the mid-day sun radiating off the dented hood in waves in spite of the cool air. Overhead, a pair of bald eagles traced the tight circle of a thermal as two dust-covered cruisers from the Sheriff's office turned onto the highway below, lights flashing, and disappeared behind a low hill. San put the key into the ignition, turning the engine as he glanced at Johnson.

"You sure had that young feller scared. I appreciate what you did for me down there."

"He was easy to catch. He made a lot of noise."

"You made it look easy. How old are you Johnson, if you don't mind my asking?"

"I am eighty-three."

"You get around well for a man up in years."

"I have pains in the mornings but my plants and herbs help some."

"How did you find out about herbs and the like?"

He thought for a moment. "As a boy I got interested in folklore and studied anthropology for a short while in college. That was before my father got sick and I had to leave school to take care of the family. For many years after that, I drove a truck delivering propane gas to people around this part of the state. They use the gas for cooking and heating. Many of the people I delivered gas to were old widows who would ask me into their houses to visit. They told me many things about the old remedies, what to grow and where to find useful plants. I began to collect herbs and other plants as I traveled around delivering the gas.

"I always liked to read, ever since I went to college, so I researched the plants and remedies the old ones told me about. When I retired I started making teas and tonics for people. It gives me something to do and I like helping people."

"You're just one surprise after another, Johnson." He chuckled. "Since you mentioned helping people, I have another favor to ask of you if you're willing."

"I think I am willing."

"Do you know a man by the name of William Rivers?"

"William is like a brother to me. I have known him my whole life. Once, he took me trapping on the Canadian river when I was young. I think we were poaching but he didn't care. He was older than me and a sort of renegade in those days."

"Would you show me how to get to his place? I have the address right here." He took the card from his shirt pocket.

"I will show you." He waved off the card. "I know where William lives."

"Let me buy you lunch first."

"I know a place we can go that is not far from William's house."

They parked in front of the Cowgirl Café, in the small town of Channing, and walking across the gravel parking lot and through the door. Photos of women roping steers, branding calves and barrel racing covered the walls. A chalkboard detailing the chicken fried steak special hung over the window into the kitchen. Beyond, a bearded man sweated beneath a cook's hat. A waitress with short gray hair wearing a sleeveless denim shirt, well-worn jeans and a broad smile approached the table, pulling a pad and pen from her apron. They each ordered beef enchiladas and iced tea, and while they waited for their meal San counted twenty-three cattle trucks on their way to or from the feed lots further north.

The smiling waitress returned, placed the steaming plates before them and left. Only then realizing how hungry he was, San picked up his fork, finishing half the plate before looking up. Enchiladas had never tasted so good.

"So Johnson, you like to read then. I saw that wall of books at your house. Have you read them all?"

"I have read them all, Shakespeare, Hugo, Tolstoy, even Darwin."

"I went for years without reading much beyond the occasional sports page but a friend gave me a book Darwin wrote about his voyage around the world when he was a young man. Have you read it?"

"I have read about it in other books. Darwin understood the world has much to teach if you will listen."

"I'll send it to you when I'm finished."

"I think I would have read many more books if I had stayed in college. But my life went another way."

"Your family needed you at home."

"Yes, and then I met my wife and soon I had another family to take care of." Johnson set his iced tea on the table and sat back. "What is your family since your aunts passed on?"

San looked at him for a moment before answering. "That's why I asked you to show me where William Rivers lives. He's my great uncle."

"You are related to William?"

"My mother was his niece. She was adopted by my aunts' family and then died when I was an infant." He shook his head. "My aunts never told me the family had adopted her. I can understand not telling me when I was a boy but it's harder to understand why they wouldn't tell me when I was grown. I'm fifty-three and I just found out."

"They must have had a reason."

"Can you tell me anything about William Rivers?"

"Some say the family is related to Quanah Parker but William is Choctaw not Comanche so I don't believe that. I have known William almost all of my life but I will let him tell you what he likes." He stood. "Let me show you where he lives. It is not far."

They drove west, the road briefly following the level plain and then dropping into a broad canyon streaked with orange and cream and dotted with cedar. The narrow blacktop leveled as it wound past sloped canyon walls before dropping again as they headed toward the meeting of the Punta de Agua and Rita Blanca rivers. Huge cottonwoods towered above the distant river bank, their broad leaves flickering in the clear air. A split rail fence containing a thick stand of Scotch pines appeared from behind a low mesa. Johnson pointed toward the trees.

"There is William's house, behind those pine trees."

San turned through a metal gate and onto a dirt road that had been grated through the river bottom, stopping before a heavy wooden gate. Following Johnson through the gate and down a path between the trees, he stopped as Johnson paused before a tall brick column. A brass ship's bell hung in an arched opening near the top. Johnson gave the attached rope a quick pull, sending the bell ringing. Startled doves bolted from the trees.

"That bell is loud for its size." San yelled above the noise.

"William served in the Navy and has loved the sound of a bell ever since. He is often in his workshop and the bell lets him know he has a visitor."

"They could probably hear it in Amarillo."

"He is a little hard of hearing."

"I would be too if I lived next to that bell." San looked around. "Did you say there's a house in here somewhere?"

The dense stand of pines, their limbs touching the ground, obscured everything other than the bell tower. Just ahead, the walkway turned sharply to the left, a thick carpet of pine needles giving a hushed calm to the path as the trees blocked the ever present wind.

"William intends this to be a peaceful place. He says it is his sanctuary." Johnson picked up a pine cone, handing it to San.

"It does feel a little like a church. Or, what I remember of a church. I haven't been for some years now."

"The natural world is a church for some people."

Another bell sounded through the trees.

"I hope that's not dinner. We just ate." San turned to Johnson. "What do we do now?"

"We go on to the house."

They continued on the path, eventually coming to a low frame house with a deeply shaded porch. Painted blue-green, the house seemed to meld with the surrounding trees. A stone statue of Saint Francis stood to one side of the stairs, a Greek goddess to the other. The bust of a bearded man sat on a small table by the front door. Johnson knocked loudly.

"Who's that?" San pointed to the carving.

"That is Socrates, the philosopher. William is an artist."

"You seem to know a lot of artist types, Johnson."

The door opened and a small, wiry man peered at them, his eyes large behind aviator goggles, his arms, face and hair covered in fine white powder. After a moment, he removed the goggles and broke into a broad smile.

"Why, it's Johnson Beaver." He opened the screened door, stepping aside.

"It is good to see you, William."

San followed Johnson through the doorway and into a large room. Floor to ceiling windows covering the far wall looked onto a dense garden of fruit trees, grape vines and trellises. Beyond the garden, a gravel path led to the oversized open doors of a workshop, a large block of stone standing just inside the doorway. William looked from Johnson to San and back, as if waiting for someone to speak. San waited but Johnson said nothing, instead looking out the window so he finally spoke.

"I'm San Turner."

"Welcome to my oasis on the high plains." They shook hands.

"You have a nice place, Mr. Rivers but it is remote. I asked Johnson to show me how to get here. I doubt I would have found it otherwise."

Johnson turned from the window. "William, I have brought San here because he wanted to meet you. I will let him tell you why."

"Let's have us a drink first. It has been too damn long since we last saw each other, Johnson, and I'm thirsty. When you get to be eighty-seven years old and you don't know how many more times you'll get to talk with your old friend, well, it makes you thirsty." He turned to San. "Some of the best discussions I've ever had were when Johnson and me drained a bottle and debated philosophy. Neither of us can drink like that anymore but I enjoy the talk as much as ever. I don't know anyone else who cares a hoot about Plato or the Stoics."

William waved them to a rough wooden table the color of coal and poured three glasses half full from an unmarked bottle. Grabbing two limes from a ceramic bowl, he cut them into quarters and set them on the table. San eyed the amber-colored liquid and waited for Johnson to take a sip. Instead, he downed the entire glass in one swallow and set the glass in front of William for a refill while he sucked on a wedge of lime.

"I thought I was thirsty but Johnson has me beat." He noticed San had yet to touch his glass. "This here is handmade tequila from over near Romero, just across the New Mexico state line. A man by the name of Contreras has a big patch of agave cactus over there and taught himself how to make tequila. I helped him weld a metal stock tank and he gave me a case. It's the best tequila I've ever tasted. He doesn't sell it but he'll trade for it. Give it a try. You won't go blind."

San took a sip, expecting his throat to catch fire but instead found the liquor smooth and surprisingly flavorful. He took a larger swallow. William nudged Johnson and looked on expectantly. San felt his shoulders loosen as

William's casual hospitality and the tequila began to take effect. He sat back.

"I've tasted a lot of tequila but none like this. There's no need to chase it with a lime unless you just happen to like limes."

"You've got that right. I like limes better than I like most people but I'd enjoy this fire water without them if I was lacking for limes. That's not likely." He pointed out the window. "I have three big lime trees in my greenhouse out back."

"I'd say you're pretty well set, Mr. Rivers."

"Most folks call me William, except for the tax man."

"Alright, I go by San."

William held up his glass. "How's this batch taste, Johnson?"

"It is even better than the last bottles."

"Old Contreras is getting to be a master, sure enough." He faced San. "Some native people have trouble with the drink but Johnson and I have always enjoyed imbibing a bit. Johnson's too much of a philosopher to ever be a drunk. I guess I got my taste for tequila from my Mexican grandfather, huh Johnson?"

"You have a little white in your ancestry too."

"That's true, Johnson. I'm from a mixed breed family if there ever was one. I think that's why I'm so hardy." He chuckled. "Or maybe it's because I take a nip of whisky with my coffee every morning."

"When you're eighty-seven years old you can do what you want."

"I have to agree, Johnson but you have to be careful when working with stone. One slip of the chisel and you've ruined the entire sculpture."

"What are you working on?" San emptied his glass.

"An oil-rich widow in Amarillo, Mrs. Granger, is building a big garden behind her new house and wants three dancing figures placed around a large fountain. She was a dancer in her younger years." He bit into a wedge of

236

lime. "Nowadays I paint more than I sculpt. There are a couple of galleries in Dallas and Santa Fe that handle the paintings for me. I'm too old and ugly for them to want me at openings, which suits me just fine. I don't have any toleration for those snooty types anymore. I'd rather just stay out here and work."

"It's a beautiful spot. I can understand why you wouldn't want to leave."

"When my time comes, Johnson will just have to plant me here. I don't have any family left to bury me."

"If I'm still around, I will plant you." Johnson glanced at San.

"As long as you keep drinking old Contreras' tequila, you'll live to be a hundred." William turned to San. "San, you're a patient man. Johnson said you wanted to meet me but you've yet to say why. What brings you way out here?"

"Well, William, it turns out we're related. You are my mother's uncle."

He stared at San. "You're Callie's son? I remember she was killed in an accident somewhere down in Texas. That's what we heard from her adoptive sisters. I never heard she had a child. Your mother's adoptive family asked that we not contact her. So, you were her son. And I was just saying I had no family left. How do you like that?"

"The truth is, William, I just found out myself."

"So, I have kin after all." He slapped the table.

"Better late than never, I reckon." San set his glass down.

"Well hell, have another drink then. Mrs. Granger's sculptures will have to wait. This calls for a celebration." He refilled their glasses.

"You didn't know your mother was from the reservation? That must have been a surprise."

"My aunts never told me that my mother had been adopted."

"We all have our secrets. When I was a youngster, during the prohibition times, I got arrested for running liquor across the Oklahoma border into Texas. My parents had a fit but never told another soul, they were so embarrassed. For a time, I did plenty of other things I'd like to forget but then times got hard and I had to help my parents with your mother's brother. Your aunts were a great help to us during those times."

"I just found out about that too. You took care of him for a long time."

"I did what I had to. I taught at the college in Amarillo and hired students to help. Eventually, I could afford to pay for him to live where he'd get the proper care. The money your aunts provided made that possible."

"Is it true that you have no other family left?"

"Oh, there may be some distant parts of the Rivers clan still around but I never had much to do with them. Your grandmother, your mother's mother, left one day years ago and we never heard from her again. So, I thought I was the last of the Rivers family left on this earth until today. But then again, I don't believe family is limited to blood relations. Sometimes family seems like strangers and it's friends like Johnson here that are your true family. That's been the case for me. Unfortunately, when you live as long as I have most of those good friends are passed on.

"I can tell you that your great grandparents were good people, San. They did their best to raise us right. Your mother's mother was a sweet girl and a good sister, but she got involved with the wrong group and went downhill from there. She was too young to handle what life handed her." He set down his glass. "Do you have any children, San?"

San shook his head. "Kids weren't in the cards for me."

"They weren't for me either. I never even married. I guess I was too independent to get hitched."

"Or too ornery."

He smiled. "Johnson would know. He's seen my ornery side a time or two."

San chuckled. "So that's where my short temper comes from."

"I'm glad I could oblige."

"William, does the name Nitakechi mean anything to you?"

"He was a Choctaw chief known for his bad temper. Why do you ask, San?"

"It's my middle name and I always wondered about it. When I asked my aunts, they wouldn't say much except it was an old family name."

"It could be they were right. There was talk in the family about being related to him but no one knew the details. It's probably another one of those family secrets."

"Probably so." San held up his glass. "William, I thank you for your hospitality, but Johnson and I have to be going. Here's to family and friends, living and gone."

"You're welcome to my sanctuary on the plains any time, San Turner."

They drained their glasses.

San pulled up to Johnson's house, setting the brake. His car, now repaired, sat opposite, making him anxious to head home. He stared out the windshield for a moment and then turned to Johnson.

"Johnson, I can't thank you enough for your help. You've been a true friend. If there's anything I can ever do for you, just say the word."

"When you get old like me you start to feel like the world has no use for you anymore. You become invisible. You walk past people, even greet them and they do not see you or hear you, as if you no longer exist. But today I did not feel that. I thank you, San Turner. That is your gift to me."

"You were useful alright." He blew through half-closed lips. "If you hadn't been there I might have ended up next to that deputy. Instead, we had that young feller right where we wanted him. I wish my aunts could have seen that."

"I would like to meet your aunts in the other world. They must have raised you well for you to search so hard to find out what happened to them. Their spirits can be proud that the truth has been told. Now they are at peace and you can rest easy for them."

San sat back. The words seemed to linger in the air, feeling as if he could take them in with each breath. He sensed that something, a place in him, had given way like a dam breaking.

"They deserved justice like anyone. They were good, honest people who took in a boy and raised him when they didn't have to." His throat tightened with emotion. "I owed it to them to find the truth."

"You are lucky to have known such people. You will carry them with you always."

"So, you believe in a life after this, Johnson?"

Johnson reached beneath the neck of his shirt and pulled out the clay figure of a turtle on a rawhide cord. He held it to the light.

"This belonged to my wife. The turtle was her protective spirit and she wore it always. Last night, a hoot owl woke me and so I put it on to be closer to her. If something happens, I want her to reach out and pull me to her. She will find me if I wear this." He rubbed the figure with his thumb.

"That must help you rest a little easier."

"Yes. I miss her very much." He put his hand on San's shoulder. "But I must go now, my friend. I would like to hear more of Darwin's travels and other stories you have."

"I'd like that too." He shook Johnson's hand. "Until then."

"Until then."

Thirty-eight

San drove into Lander just before noon, having traveled through the night. Before leaving he had given Johnson his address, inviting him to come for a visit and bring William if he could. He tried to give Johnson his phone number but he said that he and William had given up their phones a year before because they disrupted the contemplative life Aristotle said was the only one worth living. He encouraged San to consider doing the same.

San crossed the metal bridge spanning the river and on past the town square, feeling like it had been months instead of days since he had left with Nora in the middle of the night. He felt changed, as if the person he had been before that night no longer existed. The autumn sunlight appeared clear and vivid across the cloud-free sky, cerulean behind the tan stones of the courthouse clock tower, shining like a polished jewel as the transparent air cast deep shadows beneath the trees.

He turned, following the drive through the front pasture and on to his house, which now seemed small against the rising hill. He had always liked the modest and unassuming look of the house, the way it reflected in physical form his aunts' spirit, but he saw a vulnerability to it he had never before noticed as he stopped near the stables.

Nina was at his door before he had even cut the engine, smiling at him through the window. He waved and awkwardly spelled her name even though he knew a single sign of the letter N against his chin would suffice. A sudden sadness passed through him as he looked at her and he wondered at the unexpected feeling as he stepped out.

Nina grabbed his hand, dragging him across the drive and into the stables while signing wildly. She led him across the room and to an empty stable. In one corner, an

241

exhausted-looking cat nursed three calico kittens amid a pile of rags and horse blankets. Nina looked up, still holding tightly to his hand. He studied her for a moment and without thinking brushed the hair from her face.

"I'm as tired as that cat." He said aloud.

"You look worse but you don't have her excuse." Nora's voice came from behind him.

He turned. "It's nice to see you too."

"Oh, I can see you've already had a king's welcome so don't pout." She smiled. "Nina's never that glad to see me."

"She's just proud to have a new cat."

"That's not her cat, it yours."

"That's my cat? I've never owned a cat. They don't take to me."

"You have one now. She adopted you while you were gone. Linder told me."

"Linder told you?"

"You just missed him. He came by to make sure everything was okay here." She shook her head. "He was a sight, all black and blue. He looked like a boxer who'd just lost the big match."

"Linder's no fighter."

"I don't know a thing about boxing but that's how Jules put it."

"What happened? Did he trip on the stairs or something else graceful?"

"There's plenty of time to talk about all that. Let me fix you some lunch."

"I don't want to be bothersome. I reckon you have plenty to do now that you're back at home."

"Are you always so hard to be nice to? Come inside this minute and eat with us. We're hungry, right Nina?"

Nina nodded and promptly led him up the back steps, through the door and into the house. He sat, looking around the wide kitchen while Nora set the table, feeling as if he was seeing the room for the first time. He had never

242

noticed the small designs in the blue checkerboard tiles above the counter though he had seen them countless times. The glass-fronted cabinets filled with crystal bowls and porcelain tea cups seemed both familiar and somehow new. Without effort he could see Gert and Mattie moving about the counters just as Nina and Nora busied themselves now.

Nora glanced at him over her shoulder and smiled. He watched her body move beneath her dress. She looked different too. She had a warmth to her gray-green eyes that made her even prettier than he remembered, and he found himself wishing she would stop what she was doing and sit next to him so he could study the light on her face, the curve of her mouth, the sound of her voice. The sadness passed through him again and he looked away.

"Are you alright?" Nora stood before him.

He wanted to tell her what he had been thinking but held back. "I was remembering my aunts. We spent a lot of time in this room."

"This house means a lot to you, doesn't it?"

"I'm just beginning to understand that. There are a lot of things I'm just beginning to realize I care about."

She sat next to him. "San, I had a lot of time to think on the way home. This is your house, where you grew up, and I can see what it means to you. There's way more room than Nina and I need. Nina and I have talked it over and we think you should move in here."

He held up a hand. "I couldn't do that to you. This is your place now."

"Let me finish. We only use a few of the rooms, and I've begun shutting up half of them because of the cold. You could have a whole half a house and we'd have the other half. We wouldn't get in your way anymore than we do now, and you'd be a sight warmer in here than out in that drafty apartment."

"I don't know, Nora. It could be awkward to have an old guy like me getting in the way of you females."

"The house is laid out perfect. Nina and I stay in the back part of the house and almost never use the front door. You could use the front bedroom and bath, and come and go through the front door. We wouldn't ever have to see each other, except in the kitchen."

"I'm pretty set in my ways."

"We'd feel safe with you here."

"Raymond Cloud won't be back."

"I'm not so sure, but that's not all." She put her hands together. "San, Dewey went to Linder's house looking for me. He pistol-whipped him pretty bad."

He glanced at Nina. "Nina knows about this?"

"Yes, she was here when Linder told me."

"What happened? Your old boyfriend is in jail now, right?"

"Not exactly, Jules showed up and probably would've been shot but Linder put an arrow through his heart."

"He did what? Linder's not up to killing someone, even a lowlife like Dewey."

"Well, he did. Jules said she has no doubt he saved her life."

"That's some story."

"You can see why Nina and I might not be feeling too safe these days."

"The apartment isn't far."

Nora turned to Nina. "You tell him, Nina."

Nina looked into his face, signing emphatically. "You belong here, with us."

San looked at them both. He realized he no longer had a clear idea of what he wanted or what he should do. It was as if he had lost his bearings and the usual landmarks were no longer of help. His instinct was to resist and avoid any change yet he still had not answered her.

Nina took his hand. "Please."

San looked into her dark eyes. She's an orphan, he thought. Her father's in prison but is as good as dead to her. Nora will adopt her if she can and, in any event, she'll

244

be raised by her aunt. It's no wonder she takes to me. As if she could read his mind, she pointed at him with one hand and at herself with the other, and then brought her fingers together. San nodded.

"Okay, we'll give it a try. But you girls have to say so if you decide that a man underfoot cramps your style. I'm outnumbered, you know."

"Good, it's settled then." Nora pulled three plates off the counter. "Let's eat."

"No, everything is not settled." San took a bite of sandwich. "We still need to talk about who belongs to that cat and those kittens. We're not running a home for lost animals here."

Nora frowned at him. "Why San, you wouldn't put a poor mother and her brood out on the street, would you?"

He looked from her to the Nina. "Like I said, I'm outnumbered."

Thirty-nine

Three weeks had passed since San moved from the apartment into the house and he had fallen into a familiar routine with Nora and Nina. They shared breakfast most days, often using eggs from three hens San had bought at Nina's request. Initially skeptical of the purchase, he now looked forward to the routine of collecting eggs with Nina early each morning. Occasionally, he would pick her up from school if she needed to stay late and Nora was tied up at work. In the evenings, he and Nora would linger in the stable watching Nina tend her animals and visit the boarded horses. They had lapsed into an unspoken ease with each other. He had no other name for it.

He now had a stable full of horses to feed and tend each day, most belonging to owners in town with no room to care for an animal themselves. He often allowed Nina to assist, providing she had finished her homework, but more than anything else she seemed to enjoy helping him with his colt. The young horse was beginning to fill out and seemed to be responding well to Nina's awkward attempts at training. San would sometimes find her reading in a corner of the colt's stable.

A young girl should have a horse, he thought as he watched Nina walk with Nora past booths selling sausage and funnel cake and through tents housing jewelers, potters and other artists that were scattered across the town park for the annual Harvest Fest. He bought a beer and joined them, and he and Nora sat listening to the fine accordion work of a Tejano band from Cotulla while Nina had a pumpkin painted on her cheek. Behind the band, a brisk wind rumpled the green band of river, sending glints of sunlight skittering across the surface. They bought several ears of roasted corn, eating them along the riverbank beneath a leafless pecan tree.

After finishing, they walked back to the fair. Making it a point to avoid shopping whenever possible, San waited outside a striped tent while Nina tried on silver charm bracelets. The Tejano band had just finished their last song, a sad ballad about a gunfighter in Mexico, when Nora emerged from the tent dragging Nina by the hand, her face pale and twisted with worry.

"I just saw Jimmie Cloud." She gasped, trying to catch her breath.

"He's in prison, remember? You just saw someone that resembles him."

"But it looked just like him."

"It happens to everyone." He wanted to sound reassuring. "It has been a while since you were in a big crowd. Seeing somebody that reminds you of someone you haven't seen in a long time is common. A person can look enough like the person you know to fool you for a minute, but when you really take a look you realize you got it wrong."

"You really think so?"

"It happens. Wait here a minute." He pointed to a nearby picnic table.

San returned with a glass of lemonade in each hand. He handed Nora the drinks and turned as he felt a hand on his shoulder. Linder stood behind him smiling.

"Well, you're as pretty as you ever were." San studied his face. "But that's not saying much."

"They took the rest of the stitches out last week. You can call me scar face."

"Don't listen to San, Linder. I like it. It gives you character and sort of a rugged look."

"Linder's a character, alright. I'll give you that." San patted him on the shoulder.

"San, I need to talk to you. It's important. Do you think you'd have time later today?"

San looked at him for a moment. Linder had taken time off after his injury and San had seen little of him in the weeks since he had returned from Oklahoma. Nevertheless, he was concerned for his friend. He had killed a man.

"Why not now?"

"I don't want to take you away from the festival."

"It's okay, Linder." Nora stood. "We were about to leave."

"Linder can give me a ride to the house. I'll see you there." San handed her the car keys.

San and Linder walked down the grassy slope, sitting at a table near the river. The high-pitched whine of a steel guitar drifted from the festival tents. They sat in silence for a minute watching a flock of Canada geese in the distance making their way south. While the day was warm for late November, the geese were a living reminder of the coming winter. Linder rubbed his hands together as if thinking of the cold days to come and finally spoke.

"Those are the first geese I've seen this year."

"Could be the cold weather is not far behind."

"I hate the cold."

"I'm no fan of winter either but it'll get here whether I like it or not so I'd best get used to the idea."

"You're right. We can't wish away things we don't like."

"Not in this life."

"I killed a man, San."

"He needed killing."

"I've always been against violence as a solution but killing a man goes way beyond that. It's off my scale of what is wrong."

"No one wants to have to do it."

"I can't get used to the idea."

"Seeing a person die can make you question everything you know, Linder. There's no shame in that."

"I was trained to care for people not kill them."

"You did what you had to."

"Explain that to me. Things happen that change us forever. Why is that? You don't see them coming and then suddenly nothing is the same. Everything you thought you knew seems different, as if you were walking through a fog and then it lifted. In an instant, the world has changed."

"It's not uncommon to lose your bearings for a while when you experience something like you did." He put his hand on Linder's shoulder. "Try not to be so hard on yourself. You've never meant anyone harm."

"I'm supposed to turn to God at a time like this but I can't seem to. I can't explain to myself or anyone else why things like that happen. Why did my father abandon us? Why did my wife up and leave one day?"

"Things just happen, that's all."

"Why did you hit that slick patch on the road that night? Why were you orphaned? Why did two sweet old ladies that took you in and raised you get poisoned?"

"Not all things that change us are bad."

"It seems that way."

"Even bad things can have some good in them. If none of those things had happened, I wouldn't be the man I am now and neither would you. My aunts wouldn't have raised me and half-raised you. You and I wouldn't have grown up next to each other, both of us without fathers. We probably wouldn't have even been friends."

"I can't imagine that."

"You just need time to sort it all out, Linder. You survived a bad experience, but the important thing is you survived it."

"Jules said God was not in my house that day." He shook his head. "I'm still trying to find him."

Another flock of geese passed overhead, their familiar calls occasionally rising above the festival din. Yellow leaves, brilliant against the blue sky, scattered through tree branches on a gust of wind. Sunlight winked along the river. San realized with surprise that he had been talking to himself as much as to his friend. The world had changed and he had changed along with it. He pointed in the distance.

"Those geese are a beautiful sight. If I wanted to find God, that's where I'd look." He turned to Linder. "You're a good man and a good friend, Linder. I know you better than anyone. You're strong and you'll get through this. Give yourself the time."

"Time is one thing I have plenty of."

Footsteps approached from behind them and San turned, spotting Jules as she loped down the hill toward them, unsmiling. He turned to tell Linder when he realized something must be wrong so he stood, walking toward her as she slowed to catch her breath.

"I'm glad I found you." Jules called out as she approached.

"What's wrong, Jules?"

"A Johnson Beaver came by the office looking for you."

"Johnson is here?"

"He said he needed to tell you some guy named Jimmie Cloud was released from prison yesterday."

"I can't believe they let him out." San shook his head.

"Who is this Jimmie Cloud?" Linder interrupted.

"He's Nina's father but his parental rights were terminated a long time ago." San tried to think. "Jules, where is Johnson?"

"I told him how to get to your house but I thought I'd check to see if you were here."

"I can't figure why he didn't just call to tell me."

"He said the word is Jimmie Cloud is headed for Texas. He thinks the guy is coming to Lander. Why would this Jimmie come here if he no longer has rights?"

"Johnson said Jimmie Cloud is on his way here?" He rubbed his forehead.

"What are you thinking, San?"

"A little while ago Nora said she thought she saw him here at the festival. I figured she just imagined it."

Linder grabbed San's arm. "Where did Nora and Nina go?"

"They went home." A hole seemed to open in his chest. "We need to go now! He may already be there."

Forty

Nora turned through the gate and drove the gravel drive toward the house, still feeling foolish for imagining she had seen Jimmie Cloud. After all, the man she saw was a long way off and partially obscured by the crowd. She admitted to herself she never had a clear view of him.

As she rounded the back of the house, a green sedan came into view. She wondered if someone had come to see a horse, although she knew San was emphatic that owners let him know if they were visiting outside standard hours. She studied the car for a clue as to the owner but the dirt-covered license plates were unreadable. A voice inside her head told her to stay calm and think. She put the car into park, leaving the engine running, and reached beneath the seat, pulling out San's pearl-handled pistol and shoving in into her purse. Nina looked at her, wide-eyed.

Nora put the car into reverse, backing close to the house. She thought it would be safest to leave, but before she had a chance to shift the car into drive, the passenger door flew open and an arm reached in, tearing Nina from her seat. Nora grabbed her purse just as Jimmie Cloud bent into the car, a small caliber pistol in his hand.

"Get out, Nora." He pointed the gun at her face.

"Why are you here, Jimmie?" She held her purse as she opened the door and stepped out.

"You know why I'm here." He released his hold on Nina. "Both of you into the house now."

Johnson flew past the gate and down the gravel drive, throwing up a cloud of red dust before sliding to a stop near the front of the house. Twenty yards ahead, he recognized Jimmie Cloud's rusty green sedan. Closer to him San's car sat at an angle, blocking the drive. He got out, ducking behind his truck as a voice called from the front of the house.

"I'm taking Nina with me. She's my blood."

"You have no right to her, Jimmie Cloud." Johnson yelled back.

"Stay out of this, uncle. Just because you're old doesn't mean I won't hurt you if I have to."

Johnson stood. "So Jimmie, you know that it is your uncle talking to you. I thought you might shoot me if you thought I was a stranger. But I am your elder and you will show me the respect of your family."

"I'm going to take my daughter." He smirked. "No old man is going to stop me."

"We will see. I am patient." Johnson leaned his elbows against the truck bed.

Jimmie stepped to the front of the porch and stood holding Nina, his arm across her neck. His other hand held the small black pistol. Nora stood to the side. Without warning, he put his boot to her back, shoving her off the edge. She tumbled down the stairs, falling hard and rolling into the red dirt. Johnson stood upright, startled at Jimmie's brutality. Nora moaned, turning on her side. One cheek appeared red where she had hit the ground and her hands were scratched, but she appeared to be otherwise unhurt. Johnson realized what he would have to do.

"Alright uncle, I won't shoot you. But if you don't move your truck now, I put a bullet in the worthless whore." Jimmie Cloud stepped off the porch and down the stairs, pointing the pistol at Nora.

Before he reached the bottom stair the air erupted in an ear-piercing blast. It was quickly followed by another. The green sedan lifted slightly and then collapsed to the ground, the tires on one side in shreds. Jimmie fell back against the steps, still clutching Nina while Nora scrambled around the corner, leaning against the side of the house and trying to make sense of what had just happened. Johnson stood behind his truck, his big shotgun resting on the edge of the bed.

"You will not leave here with the girl, Jimmie Cloud." He nodded toward the highway. "But I will let you walk home."

He pointed the gun at Johnson. "I'll take your truck then. Give me the keys."

Johnson pulled out his keys, held them up and then threw them twenty yards into the tall grass of the pasture. Jimmie instinctively lurched toward them. Feeling his grasp loosen, Nina elbowed him in the groin and pulled free. Johnson saw his chance and bolted from where he stood, grabbing Nina and racing back toward the house. Jimmie turned the gun on them both.

"No!" Nora cried out.

Johnson reached the top stair, pushing Nina behind the low porch wall as he heard a sharp pop and then the unmistakable crack of a .45 caliber. He dove forward, falling hard against the floor as the crack of the .45 sounded again. He looked up as Jimmie Cloud spun around, arm extended, firing his pistol twice more before falling. Then there was silence.

San bolted from Linder's car even before it had come to a stop, running toward the house and surveying the scene as he went. A man he assumed to be Jimmie Cloud lay sprawled on his back at the edge of the tall grass. Jules bent over him, checking for a pulse as she radioed for an ambulance. Next to the stairs, he spotted Nora slumped against the house. He felt the blood drain from his face as fear of losing her gripped him. Nina hovered over her, pacing frantically as he approached, her face streaked with tears. San bent over Nora, brushing the hair from her ashen cheek. Pulling aside her blood-soaked collar, he found the wound just under her clavicle. He took out his handkerchief and pressed it against her shoulder.

"The ambulance should be here any minute." Linder stood behind him.

Nora opened her eyes. "San... not me, him... please."

"Jimmie Cloud is dead." Linder interrupted.

"No... please." Nora tried to move.

"Try to stay still." San took her hand. "I need you, Nora. Don't leave me."

Nina grabbed Linder's hand and pulled, pointing to the porch. He looked at the front of the house and shook his head, seeing nothing out of the ordinary. She pulled harder and he followed her up the stairs, where behind the porch wall Johnson lay on his back, his shirt stained with blood. Nina knelt and placed her hand in the middle of his chest as Linder squatted, finding a weak pulse.

"San, there's someone up here. He needs an ambulance now." Linder called. "I think Nina knows him."

Jules knelt next to San and took the handkerchief from his hand. "I can do this. I think that must be your friend up there."

Nora opened her eyes and squeezed his hand. "Go. Johnson saved us."

San climbed the steps and knelt next to Johnson, placing a hand on his shoulder. He stirred and then opened his eyes.

"Take my hand and put it on my chest." He whispered.

San lifted Johnson's right hand to his chest. Johnson reached into his shirt, pulling out the turtle figurine and holding it in his palm. Dark blood pooled beneath his back.

"I heard the owl call again last night. I wish I could understand owl like some of the old ones." He talked slowly, between breaths. "He talked to me so long I could not sleep so I went to the all-night diner. That is when I learned they let Jimmie go and he was coming here. I knew I had to come help you."

"Johnson." It was all San could say as he wiped his eyes.

"There is no need for sadness. I will see my wife soon and then my life can begin again. I have not lived since she left me." He closed his hand around the turtle.

"The ambulance is here." Jules called from the yard.

"Don't forget your uncle. William will need you now."

Johnson's breathing slowed, becoming a shallow rasp, and then it stopped altogether.

Nina slumped against San. After a moment she reached out, placing her hand over Johnson's and quietly crying.

Forty-one

San rested his elbows on the weathered wood of the table, looking across the green ribbon of river to the rippled horizon beyond, blue in the afternoon light. Overhead, a warm breeze tailed through the nearly bare branches of a towering pecan, occasionally sending a yellow shower of leaves to his feet. The day was unusually warm for late November but a triangular wall of thunderstorms grew in the distance, counting down the end of autumn like a huge hourglass. By this time tomorrow, he mused, it will be below freezing. Linder joined him at the table.

"Enjoy this fine weather while it lasts, Linder."

"I heard it's finally going to get cold but I'm not sure I'm ready for winter to set in. I wish it would stay warm."

"Wishing never changed a thing, remember?" He fingered the edges of a small ceramic vase. "On the other hand, it's good to have hope. A person needs to have hope or they simply exist in the world. They have nothing to look forward to. That's no way to live."

"You sound like you've been reading too much philosophy. So, what are we here for?"

"You mean on this earth? Well, we human beings have tried to answer that question for ages."

"You need a drink."

"Linder, you used to be a thinking man. I guess you gave that up." He chuckled. "Did you bring the Scotch?"

"It's early to be drinking."

"Not if this is a wake. And it happens that we're having us a wake so break out the bottle and let's have us a glass."

"Can we drink in a city park?"

"Linder, what's happened to you? You sound like you've just come from the church league."

"I don't know. Things have changed so fast." He squinted, running his thumb along his jaw. "Jules wants to get married."

San looked at Linder in astonishment. "I do need a drink."

"Now that I think about it, so do I."

"Jules is a handsome woman, Linder. I used to think she had a level head on her shoulders but now I'm not so sure. What are you going to do?"

"I have no idea." He poured two glasses and took a gulp. "Jules is amazing. I'm astounded that she'd be interested in me at all, much less want to get married."

"That I can understand, as old as you are."

"Now, hold on. I'm not so old." Linder frowned. "But I've quit my job and don't know what I'm going to do next. And now this talk of marriage comes up. Just the word makes me nervous."

"Well, we wouldn't want that. You're already nervous as a cat in a kennel."

"Let's talk about something else then." He took another long drink. "So, why are we here?"

"I told you, it's a wake." He nodded toward Linder's near empty glass. "It looks like you've started already."

"For your friend, Johnson Beaver?"

"That's right. His oldest friend, William Rivers, should be here soon. Johnson told William he wanted to be cremated and his ashes combined with his wife's so their spirits could drift away way on the current of a river." He tapped the urn. "I figured this river is as good as any."

"That's a nice sentiment."

"Yes it is. Johnson was a spiritual man, but not in the church sense."

"I would have liked to have known him. Is any of his family coming?"

"There are two sons but their religion believes cremation is wrong. They won't have anything to do with this."

Linder turned as Jules pulled up in San's car, followed by a sheriff's office cruiser. Nina helped Nora out of the back seat, walking with her to the table as Jules stood by. A blue sling held Nora's left arm. Beneath her blouse, heavy bandages stretched across and over her shoulder. Although pale, her face had regained some of its color and looked to San more beautiful than ever.

As she neared the bench, San reached out to take her hand but she pulled away. "I'm not an old lady, you know. I can walk on my own."

"I hear you're handy with a pistol too."

Her face darkened. "Oh, San."

He took her arm, helping her sit. "We won't talk about it. Everything's alright now."

Jules touched his shoulder. "I need to talk to you."

He followed her down to the riverbank. "Is something wrong?"

"I didn't want them to have to hear this, San but I got a call from a deputy I know in Oklahoma." She glanced up the slope. "They found Raymond Cloud and his mother shot dead at their place. They were out on bail for drug manufacturing and trafficking. The deputy said the bodies had been there for some time, corresponding with Jimmie Cloud's release. They also found two other men shot down on a remote road, and a former girlfriend strangled in her home. Jimmie Cloud's gun was the weapon used in both shootings."

San shook his head. "He would have killed Nora, no doubt."

"He would've killed anyone he had a grudge against or that got in his way. San, my belief is he would have eventually done the same to Nina once she failed to live up to his expectations. Nora did the world a favor."

"I don't want to think of what might have happened if Johnson hadn't been there."

"But he was." She put a hand on his shoulder. "I have to get to work."

"Thanks for bringing Nora, Jules."

"You take care of yourself, San and those two females. They've been through a lot."

San turned to see William stepping out of his truck. He held up a bottle of home-made tequila with one hand and the ashes of Johnson's wife in the other. San motioned him down the hill before calling to Linder, and soon they all stood together at the edge of the river. San held one urn and William the other while they emptied the gray-white contents into the green water. Nina leaned into San, reaching her arm around his waist. Surprised, he looked down at her and then draped his arm across her shoulder.

"Here's to Johnson Beaver, a good friend and a good man now with his beloved Mary." William raised his glass. "As Yeats said, 'I will find out where she has gone, And kiss her lips and take her hands; And walk among long dappled grass, And pluck till time and times are done, The silver apples of the moon, The golden apples of the sun.'"

They drained their glasses and stood beneath the stretching branches of an ancient live oak. William and Nina signed back and forth in animated gestures while Linder looked on. Nora stood close to San.

"William knows sign language, Nora. He keeps surprising me." San shook his head.

Nora turned to him. "When I was lying there against the house thinking I might die and worrying that Jimmie Cloud was still alive and might kill you, I realized how afraid I was something bad might happen to you. I don't know what I would do, San. I don't think I could go on."

"I know it's uncomfortable for me to talk like this but I can't help it. Nearly getting killed changes things. It makes you realize what's important and that life is fragile and temporary. All that I want is right here. It's Nina and you, San. Don't you see? I don't mean forever, just us together now."

San looked at her and then away. Having spent most of the last week by her hospital bedside, he knew he had let her and Nina become part of his life in spite of himself and was the better for it. But he also felt he had changed in ways he scarcely understood. He turned to face her.

"I do care about you and Nina. I hope you know that. But we've been through a lot, all of us." He rubbed his forehead. "I know things have changed and I have changed but I don't yet understand it all."

"You mean you need time?"

"I think we both need time."

She reached up and briefly touched his face, saying nothing. And they stood there together, watching the green river eddy and swirl under a brilliant sun, so close their hands brushed against each other lightly. Above the distant hills, the towering wall of clouds filled the horizon as Nina turned to look at San, laughing. He heard nothing yet the silence held something more than emptiness, something tangible, something real, like the touch of one hand on another.